LOVE'S MEMORY

"Brynna, tell me true. Were ye in love with me?"

After a moment, she nodded, and tears welled in her eyes. Though he was fair certain he understood what brought her so near to weeping he asked, "Are ye still?"

The tears streaming down her face answered him more eloquently than any words. He released her, and she backed away before fleeing as if he were a demon intent on swallowing her whole.

He could still feel her in his arms, how perfectly she fit against him. There was no denying it. Some part of him knew her, and his memories were strengthening by the day. Kieran could no longer ignore the truth of it.

He was in love with a woman he didn't remember.

FEARLESS

ANDREA WILDER

LOVE SPELL NEW YORK CITY

For Rob

LOVE SPELL®

August 2007

Published by

Dorchester Publishing Co., Inc.
200 Madison Avenue
New York, NY 10016

ISBN-10: 0-505-52721-9
ISBN-13: 978-0-505-52721-9

The name "Love Spell" and its logo are trademarks of Dorchester Publishing Co., Inc.

Printed in the United States of America.

Visit us on the web at www.dorchesterpub.com.

ACKNOWLEDGMENTS

No writer truly works alone. I've been blessed with many people who have supported, nudged, and applauded me along the way, and I'd like to recognize them here. First, my family and friends, for their endless patience and understanding. Next, Alicia Condon, for giving Kieran and Brynna—and me—a chance. Also, the wonderful staff of Dorchester for making me feel welcome and doing such a wonderful job producing this book. And Deidre Knight, who took me into the fold and put me in the very capable hands of Elaine Spencer.

Finally, my undying gratitude to Madelyn and Victoria. You encouraged me to follow this path and kept me going when the going got tough. I wouldn't be where I am without you.

FEARLESS

CHAPTER ONE

County Meath, Ireland, 1467

"We can surrender or we can fight."

Kieran MacAuley regarded his battered kinsmen intently. In less than two hours' time, their force of fifty had been halved. The grim sounds of ongoing battle echoed through the trees, telling him the other clans had fared no better than his own.

Trapped between the English encampment and a formidable line of cavalry, his kinsmen's choices had been reduced to two. Only the encroaching night gave them the reprieve they now enjoyed. King Edward's soldiers wouldn't venture into the darkness of the forest to be picked off like stiff-necked pigeons.

Kieran wanted to fight. Had always wanted it, since he was a boy wrestling and playing at swords. The challenges of battle fascinated him. Circling his opponent, trying to outguess him, more oft than not besting him in the end. And now, he fought against the English trying to impose their civilized ways on the wild beauty of Ireland.

But 'twas not his decision alone. If the others chose differently, he'd abide by their wishes. Death before dishonor held a more complex meaning for men with wives and children waiting for them at home.

"I don't know about the rest of ye, but I'd ruther die standing than live on me knees." Wiping his bloody sword on his woolen trews, his cousin Peter rested a hand on Kieran's shoulder. "Who's with us?"

In less than a heartbeat, every last one of them thrust his hand atop Peter's. They clasped one another's wrists in a show of unity that made Kieran's heart swell with pride.

The mark of a man's courage came when he acknowledged his fear and did what honor demanded of him. They could die like rats whimpering in some prison camp or go down screaming their battle cry. This day, the legend of the MacAuley would be plowed into the soil, carried on the wind to be heard far and wide across the Isle.

Never would they be forgotten.

Darrin crouched at his side and offered him a skin filled with water. "What's yer plan?"

Kieran took a long swallow of the cool water before answering. "First, we bury our brothers."

Beneath the blood and grime, Darrin's scowl gave way to a smile. "So, ye have no plan."

"Not yet. But this I can tell you." Kieran connected with each pair of determined eyes. "We'll not be waiting 'til dawn."

* * *

Kieran lay on his back staring up at the black sky. A few stars shone bravely through the clouds, but they blurred before his eyes. It seemed he'd lain here an eternity, listening to the prayers and curses of his wounded men. Each plea for death tore through his heart as one by one they fell silent. Now there was none left but him.

A jagged rock gouged his back, but as the feeling left his limbs, he scarce felt its bite. Still, he fought the darkness. Once he succumbed, there would be no turning back. Some paths led in but one direction, and this one he'd veered from many a time.

Not this time.

Through heavy eyes he watched as a fine mist crept along the ground. The scent of woodland flowers reached him through the stench of blood and death, and on the early spring breeze he heard quiet sobs. He imagined 'twas Ireland weeping for the loss of so many of her fine sons.

Stone fences, rolling fields, homes and families. Pride and honor. For those things, they'd fought and died. Again, he admired the dauntless courage of his men, prayed their souls would find quick passage through the gates of heaven.

Then he saw her. A slender shadow floated among the dead, knelt by each one. She bent to tenderly kiss each brow, then moved on to the next. 'Twas no place for such a delicate lass. Kieran tried to warn her away, but he couldn't summon breath enough to speak.

She glanced about as if she'd heard his thought.

Her dainty feet made not a sound as she hastened through the carnage to where he lay and fell to her knees at his side.

Tears shimmered on her cheeks as she lifted his head and pillowed it in her skirts. "This was madness. What in the name of Brigid were you thinking?"

It took all his strength to lift the corner of his mouth. Though he'd never laid eyes on her, he wished for only one thing—to die with her kiss on his lips.

And she granted it.

The ground beneath her trembled. Off to the east, Brynna Ryan heard thunderous hoofbeats and the clang of armored horses. A dozen knights broke through the trees at the edge of the glen, torches held high. Their leader was dressed in metal from neck to toes, a polished helm laid carelessly across his thigh. His face she knew well, and she shrank into the shadows so he'd not see her. He surveyed the clearing with a pained expression.

For one so triumphant, his eyes held little joy.

A massive gray destrier pushed past him, its rider clearly agitated. "Major Hawlings, when I put you in charge of this division, I told you I wanted the head of Kieran MacAuley on a pike. That's the only way I'll believe he's finally dead."

"As you can see, Lord Worcester, they're all quite dead."

"His head." Leaning forward in his saddle, the older man calmly added, "Now."

"Which one is he, sir?" another asked. "They all look the same to me."

Brynna gazed on the man clinging so desperately to life. She reached out to push aside hair the color of mahogany. Hidden beneath it she found the mark that Maire, the faery Queen of Meath, had given him at his birth. Stark against his deeply tanned skin, the tiny star at his temple glowed like its sisters in the sky.

The hope of Ireland, Maire had proclaimed him. He and others like him would lead their people out of the darkness into a future filled with promise.

Soldiers strode through the bodies, shaking their heads and muttering all manner of insults to the Irish in general. They hadn't yet noticed her, and she could easily slip away. But if she left Kieran behind, the Englishman would make good on his threat, and she couldn't bear the thought of the chieftain being reduced to naught but a grisly trophy. So she did the only thing she could.

She threw herself over his prone figure and began sobbing.

Careful to conceal his features, she kept her own face hidden in the folds of her cloak and wept as though her heart were breaking. From the corner of her eye, she glimpsed one of the knights striding toward her.

Major Hawlings stopped him with a hand on his arm. "Leave her be. We've no business with a grieving widow."

"I'd be only too happy to distract her from her mourning, sir."

"Back to your mount," he ordered, strolling to join the nobleman still astride his horse. "I'm familiar with MacAuley, and I don't see him anywhere. He must have escaped."

"Again. I swear, when I finally catch him, I'll have his liver with my breakfast."

"Remind me not to join you that morning."

With a harsh laugh, the English lord wheeled his stallion into a dignified trot. When the young officer reached his horse, he turned to look back at Brynna.

Eyes shadowed with sorrow, he dipped his head to her, then mounted and rode away. His men trailed after him, laughing and boasting about their great victory. Their voices gradually faded, but never would she forget their mocking words.

Brynna glanced about her with a shudder of loss. The wails of banshee had echoed through the surrounding hills for three nights, foretelling death in great numbers. This night, they could rest.

She heard a rustling in the brush nearby and glanced up to find two familiar forms slipping through the brambles. Apparently, not all the *sídhe* were tucked away in their beds.

Lithe and fair, with hair like spun gold and eyes of aquamarine, her mischievous half-sisters had captured the hearts of more men than they could recall. Being immortal, faeries had a great deal of time to fill.

"Oh, look," Rianne crooned, hands clasped over her romantic heart. "He's beautiful!"

"Move aside and let me see." Shela shoved Rianne out of the way. "Beautiful he is. Such a waste of Mother's finest work."

"Hush, both of you," Brynna warned. "He might hear you."

"You mean he's alive?" Rianne asked, looking quite confused.

"He is, and I intend to keep him that way."

"You kissed him, didn't you?" Brynna refused to answer, and Shela rolled her lovely eyes. "You should have let him go. When a mortal's time has come, there is no bargaining with death."

" 'Tis easy to say such things when you need never face that fate."

"You've saved one?" Rianne gestured about her. "What good is that?"

Brynna looked down, smoothed an errant lock of hair from his closed eyes. "To him, it means everything."

The three fell silent as a silvery wash of light spread over the glen. The hazy beam hovered over each man, brightened for a moment, then faded to its original appearance.

When every soul had been accounted for, the light winked out, leaving in its place a petite woman with luminous hair and sea-green eyes. Her trailing gown shimmered in the moonlight. It seemed made of jewels but in truth was fashioned of dewdrops that rippled with her graceful movements. As she strolled to join them, she looked about her with the weary expression of a mother who'd lost countless sons.

"Mother, look!" Shela knelt beside Brynna. "This one's alive. May we keep him?"

"Have you ever seen such a wonderful man?" Rianne breathed, staring at him dreamily.

"Indeed I have." Maire cast a look at Brynna that seemed equal parts anger and pride. "What were you thinking, using your skills that way? Have I taught you nothing?"

"You've taught me a great deal. I used my knowledge to help him."

"You used your knowledge to change the course of his life, and even I cannot foresee the consequences. He accepted his fate. Who are you to deny it?"

"He was prepared to die," Brynna argued. "That doesn't mean he accepted it."

As she glanced at the battered face resting in her skirts, she couldn't keep back a smile. He looked almost boyish, as if any moment he'd leap to his feet, eager to take on anyone who dared challenge him. "This is Kieran MacAuley."

"I know who he is, child. Since the day of his birth I have watched this one. Many times have I intervened, but—"

"I beg of you, do it again. I know I can save him."

"You needn't fash yourself, little sister," Rianne chided her with a dimpled grin. "We'll take good care of him while he's with us, won't we, Shela?"

Brynna glared at them both. "You'll tie him to your bed is what you'll do."

"Men love that," Shela assured her airily.

"Not this man."

When her sisters reached curious hands to his face, Brynna pulled Kieran as far away as she could. She'd never fought them before, but somehow this man was different. Perhaps it was the way he'd watched her so protectively, trying to warn her away from the hideous scene. Or the look on his face when he'd gazed up at her, giving her a crooked smile before wishing for a kiss.

Brynna steeled herself to face the powerful Queen of Meath. "He's needed here, to help his people. Please let him stay and finish what he's begun."

Smiling sadly, Maire bent and took Brynna's face in her translucent hands. "My darling one, what he's begun won't be finished in his lifetime."

"Then his sons will finish it, or their sons. But he's the last of his brothers, and without him, the line of Morgan MacAuley will all but vanish."

"I know that!" Maire straightened to her full height and glowered in a most unqueenly fashion. "They vex me to the last, and he is the worst of them all. There is no fear in this one, not even as a child."

"Leave him with me. I'll care for him and return him to his clan."

"But I want him!" Shela turned to Maire with a beseeching look. "If you let me have him, I'll share him with Rianne."

While her sisters pleaded and whined, Brynna kept silent. She'd gain nothing by voicing her objections. Her mother knew them already. Beyond that, she knew Kieran, cared for him as she did for so few mortals. 'Twas a rare human who commanded her attention, much less her continuing indulgence.

At last, Maire raised her hands to signal for quiet. "I cannot take him that way. He has fought long and hard." Pausing, she smiled at Brynna. "And he has a staunch champion, to be sure. Heal him and help him find his way home." A warning look replaced her smile. "But do nothing beyond that. You have altered the future quite enough."

"I understand. Thank you, Mother."

Maire rewarded her with a smile and a tender kiss on each cheek. Then she straightened and looked pointedly at her older daughters. "For my part, I promise your sisters shall not interfere, as they are so often wont to do."

With that, she strolled back into the mist, Rianne and Shela grumbling as they trailed in her dignified wake.

"Put him here, Grady." Brynna motioned to her small bed, then quickly removed her woolen cloak. The fire hissed its approval as she threw several dry logs onto the embers. "I couldn't have managed him alone. I'm grateful for your help."

"Anything for you, Mistress Brynna," the farmer assured her as he limped across the room and settled Kieran atop the covers. "After saving our little one this winter, 'tis a lifetime of debt we owe to ye."

"And how does Kathleen fare these days?"

"Sturdy as any lamb on the farm." He unbuckled the scarred leather scabbard from about his waist. "He'll be wanting his sword, I'd wager."

"No doubt. Thank you for bringing it."

His eyes went to the still figure in her bed. "'Tis him, is it not? Kieran MacAuley?"

"I didn't ask his name," she replied, hoping to still his curiosity.

"I met him once, just before one of the dawn raids a few miles east of here. He went around that camp, spoke to every man face to face. Laughing, telling us to eat hearty." He swallowed hard, pain etched deeply around his eyes. "When next I saw him, he wasn't laughing. He dragged two of his brothers back behind our lines and returned for half a dozen more men."

"One of them was you," Brynna surmised as she handed him a cup of mulled cider.

Grady took a long drink and grimaced. "Aye. Were it not for him"— he nodded to the man he so obviously admired—"my Meg would be a widow and Kathleen just a fond wish in her mother's broken heart."

And now, by asking Grady for his help, she'd put them all in danger. Aiding the enemy didn't set well with the English who ruled this portion of Westmeath.

Aiding the infamous chieftain carried a death sentence.

"I'll not tell a soul," Grady assured her. "Not even Meg. I owe him that much and more."

"Thank you, Grady. I think it best that I not tell him about you, either."

"He'd not remember me, even if ye did. We're not kin, so I was nothing to him." He rubbed the back of his neck and chuckled. "I said as much at the time. He clapped me on the shoulder and laughed. Said I was defending Erin, and that was good enough for him."

Brynna was beginning to understand how the legend of the Fearless One had blossomed so quickly. Kieran's loyalty and courage inspired those traits in others, and where he led, they followed. Not out of blind acceptance, but admiration and trust. Such a remarkable man was he. Little wonder her mother doted on him.

She went to the pot hanging over the fire and dipped some warm water into a small wooden bowl. From her herb drawers, she added a good amount of crushed healing yarrow. When she pulled out her needle and several lengths of sinew, Grady paled.

"Will ye be needing help holding him?"

Taking pity on the poor man, she shook her head. "You've done more than enough. Your family will be missing you."

"Right y'are. A peaceful evening to ye, then." Donning his cap, he made for the door as quickly as his lumbering gait would carry him.

Once the door closed, she pulled a chair up beside the bed and focused on Kieran. Not powerful enough to heal him completely, her kiss had sustained him while Grady carried him through the woods to her sod hut. Though she'd taxed her own strength, she deemed it a worthy trade.

She removed the studded jerkin he wore, frowning at the deep cuts rending the sturdy leather. Then she took off his boots and blood-soaked *léine*. Slashed to ribbons, the tunic was beyond repair, and she tossed it into the fire. The injury that vexed her most was a long gash that traveled from his right shoulder past the waist of his leather trews. They were drenched with equal shares of sweat and blood, and she stripped them away, averting her eyes until she'd pulled a blanket over him.

"My apologies for the indignity, Chief MacAuley, but there's simply no help for it."

Whether he heard or not, he made no response, and she turned her attention to cleaning his wounds.

Considering many of the Gaelic tribes fought on foot against the mounted English, 'twas a miracle he'd sustained no lethal injuries. He might still have bled to death in the forest, but Maire's generosity had spared him that lonesome fate.

Glancing out at the crescent moon, Brynna smiled. "Thank you, Mother."

She felt a light touch on her cheek, and began the grueling task of mending the hope of Ireland.

"Darrin!"

Kieran's thrashing startled her awake. Brynna jumped up from her pallet on the hearth and hurried to his side. Raging with fever, he called out to several more men, his left hand sweeping an invisible sword.

Bracing her hands on his uninjured shoulder, she pressed with all her might, but he struggled against her, cursing in a rough growl. If he didn't stop, he'd tear the stitches closing the right side of his chest. Since she hadn't the strength to restrain him, she hoped a gentle voice would calm him.

"Kieran, the battle is over. 'Tis time to rest."

"Peter," he groaned, features contorting with anguish. "Amalie."

Some woman named Amalie had lost her husband this night. Tears wet Brynna's cheeks while she bathed Kieran's forehead with cool water. As he choked out one name after another, she could only imagine the horrific visions haunting his restless sleep. Dozens of men had she seen, bearing the crests of many clans.

But only one had she been able to save.

CHAPTER TWO

At last he was warm, and that blasted rock was gone. He lay not on the ground but in a heavenly bed, blanketed by throws soft as down. Dyed various shades of green and rose, they brought to mind his mother's resplendent summer gardens.

Aileen O'Connell MacAuley had surrendered her husband to the cause of freedom, and now her last son she'd lost, six in all. He prayed she'd heard the words he'd murmured to her while he could still speak.

Best love to you, Máthair. I'll be waiting for that lashing you threatened me with before I left.

She'd entreated him to stay behind in Dunsmere, settle the backlog of disputes and supervise the spring planting. When he refused, she saw him off with the empty threat but no tears. She'd nursed all her sons on Gaelic pride and lullabies, and her fierce blood ran through them, hot as their father's.

Now someone else must be found to lead the

MacAuley, Kieran mused through his contented haze. Cozy it was in heaven, and he smelled—rabbit?

His addled mind was still pondering that when he felt a tug at his right shoulder. Moving his head was no small feat, but he craned his neck to find a lass unwrapping a length of linen from his upper arm. She swabbed something over the neatly stitched gash that ran the length of his chest. While she bent over her task, a tendril escaped the chestnut braids coiled about the crown of her head. The long curl tickled his skin, and 'twas then he understood.

"I'm not dead."

She tilted her head as her cheek dimpled with a smile. "No, you're very much alive."

She hadn't yet looked up, and he found himself longing for a glimpse of the face that accompanied the melodic inland brogue. "I thought ye were an *aingeal.*"

In the dim light of the tiny hut, the bright sound of her laughter was like sunshine. "Not an angel, to be sure. But thank you, all the same."

When at last she lifted her head, he dared not believe his eyes. Loathe to frighten away the vision before him, he fingered a nearby fold of her skirts. The coarse rasp of wool on his skin assured him she was real, and he drank in the sight of the woman he'd thought a dying man's dream. "And who might ye be, lass?"

"Brynna."

He repeated the unusual name, savoring the way it rolled from his tongue to echo pleasantly in his ears. When she resumed her washing, he noticed her fingers were stained a dull russet nearly the color of her overlarge gown. His blood, he realized. Not a drop did he see on himself, telling him just how devoted she'd been.

" 'Tis blessed I am to be in the care of such a skilled healer." Reaching for one of her dainty hands, he lifted it to his lips. "I'm Kieran MacAuley."

"I know," she replied with an impish smile.

When he smiled in return, she flushed a becoming shade of pink. Her sudden shyness made him chuckle. " 'Twas you who kissed me."

"I'd no idea you remembered it," she stammered, her blush deepening to crimson. "I apologize for taking such liberties."

"Ye saved my life, Brynna. You've my permission to take as many liberties with me as ye like."

Her face had gone the color of claret wine, and he barely quelled a smile as he released her hand. He decided not to mention that her kiss was the very thing he'd wished for when he thought he'd taken his last breath. "Where am I?"

"In the forest near Westmeath."

She seemed disinclined to offer more information, so he contented himself with assessing his surroundings. A three-legged table and single chair occupied the space before a modest hearth. Two small windows and a door broke up the sod walls, and a simple chimney carried away smoke from the fire.

"You're alone?" he asked. When she nodded, he frowned. He distinctly remembered faces ringed by golden tresses, gowns of pale silk garnished with jewels. "Did I imagine the other two?"

" 'Twas my sisters you saw."

"They live nearby?"

"Aye."

Kieran's stomach rumbled insistently, and she laughed. Such a lovely sound it was.

"Hungry, are you?" she asked.

"A bit."

"Once I've finished dressing your wounds, I'll fetch you some coney stew."

"It smells delicious."

As he tentatively moved his unfettered arm, he felt the pull of sinew closing the many sword blows he'd taken. She'd fairly stitched him back together, bless her generous soul. It must have taken her hours.

Even though he was lying prone, his head swam from the blood he'd lost. "How long have I been here?"

"Since last night."

The night that had rained disaster on the allied clans of Meath. Kieran's heart twisted with guilt for surviving the battle that had killed so many. He should have died with his kinsmen, but for some unfathomable reason here he lay, cradled in soft wool, being tended like an ailing child.

"Which clan do ye hail from, lass?"

"None. 'Tis only me."

That made no sense at all. "What of your sisters?"

"They're my half-sisters, and I'm not welcome in their home. Their father dislikes me."

When she didn't continue, he decided to let the matter rest. She'd shown no desire to confide in him, and after all she'd done to help him, he didn't wish to upset her.

While she applied a poultice to the angry bruise at his right shoulder, he smelled spice of some kind. "What is that?"

"Marjoram, to help with the swelling."

Kieran honestly didn't care if the shoulder bloated to twice its normal size and his arm fell off. He'd rushed into the thick of the fight to die with honor, not live out his life as a crippled wastrel.

"In time, you should regain full use of your arm," she told him, as if she'd somehow divined his angry thoughts. "You're most fortunate. None of your injuries should hinder you for long."

"I lost forty-nine kinsmen yestreen. I feel anything but fortunate."

Deflecting his bitterness with a patient smile, she smoothed a hand over his brow. "I've not been able to bring your fever down all night. If I brew some tea, will you drink it?"

A wave of fatigue swept over him, and he nodded. He closed his eyes, only to find that the scenes playing behind them resumed where he'd left them. Grim determination showed on the faces of men who would forever be his heroes. Courage and fortitude they'd carried with them, weapons that had sustained the Irish through centuries of war. But they'd proven no match for treachery and suits of steel.

Someone had contrived their defeat at the hands of the English, of that he was certain. If it took the rest of his days, he'd discover who was responsible for it and tear the bastard apart with his bare hands.

She sat in the chair beside the bed and handed him a steaming cup. "Drink this."

He sniffed at it, expecting the bitterness of most healing mixes. It smelled of flowers and honey, so he took a cautious sip. "Even your medicine is sweet."

"Thank you."

The compliment seemed to unsettle her. In his lifetime of five and thirty, he'd known more than his fair share of women, but never had he encountered one like Brynna. Unusual, to be certain. Then again, living alone in the forest could do that to anyone.

That thought led him to a question. "How did you bring me here after the battle?"

"With some generous help."

"Does your helper have a name? I should thank him."

"I think it best if you didn't."

Dropping his head back into the plump pillow, he glared at the dried herbs above his head. "Good God, I'm in *English* Westmeath."

"A bit."

Summoning his fleeting patience, Kieran turned his head to look at her. "How far?"

She nibbled at her lower lip, but her eyes never left his. "Far enough."

"Then the English must know I'm here."

"No, they don't."

"What about the man who helped you?" he

pressed. "He might have told them. There are spies aplenty hereabouts."

She said nothing but took the cup from his hands and tucked the blankets more closely about him. Her reticence troubled him greatly. As he considered what she might be hiding, his mind began to blur and weakness stole through his body.

Alarmed by the disquieting sensation, Kieran struggled to sit. His muscles refused to obey, and he fell back into the small bed.

"Brynna, what the devil have ye done to me?"

She was so stunned by the accusation, it took her a moment to summon her voice. "Nothing. 'Tis only a mixture of herbs to help you sleep."

"Meantime, you've left me helpless."

His voice trailed off, his eyes drifting closed as if he no longer had the strength to keep them open. By the saints, he was stubborn. She wanted only to heal him, yet he fought her at every turn.

He was accustomed to fighting, she mused as she studied her notorious guest. Scarred with reminders of countless battles, his was not the handsome face of a romantic poem but the visage of a man who challenged life as it came. One in his position hadn't the luxury of trusting anyone.

'Twas a feeling she knew all too well.

Careful not to disturb him, she tidied the little house, her mind on things other than firewood and simmering stew. Kieran's mistrust had dredged up memories too disturbing to ignore. After ensuring he slept soundly, she picked up the empty water bucket and slipped out the door.

How she loved the forest. Under a shroud of interwoven branches, it was a living, breathing thing teeming with all manner of creatures. Here, the fabric that separated her from her mother and sisters was most easily drawn aside. Though she wasn't permitted in the fae realm, they often stepped through the curtain to visit her.

She wasn't surprised to find Maire waiting for her near the spring. "How does our warrior fare?"

"Well enough." Brynna bent to fill the bucket, then saw it was brimming with water. She smiled up at her mother. "Thank you."

Maire waved away her gratitude, then patted the rock on which she sat. "Come. Join me for a bit."

Brynna glanced back toward the soddy. "Kieran—"

"Will sleep a while longer. I wish to speak with you."

Once Brynna had settled beside her, Maire continued in a somber tone. "I have discovered something that distresses me greatly."

"Father helped the English plan this attack."

"How could you know that?"

Brynna frowned. " 'Tis no different from two years ago, when he pledged his support to the clans and withdrew his cavalry at the height of the battle."

"He walks a dangerous path."

Maire's ominous warning sent a chill over Brynna's skin. "Is he truly destined to become High King of Ireland, as he claims?"

"The throne at Tara has not lain empty all these centuries by happenstance."

The cryptic answer, so typical of the *sídhe*, only made Brynna more curious. She drew up her legs and wrapped her arms around them. "Father told me the Ryans once ruled Ireland. Is that true?"

"Long ago," Maire replied with a nod. "They lost their position to one with more cunning, and he in turn lost it to another. Now your father seeks to regain what he feels is rightfully his." She rested a hand over Brynna's. "I never considered he might try to coerce you to use your skills to help him. I wish I had known."

"To what purpose? He does as he pleases, and you have worries enough. Leaving Ferndon was the best thing I could do." Brynna smiled. "Beyond that, I know you watch over me."

Maire drew herself up haughtily. "I do no such thing."

"Mother, please." She laughed. "I sense when you're nearby, or Shela or Rianne. Whether or not you speak to me, I know when one of you is about."

The momentary pique faded, and the queen gave her a proud smile. "I had no idea you'd honed your intuition so well."

"Father's men are constantly searching for me, so I had no choice but to learn to use it. 'Tis the only weapon I have."

"Perhaps I should have taught you more when you were a child."

Brynna firmly shook her head. "Because I loved him so much, I'd have done what he asked. How much suffering might I have caused simply because I knew no better?"

"Instead, you help those he seeks to harm. He will not be pleased to learn that Kieran is alive."

"I'll manage that if I must. My only concern is to heal Kieran and get him home. Ireland needs him greatly."

"That she does." Maire's gaze roamed through the forest, then settled on Brynna. "But mortals must be allowed to live their own lives. Much as I cherish Kieran, I shall not intercede on his behalf again."

"And me?"

Maire took Brynna's face in her elegant hands and placed a motherly kiss on each cheek. "I leave you to your choices, my precious one. Be certain to weigh them with your mind as well as your heart."

Then she was gone.

Kieran awoke to the crackling of a fire and the smell of vegetable pottage. He held his eyes closed for a few moments, then opened them a crack.

The hut was empty.

Just the opportunity he'd been waiting for. Brynna had baffled him from the first moment he saw her. Well-spoken and finely mannered, she dressed in rags. She was delightful company, yet she lived alone in the forest. Instinct told him it was important he solve the mystery of her, and quickly.

Ignoring the protest of his stiff limbs, he pushed the covers aside and sat up. A quick look about showed him a few places in which a clever woman might hide things.

To begin, he slid his arm beneath the grass-filled mattress and was pleasantly surprised to find his sword. He drew it out, closing his hand about the hilt as he unsheathed the blade to assess its condition. It needed a thorough cleaning, but otherwise it appeared to be sound. He'd assumed the English had taken it after the battle, and as he returned it to its hiding place, he smiled. 'Twas good to know he wasn't unarmed.

Nothing else presented itself, but near the base of the fireplace he located a loose stone. When he moved it aside, he found a carved wooden box. Beneath the cover were several filigreed silver hair combs, tarnished but meticulously fashioned. They were the sort of thing a lady might wear with a silken gown, and he wondered how Brynna had come by them.

The leather-bound book of poetry intrigued him even more. He flipped through the mildewed pages but found nothing beyond lines of hand-copied French text. The volume was well-worn, as if it had been read many times.

"And what is it you think you're doing?"

Skilled as he was at inventing plausible explanations, none came to him. Like a boy caught with a forbidden treat, he slowly lifted his gaze from the book. The eyes that met his flashed emerald fire, rivaling the heat of the flames behind him. She set down a full bucket of water far too heavy for so delicate a lass to carry.

"This is my reward for helping you?"

"I meant no offense," he began, holding up his hand in a placating gesture. If he could only get to his feet, he might scrape together some dignity.

"Men never do."

She spat the words as if they tasted bitter on her tongue. All thought of standing left him, and he simply stared at her. Before his disbelieving eyes, the sweet *aingeal* who'd rescued him had become a sharp-tongued harridan. Until he determined her true nature, he'd best tread carefully. "My apologies for insulting you."

"You think I'm a spy, is that it?"

"I wasn't certain what to think." Hoping to calm her, he shrugged his good shoulder and summoned what he hoped was a sheepish grin. "Ye canna blame a man for being curious, can ye?"

She snatched the book away from him, cradling it protectively against her. "You might have asked me."

"I suppose if ye were a spy, you'd have told me." Kieran got to his feet, bracing himself with a hand on the sod wall to gain his balance.

"Why would I save your life only to turn you over to the English?"

" 'Tis difficult to execute a dead man."

The room began to spin, and he shook his head in an attempt to clear it. The sensation worsened, the hum in his ears blocking the sound of Brynna's voice. She caught him just as his legs gave way.

"You mustn't overtax yourself this way," she chided as she eased him onto the bed. Swallowing hard to keep from retching, he stretched out with a groan.

She opened her mouth to continue her scolding, then turned her head and stared out the open door. Kieran followed her gaze but saw nothing.

"What is it, Brynna?"

"Riders, coming this way."

She needn't tell him they were English. Even as he tried to sit, she pushed him back down. That she could do it infuriated him, and he growled at her. "Let me up. They'll kill us both if they find me here."

"I won't let that happen, but you must listen to me."

"Have I a choice?"

Eyes sparking angrily, she took a deep breath but kept her voice calm. "Lie very still and no matter what happens, stay absolutely quiet."

Before he could reply, he heard the rumble of horses in the distance. "How did ye know they were coming?"

"Hush, now." Tucking the blankets more securely about him, she gave him a heartwarming smile. "And stay hushed. You can trust me. I won't betray you."

He watched her pluck at the flawless braid encircling her head. From the foot of the bed she took a blanket. Draping it about her shoulders, she hunched over until she resembled a bent old woman. Her sweet smile fell into a frown, and the lively sparkle in her eyes dulled to the flat color of a stagnant pond.

Something else had changed, something he couldn't define, but she'd done more than disguise her appearance. Somehow, she'd transformed herself into a weary-looking hag, defenseless and harmless. But such a thing was impossible.

When she turned to go, he reached out and caught her slender wrist. "Be careful."

"I'll be careful if you'll be quiet. Agreed?"

He nodded and watched her hobble outside, leaving the door open behind her. Nothing to fear, nothing to hide, the gesture plainly said. Lying as still as he could, he wondered how she'd convince the soldiers to leave.

From his position, he saw nothing but the slats of the wooden door. The vulnerability of his situation raked over his already raw nerves, and he strained to hear what was happening outside.

"*Fáilte,*" she welcomed her visitors in a cracked voice. "What can I be doing for King Edward's men this fine morn?"

"We're looking for a dangerous outlaw," a man answered, his cultured tone dulled by fatigue.

They'd been hunting for him, had they? The Earl of Worcester must be cursing up a storm. He'd been sent to gain control of the "Irish problem," a laughable term. Beyond ongoing feuds, famines and the occasional outbreak of plague, the only problem the Irish had was the unending stream of Englishmen invading their country.

But this time, the king's emissary had come with a sobering credential. During the Wars of the Roses, he'd been dubbed the Butcher. The clans soon discovered just how well the appellation fit him.

"An outlaw?" Brynna echoed, sounding a bit frightened. "And who might he be?"

"Kieran MacAuley. Do you know him?"

"Aye." She spun out the word on a long breath. "We all know the Fearless One. What crime has he committed?"

"Too many to count. But two nights past, he

slaughtered a score of my men and vanished into the woods."

"Did he, now? Why would he do such a thing?"

"Have you seen him?" the man asked impatiently.

"No, I haven't, but I've no objections to you looking about the place."

Kieran couldn't believe what she'd done. She could have sent them off with memories of a slightly mad woman who lived alone in the dense woods. Instead, she'd invited them inside the hut to find him flat on his back like a carcass ready for the cleaver. That thought conjured a vision of the Butcher carving him up with great relish. After the havoc he'd caused, they'd not have the decency to slit his throat first.

"That won't be necessary, madam, but you should be on your guard. We have this area surrounded, but MacAuley is well-armed and desperate to escape."

Kieran bristled at the implication that he'd harm a woman, and an Irish one at that. Silently, he assailed the soldier with one heartfelt Gaelic curse after another. If Queen Maire truly favored him, as his mother insisted, the man would not only return home in a box, he'd be minus a few of his appendages as well.

"I'm grateful for the warning, sir. *Slán.*"

"And farewell to you."

Damned polite for an Englishmen, Kieran grumbled to himself. Brynna now stood within his view, waving as the soldiers' horses cantered away. After the last echo of hoofbeats faded, she shook off the

heavy throw, her back straightening to its customary regal bearing. Never had he seen a woman
saunter as she did now, and she wore a triumphant
smile as she walked back inside.

Braced to fight if necessary, he fell back as she
closed the door behind her.

" 'Twas a foolish thing to do," he gritted through
clenched teeth.

"It succeeded, did it not?"

He stared at her incredulously. "Are ye daft?
What if he'd accepted your gracious offer to search
in here?"

She lifted a careless shoulder and tossed the blanket at the foot of the bed.

"You're either the most clever woman I've ever
met or the most fey."

Arching a graceful brow, she smiled. "Or perhaps a bit of both."

There he lay, helpless as a bairn, hidden in plain
sight.

If he didn't miss his guess, the next patrol would
give the soddy a wide berth. The English thrived on
order and conformity, and anything outside the
scope of their well-ordered culture unnerved them.
'Twas why so few of them understood the ways of
the Irish.

Somehow, Brynna knew that and had used it
against the weary captain, presenting him with a
harmless oddity he could easily ignore. Such a
quick mind in the head of a beautiful woman, he
mused with a grin. A volatile combination.

"Now you smile at me?" she asked as she sat in
the little chair beside the bed.

" 'Tis what I should have done from the start." He took her hand and raised it to his lips. "I pray you'll forgive me for thinking ye were a spy."

She granted him the most beautiful smile he'd ever seen. "Of course I forgive you. But for now you should rest. 'Tis what you're needing."

"I'm not tired," he lied. In truth, he couldn't bear to close his eyes and relive the battle in his nightmares.

"All right, then. I'll fetch you some porridge."

"No, thank you."

"You'd prefer something else?"

"Redemption," Kieran spat without thinking. "Can ye brew a batch of that for me, Brynna?"

"You've done nothing to be redeemed for. Those men knew what would happen if they fought. They also knew the consequences if they didn't. They chose to follow you of their own free will."

There was but one way she'd know that. "You were there."

She made no response, but he saw the answer in her eyes. "How could ye be so foolish? 'Twas no place for you, and well ye know it."

"I wanted to help if I could. By the time I thought it safe to come out—" Her voice trailed off into a choked whisper, and he swore under his breath.

"What ye saw, no woman should ever see." A hazy memory cleared a bit in his mind. "'Twas your weeping I heard."

"Aye." She began rubbing salve over the gash on his left wrist. "It made me sad to see so many men slaughtered that way."

"None of the others could ye save?"

"No."

Her tone echoed with remorse. She focused on rebinding his hand, and Kieran swallowed hard to quell his emotions. He dreaded returning to Dunsmere, facing the mothers, wives and children of the men who'd been lost. The wrenching task made him consider staying in the forest, living out his misery until death came to free him.

Was that what kept her here, scraping her existence from the forest floor like a squirrel? Had she run from some tragedy too overwhelming to bear?

Her intriguing eyes lifted to his, the gold in them glinting in the muted sunlight. He fancied they saw a great deal more than his face, and he turned away.

"Kieran, look at me."

When he met her gaze, the compassion he saw nearly undid him. As her thumb brushed his cheek, he stiffened. "I don't know what ye think you're doing, but stop it."

"I was putting salve on this cut. I didn't mean—"

"Please forgive me, lass. Ye must think me an ungrateful bastard." Sighing, he dropped his head back to the wall that formed a headboard of sorts for her bed. "Forgive me again. 'Tis not like me to speak that way in front of a lady."

"You've no cause to hold your tongue with me. I'll not tell a soul."

She didn't chide him for his black mood but pressed a hand to his brow. Though he understood she was gauging his fever, her gentle touch seemed to reach beyond his skin. He wondered if she were attempting to heal the wounds festering where no one could see.

"You need to rest," she told him again.

"I canna sleep. I keep seeing them, hearing them. They were my men. I should have died with them."

"Were they here now, would they say the same?"

He spun his gold chieftain's ring about his finger while he considered her question. The oak leaf, symbol of the MacAuley, reminded him of the resolute strength of all those who'd worn it before him. "They'd say I should heal up and get me home."

"That's what we'll do, then, out of respect for your men."

The corner of his mouth lifted in a half-smile, and he nodded. "Aye. For my men."

"Tell me about them," she urged, curling up in the little chair. "Start with Darrin."

"He's my—" Kieran paused a moment to steady his voice. "Was my mother's cousin. Couldn't carry a tune but loved to sing. I swear he could talk to animals, he mimicked them so well."

"And Peter?"

As he relayed stories of the kinsmen he so admired, the leaden weight on his heart began to ease, and he found himself laughing with her over their many escapades. His heroes ceased to be dead warriors and became men again. Somehow, Brynna resurrected them, sealing them in his memory as flesh and blood rather than lifeless bodies scattered through the forest. Should he live to be a hundred, he'd never forget what she'd done.

CHAPTER THREE

Kieran awoke to the sound of quiet humming. Seated near the open door, Brynna was repairing a seam in her linen nightgown. He'd seen her wearing it while she tended him in the midst of the night, and he realized she must own no others. Clearly well-bred and educated, she was no doubt familiar with fine needlework, yet she seemed content with the menial task before her.

The stitches in his chest pulled a bit as he rolled onto his side, reminding him just how skilled she was at mending things. As he studied her, his fascination deepened by the moment.

The early sunlight glistened in her hair, burnishing the curls about her face to a deep auburn. Though the ill-fitting woolen gown disguised the shape beneath it, nothing could mar the beauty of her sweet face. And those eyes. As they lifted to his, he couldn't help smiling.

"Good morn to you, Kieran. I trust you slept well."

"Aye, for the first time in a sennight. And you?"

"I did, as well. Would you care for some breakfast?"

Smelling of springtime, the gentle breeze called out to him. "Actually, I'd like to go outside."

" 'Tis a fair morning," she agreed as she got to her feet. "Perhaps some fresh air will do you good."

"I think it will."

She fetched his trews from the drying rack by the fire and handed them to him. "Would you care for my help with these?"

"I can manage."

She watched him with an expectant look. During the time she'd been caring for him she'd seen a good deal, but he felt awkward dressing in front of her. He was far more accustomed to shedding his clothes in front of a woman than putting them on.

Apparently reading his hesitance, she smiled, her woolen skirt swishing over the dirt floor as she spun to face the other way. Kieran's bound shoulder impeded his movements. He pulled his right leg through the trews and groaned, leaning against the bed while he waited for the throbbing in his chest to subside.

"Not yet," he warned as she began to turn.

"But you're in pain."

Her empathy made him chuckle despite the burning in his side. " 'Tis nothing I canna bear."

He finished with his trews, then stared down at the lacings like an imbecile. He couldn't tie them one-handed. Much as he hated to do it, he had no choice but to ask Brynna for her help.

Before he could utter a word, she hurried over and knelt before him to knot the leather thongs. 'Twas not the first time she'd seemed to divine his thoughts. Could it be this mystifying nymph had the power to discern what he was thinking?

She stood and backed away, but he grabbed her wrist and pulled her against him. He forced a cruel thought into his mind, watched her blanch with fear.

"Ye know what I'm thinking, don't ye, lass?"

"Of course not. That's impossible."

"Is it, now?"

Her eyes narrowed, then softened as he focused on a tender thought and ran his fingertip along her jaw. Her lips parted, as if she sensed his sudden desire to kiss her.

With great restraint, he brushed his lips over her forehead. "'Tis a remarkable gift. One ye should be most careful with."

"I usually am, but you needed my help and wouldn't ask me for it. You're a stubborn man, Kieran MacAuley."

"Aye." After stepping into his boots, he bowed stiffly and offered her his arm. "Many a woman has faulted me for it in the past."

She laughed. "I think for one such as you, it must be a virtue."

"One such as me?" he asked as he opened the door for her.

"A man needs many weapons for the battles he fights. Swords and dirks serve their purposes, but he needs determination as well, does he not?"

"True enough."

They made their way to an oak branch that had

fallen nearby. He looked back at the little house and saw it was nestled in the roots of a massive willow, with a small pool on the far side of the sod walls. 'Twas like a snug rabbit's warren, but to his mind she didn't belong there.

"Brynna, might I ask you a question?"

"Of course."

"Why do ye stay here all alone?"

"Where else would I go?" she asked with a puzzled frown.

"To one of the settlements. Any man would be proud to have you."

She rose from her place beside him and moved a few steps away. "I've little use for men," she said, running her hand over the knobby bark of a pine.

Intrigued by the remark, Kieran joined her. "Is that so? Perhaps you've just not come across the right one."

"Perhaps."

Her smile washed over him like sunshine, and he cradled her cheek in his hand. Her skin felt whisper soft to the roughened pad of his thumb, evoking the image of her lying in his bed, the petals of dozens of roses sprinkled over her body.

Just the thought of it could bring a man back from the dead. Then again, she'd already done that once.

Caressing her cheek, he gave her a lazy grin. "If I kissed ye, would ye scream?"

"I might."

He'd come to adore this woman with the emerald fire in her eyes. His hand drifted down to rest lightly at her waist, and he drew her to him, allowing her time to pull away. As he'd guessed, she didn't retreat, instead tipping her face up in unspoken invitation.

He meant to kiss her gently and release her, but when their lips met, mindless heat flooded every part of him. She draped her wrists about his neck, and he gathered her closer. Her lips parted beneath his, and as his tongue delved into the sweet warmth, she let out a heady sigh.

His kisses wandered down her slender neck to the racing beat in her throat. The scent of wildflowers greeted him, unleashing memories of the night he'd thought would be his last. The night a fearless lass stepped from the shadows and gave him a reason to keep fighting.

When he tried to pull away, she brought his mouth back to hers for another searing kiss. Passion flowed from her like quicksilver, surrounding him in an undeniable current. Tentatively, he ran a finger along the upper curve of her breasts, delighted when she pressed herself into his hand.

Suddenly, she jerked back. "Someone's coming."

Tugging at his hand, she led him away from her house. The forest engulfed them, and she hastened to the foot of a gigantic pine. "Can you climb?"

"Aye."

First, he boosted her into the lower boughs, then watched her scramble a bit higher. Even from beneath the tree, she'd have been invisible if he hadn't known she was there. Climbing one-handed was difficult, but in a few moments he settled on the branch below her, trying to quiet his breathing so he'd not alert the intruders to their hiding place.

Then he heard it: horses. Keen as his ears were, he'd not heard them until now, and instinct told him Brynna hadn't heard them, either. Somehow, she'd sensed their approach and sprinted for cover like a rabbit fleeing a hawk. She sat with her arms locked about her bent legs, her forehead resting on her knees. She looked even smaller than usual that way, waiting for whatever threatened her to go on its way.

How many times had she done this? Lovely as a forest sprite, defenseless as a bairn, she presented an irresistible temptation to any male over ten and two. When the hoofbeats drew closer and halted nearby, he knew the riders had come across the sod house. After a few short raps on the door, he heard the creak of leather hinges. He gave thanks that he wore his trews and boots. They'd have betrayed his presence, putting Brynna in grave danger.

One of the men gave a disgusted snort. "She canna possibly live here. 'Tis little more than a hole in the ground."

"The old man seemed quite certain we'd find her here," his companion argued in a confused brogue.

"I pray he's wrong. Her father would be furious."

"No doubt he's waiting at the gates for us." The other one sighed. "We'd best report back."

The door closed behind them, followed by the sound of hooves rustling through the dry leaves. The men passed beside the tree, then picked up the path that led east.

After several moments of silence, Brynna lifted her head. "They're gone."

"Why does your father have men searching for you?"

She'd begun to climb down and appeared not to hear his question, but Kieran knew better. Once they were on the ground, he grasped her arm before she could move away. "Brynna, tell me: Why are ye hiding from your father?"

" 'Tis safer that way."

"What sort of man threatens his own daughter?"

Biting her lower lip, she frantically searched for a response that would satisfy him and protect her, as well.

"Don't." He rubbed her chin with his thumb. " 'Tis enough to know you're in danger, with no one to defend you."

Much more did she see in his eyes, and she pulled away from the perilous edge of his emotions. "We should go back now. I want to make certain our climb didn't rend your stitches."

"Brynna—"

She fled before he could say anything more.

While she sliced a loaf of fresh bread, the ringing sound of an ax reached her through the open door. Brynna glanced up to find Kieran with her hatchet in his left hand, pounding through a log with one swing. He tossed the pieces onto the growing pile to his right and reached for a longer limb. This he quartered before splitting the remaining pieces into kindling.

Even as she admired his expertise, she sobered at the unpleasant thought that he must have gained it wielding a battleax. She poured water into two wooden cups, picked up the bread and went outside. Kieran angled the hatchet into an uncut log and wiped a cloth over his face.

" 'Tis glad I am to see ye." He grinned as he strolled to join her. "The smell of your baking has my stomach growling."

She sat on a stump and handed him one of the cups. "I thought you might be thirsty, as well."

"Parched." He drained the cup in two long swallows. When she offered him the other, he chuckled. "How is it ye know what I need before I do myself?"

"Chopping wood is hard work."

"Aye, and well ye know that. Too well, I think," he added with a disapproving frown.

" 'Tis the price of my freedom."

With dark eyes unreadable even in the bright sunlight, he studied her for an endless moment.

"I canna leave ye here, lass. Come with me to Dunsmere."

When she gaped at him, he gave her a boyish grin. "I think you'd like it there. The MacAuley would welcome such a skilled healer, and the way ye handle me, my mother would adore you."

"She'd not object to you bringing a guest she's never met?"

"Brynna, I've been gone a fortnight, and none of the others have returned. She must think I'm dead. I could bring the Devil himself with me and she'd not care in the least."

"You know nothing about me."

He took her hand, cradling it gently in his own. "I know you're generous and kind, that ye care for those in need. Beyond that, you're lovely and sweet, and clever enough to outsmart any man I know. Buried here, you're missing so much. Let me show you what's beyond the forest."

She longed to accept what he offered her, escape her solitary life and live among people again. He seemed confident his clan would accept her—welcome her, in fact. Once again, she'd be warm and safe.

And she'd be with Kieran.

"If I went with you, what would you show me?"

In answer, he rested her hand on his chest, covering it with his own. Under her fingers, she felt the beat of his heart, the enduring force of a man who fought not only with his body but with his soul.

The way he'd love the woman who matched him.

Startled by the unexpected glimpse of his deepest desire, she tried to pull her hand away. He held it fast, smiling as he raised it to his lips. No woman could repel such a tender gesture.

"Come home with me, Brynna. I swear you'll not regret it."

Never had she wanted anything as much, and the intensity of it frightened her. In self-defense, she pushed herself to her feet. "If this is how you treat your women, I see why you've not married."

His grin vanished, and shadows clouded his features. "In truth, it's been my choice not to marry. It dismays my mother to no end."

"I can well understand that. A man of your age in such a high position should be wed and a father many times over."

"A warrior has no right to claim a wife, only to

leave her at home while he fights battles that never end." His voice broke, and he swallowed hard. "Children deserve a father, not a ghost the bards spin their legends around."

"And if the battles were to end?"

"They won't."

Grim certainty girded his words, and her heart ached for him. Before she could say anything more, he rose from the log and strode into the woods.

The evening she removed the stitches from his right arm, he behaved as if she'd granted his fondest wish. He jumped up from the chair and began testing his range of movement.

"Go gently, Kieran. Fresh scars tear easily."

"I'll be cautious," he assured her as he flexed his hand. "Ye do fine work, Brynna. How can I ever repay your generous care of me?"

She handed him the tunic she'd begged from Grady and tucked the sharp dirk away in her healing chest. "That's not necessary."

"Brynna, look at me." When she did, he smiled. "Why is it other women flutter when I compliment them, but you act as if I've insulted you?"

"I'm not accustomed to hearing praise, I suppose."

"What is it ye do hear?" he asked as he pulled the *léine* over his head. Grady was far broader than he, but once he fastened his studded belt at his waist, Brynna decided it fit him well enough.

Hesitant to complain, she didn't respond. When he repeated his question, she sighed in resignation. "How unusual I am."

"Many times have I heard that myself." Tapping the star that marked him, he grinned. "No doubt you've noticed this."

"Maire's kiss."

"So my mother tells me. Beyond that, I'm left-handed. And since my boyhood I've had a talent for getting out of trouble."

" 'Tis fortunate, since you also have a talent for getting *into* trouble."

"True enough." He turned a sober gaze on her, though his eyes sparkled with humor. "What I'm needing is someone to look after me."

"You must be surrounded by women anxious for such a task."

"Aye, but I've no taste for fawning and clinging." Drawing her into his arms, he gave her a long kiss. "I've a taste for bread and honey, with a bit of raspberry tea."

"Have you, now?"

"I could beg ye to go with me, if ye like."

She laughed. "You wouldn't know how." As he nuzzled into the curve of her shoulder, she realized he was gently demanding a decision of her. "You're leaving."

He drew back his head and grazed her cheek with his knuckle. "On the morrow. I'm well enough to travel, and my clan must know their chieftain is alive. Please say you'll come with me."

"But my father—"

"Hang your father! I'll keep ye safe, Brynna, I swear it." When she hesitated, he grinned at her. "If ye don't agree to come, I'll have no choice but to toss ye on my shoulder and carry ye every step of the way."

"I should like to see you try," she retorted with a toss of her head. " 'Tis several leagues to Dunsmere."

Gripping her thighs, he lifted her just as he'd threatened, laughing while she kicked and squirmed. "Do ye cede?"

"No, I do *not* cede." Struggling harder, she summoned her mother's imperious tone. "Unhand me at once."

"I rather like my hands as they are," he taunted, swatting her lightly.

"Kieran, let me down."

"Will ye walk to Dunsmere, or shall I carry you?"

Sighing, she rolled her eyes. "I suppose I could consider walking."

"Such an amiable lass y'are," he crowed as he lowered her to the floor.

She muttered a nasty curse under her breath, and he canted his head with a maddening grin. "What was that?"

"Nothing."

Kieran returned from his walk with an armload of wood only to find the little house empty. A companionable fire crackled on the hearth, but Brynna was nowhere in sight. 'Twas not the first evening she'd gone off on her own, but this night he set about discovering where she could be. It wasn't safe wandering in the forest after dark.

While his eyes grew accustomed to the dim surroundings, his ears caught the sound of the voice that had comforted him during the darkest time he'd ever known. Following the lilting melody of a romantic folk song, he found his way through the underbrush to the bank encircling the little pool beyond Brynna's hut.

And there he stopped.

Wisps of fog rose from the water, disappearing in the cool air as if they'd never existed. He'd seen such heated springs, but none of them had held the vision before him.

Free of the ugly russet gown, she was breathtaking. Moonlight caressed the graceful lines of her body while she swam. Unfettered, her hair trailed behind her in glorious waves. She paused in her play, resumed the song as she stood to smooth water from her face. Droplets sluiced along her throat and between her breasts, flowing down her back in a sensuous waterfall.

Kieran envied the water's intimate contact with her skin. He considered joining her, discarding the notion when his entire body tensed like a panther ready to attack.

He couldn't recall ever wanting a lass so desperately. Lovers came and went, one as pleasing as the next. But Brynna was the sort of woman a man fought for, claiming her with his heart as well as his body so no other man would even consider touching her.

Their short time together had given him a glimpse of something he'd never dared hope for—a wife by his side, bonny wee ones playing at his feet. In the endless expanse of the forest, he'd been felled in the very place where she might find him.

Though his educated mind rejected the concept of fate, his Celtic soul embraced it without question. Some things couldn't be explained by reason but must be taken on faith. Once she'd settled in Dunsmere, he'd have time to unravel the mystery of her. Perhaps then he'd understand why he felt so drawn to a woman he scarcely knew.

Before he could follow his impulse and slip into the inviting water, he went back the way he'd come, leaving her untouched in the moonlight.

Brynna watched him go. She'd sensed his concern for her, heard his quiet footsteps on the path that led to the little pool. Ignoring his approach, she continued as she'd been, heart fluttering at the thought that he might decide 'twas a pleasant evening for a swim.

But he hadn't.

Odd behavior for a man, she mused, as she climbed from the water and dried herself with the woolen throw she'd brought. Pulling on her shift, she wrapped the throw about herself and hastened back to the warmth of her burrow.

She opened the door to find him slouched in her lone chair, staring into the fire. Long legs stretched out before him, he sat with chin in hand, his gold chieftain's ring reflecting the flickering light.

Thinking him lost in thought, she quietly closed the door behind her. Then his dark eyes swung to her with a look so intense, it nearly knocked her backward.

"Good eve to you, Kieran," she ventured.

"And to you. What were ye doing out there?"

"Swimming," she retorted in the sassy tone his nieces used to vex him.

"I saw that. I meant, what were ye doing out there alone?"

" 'Tis safe enough. Most are afraid to go into the forest at night."

Frowning, he sat up in the chair. "Wolves? Panthers?"

"I'd hear them if they were about."

"I surprised you easily enough."

"Nay." She laughed, wringing water from her hair. "I ignored you."

"Why would ye be doing such a thing?"

Over her shoulder, she gave him a winsome smile. "I hoped once you saw me, you'd come for a swim."

"Did ye, now?"

Kieran shed his brooding in favor of a smile. 'Twas pointless to deny it. As fascinating as she was beautiful, Brynna had enchanted him the moment he first saw her.

Stepping up behind her, he wrapped his arms about her waist and dropped a kiss on her bare shoulder. "Now I have you. The only question, my lovely water nymph, is what shall I do with you?"

With a silvery laugh, she spun to face him. "I shall grant you one wish," she told him, following the ancient faery story. "What do you want?"

Kieran's grin faded, and flames danced in his dark eyes. Fire shot the entire length of her body and back again, stealing her breath along the way. His gaze heated dangerously, and he cupped the nape of her neck to bring her face to his.

Once he took her mouth, he refused to surrender it, one moment crushing, the next caressing. Powerfully male, he engulfed her, blocking out any thought, any sensation but the feel of his hands, the drugging effect of his kisses.

Toying with her tongue, he growled deep in his throat as his hands molded her body through the damp shift. His lips wandered along her throat, lowered to trace the swell of her breasts with whisper-soft kisses. He spanned her waist with his hands, skimmed over her hips and pulled her to him.

"God help me, lass. There's something about you that drives me mad."

Curious, she dangled her wrists over his well-muscled shoulders. "Something about me?"

"*Everything* about you."

His admiring gaze warmed her from the top of her head to her toes; then he set her away and took a throw from the bed. After looping it about her shoulders, he snugged it under her chin and kissed the tip of her nose. "You'd do well to get some rest. We've a great deal of walking to do in the morn."

"I've told you I won't go to Dunsmere with you," she reminded him curtly.

"And I've told ye I won't leave ye here." He flashed her a devilish grin. "But I'm a reasonable man. If you've another suggestion, I'll gladly listen."

Of course she didn't, and his grin only widened. "I thought as much. This night, I'll take the hearth."

"But your shoulder—"

"Is well mended, thanks to your fine care." Chuckling, he spun her about and gave her a gentle shove. "Off to bed, now. I set a quick pace, and I'll expect ye to keep up."

Brynna sat in her bed, staring into the darkness while her mind wrestled with her heart. She yearned for all the things Kieran offered her: a home, people who would embrace her, a man who would treasure her the rest of her days. Though he'd not voiced his feelings, she'd seen his growing affection for her in his eyes, glimmering like stars in a clear night sky.

She couldn't bear to see it give way to hatred, as it surely would when he learned the truth about her. To a man who'd fought and bled for Ireland, treason was the highest crime of all.

The decision made, she put her few belongings into a shoulder pack. Reaching beneath her mattress, she withdrew Kieran's sword and left it atop the bedcovers where he'd be certain to find it. Finally, she settled on her knees beside him and touched his forehead to ensure he'd not awaken anytime soon.

Framing his wondrous face in her hands, she whispered, "I love you, Kieran MacAuley."

Even as she lowered her mouth to his, tears streamed down her face. After a few moments she stood and shouldered her pack. Standing in the doorway, she took a long look back at Kieran, drinking in the sight of him to lock it forever in her memory.

Then she left, closing the door behind her.

Chapter Four

Kieran sat up, yawning as he rubbed the sleep from his eyes. A glance around showed walls, a few crude pieces of furniture and no sign of anyone but him.

"Hello?"

His voice echoed back to him, and he stood to peer out one of the tiny windows flanking the door. A modest pile of wood sat just outside the hut, alongside a pile of logs ready for splitting. As he looked over the room again, he noticed the small bed tucked beside the fireplace.

On top of it lay his sword.

Someone lived here, surely enough, and they no doubt knew who he was. That knowledge should have troubled him greatly, but for some reason it didn't. He folded his arms to consider the situation more carefully and felt the stretch of newly mended flesh near his right shoulder. He pulled aside the neck of the large tunic to find a neat line of stitch marks that reached from his shoulder to his waist.

What the devil was going on?

He focused every one of his senses but detected no threat, seen or otherwise. How was that possible? In a strange place, under a stranger's care, he felt no danger whatsoever.

Searching his memory, he discovered that he recalled nothing after his last message to his mother. He should be dead, like the others. So why wasn't he?

Satisfied that he was safe enough, he unsheathed his sword and cracked open the door. Dense forest surrounded the little soddy, which was nestled in the roots of an enormous willow tree. Beyond it was a small spring, and he heard the myriad sounds of birds and the occasional yip of a fox.

"Is anyone here?"

Again, no response. He stepped through the door and began a thorough search of the area just outside the clearing. A marten hissed at him for coming too close to her nest, but other than that, he saw nothing.

He rested the flat of his blade over his shoulder while he considered what to do next. It seemed whoever had helped him was gone, and he had no idea how to find them. Meantime, his kinsmen must think they'd lost their chieftain. Though he worried about his mysterious host, his first responsibility was to his clan.

By way of thanks, he chopped and stacked the last of the wood before heading for home.

"Kieran?"

An enormous man sprinted up the hill and grasped his shoulders. Squinting into his face, Devlin beamed like a love-struck fool. "Saints be praised, it *is* you!"

"Aye, 'tis me." Wincing, he rubbed his right shoulder. "Have a care, Dev."

"We thought ye were dead," his cousin went on, fairly dancing on his giant feet. "Your mother will be right glad to see you."

"I'm hoping she'll thrash me *after* I've eaten."

They both laughed heartily and started walking toward the village. But something tugged at Kieran's mind, and he stopped. Turning back, he skimmed the dense trees, though he had no idea what he might be searching for.

"You see something?" Dev asked him.

There was a flutter of movement, but the brush quickly stilled: some animal chasing after a meal.

"Nay." Yet a lingering uneasiness followed him down the hill to the stronghold of Clan MacAuley.

More fortress than castle, the keep had an outer bailey ringed by imposing walls of rust-colored granite. Guards patrolled the raised wall walk, and a massive iron portcullis guarded the main entry inside the stout barbican.

In times of peril, which occurred more often of late, the entire clan could be accommodated inside. The walls of MacAuley keep had never been breached and by virtue of the deep-water lough on whose banks it had been built, no enemy had ever succeeded in taking it by siege.

Quite simply, it was unassailable, and Kieran's chest swelled with pride at what his long-ago ancestor had accomplished. Thoughts of Morgan prompted him to twist the ring he wore with such great honor.

As he strolled along the main thoroughfare with Dev, people stopped their work to gawk. A woman dropped her washing, and the metalsmith howled as he bashed his thumb with a hammer. One by one, several more found their tongues to welcome him home, then fell in step as he and Dev strolled into the great hall.

His mother was occupied with some matter or another and didn't acknowledge the interruption. "I've told you many a time, Blaine, you must keep your father's sheep away from Daniel's. He has no wish for his ewes to be bearing the wrong sort of lambs."

The poor lad twisted his cap in his hands. "I know it. And I try, really I do. But the Herding Boys keep playing tricks on me."

Aileen's amber eyes crinkled a bit at the reference to the mischievous *sídhe* folk who made a sport of bedeviling unwary shepherds. Having raised six headstrong sons of her own, she had a soft spot for their troubles. "Be that as it may, you must devise a way to control your sheep. Another infraction and I will instruct your father to find someone else to tend his flock."

Her eyes went to the man standing behind Blaine, and he nodded. " 'Tis fair enough. I told him as much myself."

With a hand on his son's shoulder, Conor left the dais and limped toward the side door. When he spied Kieran, his eyes shot open and his mouth quickly followed. Kieran laid a finger over his lips and winked at him.

"Next!" Aileen called out, eyes fixed on the notes she was writing. Careful records were kept of clan disputes and the resolutions meted out. Many problems came up time and again, and the history of the manor court proved invaluable.

Kieran strode toward the dais and went to his knee, head deeply bowed to conceal his face and the wide grin he wore.

"What complaint have you this day?"

" 'Tis hungry I am." Behind him, he heard Dev's barely suppressed laughter.

"Silence. Raise your head and state your name for me, lad," she added in a sympathetic tone.

He did as she bade, and watched her indulgent expression blossom into a disbelieving smile.

"Kieran?"

She leapt to her feet, and the high-backed chair clattered from its perch. The inkwell toppled and splattered her gown, ignored as she fled the dais to wrap her arms about him.

"Oh, my boy, my boy," she crooned, kissing one cheek and then the other. Her eyes never left his face, as though starved for the sight of him. "How can this be? You've been gone so long, I gave up hoping. I buried you."

"I suppose you'll have to unbury me."

Glaring, she smacked the side of his head. He laughed and whirled her about in a hug before setting her back on her feet. "I came home for my lashing, but I'm rather hoping you'll feed me first."

Her hand went to the scar on his neck, and she pushed aside the ill-fitting tunic with a gasp of dismay. "What did they do to you?"

For her sake, he forced a careless grin and shrugged. "Not as much as they'd like, to be sure."

Dev came forward to drape an arm about his shoulders. "Come now, Aunt Aileen. The man's about to expire. You can interrogate him later, can ye not?"

"There will be more than me to deal with. The council will want to speak with you as well."

He wanted nothing more than a quick meal and a long bath. At least his own clothes and a shave would help steel him for the inquisition he surely faced. Though people were elated to see him home, he shared their grief for those who'd not returned. In the past, he'd have vaulted onto a table and rallied them with inspiring words, urging them to fight out of respect for those who were gone.

But for some reason his heart had grown weary of battles. He yearned to stay in the valley and— what? Shaking off the unsettling feeling, he leaned in to kiss his mother's tear-dampened cheek.

"Give me an hour, Mother. I'll be ready."

Kieran sank into a bath of steaming water scented with one of Aileen's soothing mixtures. He looked about himself with the pang of remorse he always felt when he allowed himself to contemplate the richly appointed chambers. Though he'd been chieftain for nigh on two years, he still considered these rooms his father's domain.

Panels of age-darkened oak reflected the firelight, and his mother's fine tapestries lined the walls. Books filled the tall shelves, complemented by things his parents had collected during a lifetime together. Small statues, sketches, Celtic crosses and jeweled rosaries. Carved boxes filled with all manner of treasures Magnus had discovered in his travels from Dublin to Connacht and home again.

None of the trinkets belonged to Kieran. He'd kept everything just as it had been when his father paced the wide plank floors and took his rest in the massive tester bed. His mother had offered many times to decorate the chambers anew, yet Kieran couldn't bear to put away the past and replace it with the present.

This day, however, the surroundings that had always conveyed stability and tradition irked him. He envisioned hues of summertime—blue, lavender, rose and green. Flowers on the mantel instead of swords, books of poetry rather than military strategy on the shelves. Children's primers stacked on the low tables now dominated by battle maps.

On the bed, a linen coverlet strewn with rose petals.

Where the devil had that image come from?

Frowning at his foolishness, he soaped a cloth and began scrubbing. Not long ago, the large tub had been filled to the brim with wine to celebrate the marriage of his brother Adam. A year later, Maureen had laid him to rest beside his father and brothers.

So many had they buried, too many for even Kieran's agile memory to recall. That thought led to others, and he began pondering the events clearly missing from his mind.

How in God's name had he survived the raid? One moment he lay on the verge of death, the next he was home. He fingered the healing scars on his chest, closed his eyes to search for some hint of who might have helped him. Nothing did he see, but into his heart drifted a melancholy whisper.

I love you, Kieran MacAuley.

He strained for more, but nothing came. Frustrated beyond measure, he pounded the side of the tub with his fist and dropped his head into his hands.

"Remember," he commanded himself, but his traitorous mind refused to comply. At a quiet knock, he snarled, "What?"

His mother opened the door. "I heard banging and thought you might need help."

Kieran swallowed a vile curse and summoned a bit of patience. "I'm fine, but thank you all the same."

She entered his chamber and closed the door behind her. "Will you answer a question for me?"

"Of course."

Her eyes went to the fresh scars that crossed his chest. " 'Twould seem you were in the care of a skilled healer."

"Aye."

"Might I ask who she was?"

"Ask all ye like, but I canna tell you."

"Indeed, you can," she chided him. "I don't wish to bandy her name about the valley, only to thank her."

"I meant that I don't know who helped me."

She gave him a puzzled look. "I don't understand."

"Neither do I." He sank against the back of the tub with a heavy sigh. "The council is waiting?"

"Everyone is waiting. I had the tables removed from the hall, and still a cat could scarce sneak through."

He dredged up a halfhearted chuckle. "Tell them I'm wet but on my way."

Aileen nodded and left him to dress. At the end of the corridor, she paused before a narrow window that looked out on the placid waters of Lough Dunsmere. A bow-shaped moon shone in the twilit sky as the sun dipped below the far shore. Somewhere beyond the hills lived a woman who had rescued her last remaining son and sent him home to those who loved and needed him.

"I don't know who you are, dear lady," Aileen whispered to the early stars, "but I thank you with all my heart."

Brynna's ankle twisted, and she went down hard on the rocky path. Though the stones hid her footprints, they made for tough walking, and she'd fallen twice already. Thank God she had no looking glass, she groused as she struggled to her feet. What with the mud and the brambles tearing at her skin, she had no desire to see her reflection.

The gentle tap at the back of her mind grew more insistent, and she tried to hasten her limping stride. "I know, I know. They're getting closer. I'm going as fast as I can."

How could she possibly outrun them? If they

were her father's men, they'd not harm her, only return her to him and accept his gold. But if they were English . . .

She banished the thought, as it served no purpose. The men tracking her were too far off for her to discern their intent, and she simply couldn't allow them to get any closer. Exhausted, she ignored her throbbing ankle as best she could, but she wouldn't be able to evade them much longer.

A branch grabbed at her hand, and she turned to free herself from the gnarled tree. While she dabbed at the bleeding scratch on her palm, she noticed the faint outline of rocks buried within the undergrowth.

Biting back an elated shout, she slipped into the tiny cave, careful not to disturb the thick vines that covered it. Inside 'twas murky gray, as very little sunlight penetrated the broad leaves. But soft moss covered the floor, and before long the heat of her body warmed the space.

Wrapping her cloak more tightly about her, she pillowed her head on her pack and fell asleep.

Kieran paused at the bottom of the stairwell, drinking in the sensations of home. Warmed by two huge fireplaces and several score of his kinsmen, the great hall reverberated with many conversations, punctuated here and there by laughter and good-natured debate. The scent of spiced apples and mulled wine reached him, and he closed his eyes to savor them.

Peaceful moments such as this came too seldom to let them slip by unappreciated.

Much as he did before a battle, he took a deep breath and entered the hall with a measured stride. As he'd expected, the merriment dwindled to near silence, hundreds of eyes following him as he mounted the dais that held the clan council. But he'd not sit with the elders, adding his opinion to theirs.

This night, he would stand before his kinsmen while they judged their chieftain, decided if he was still fit to lead them. He'd left Dunsmere with forty-nine seasoned warriors and returned with nothing but his sword and the clothes on his back.

Eamon, the eldest member of the council, glanced to his left, then his right, before casting a fatherly smile on Kieran. "First and foremost, I wish to express the joy we all feel to see you safely home. You were greatly missed during your absence."

"Many thanks." He turned to look over the hushed assembly. "I missed all of you, as well."

"If you would," Eamon continued, "tell us what happened in the time you were gone."

Kieran relayed the story of the combined raid, omitting the most horrific details out of respect for the women and children. Husbands, fathers and sons were missing from almost every hearth, leaving behind misery no woman should ever face.

Amalie, heavy with his cousin Peter's child, called out, "Ask him how he survived when so many died!"

The crowd broke into restless muttering, some chastising her for her insolence, others adding their opinions to hers. Kieran searched his mind for a response that would satisfy them, but all he had was the truth.

Holding his head high, very clearly he said, "I don't know."

The muttering intensified, and Eamon called for quiet. "Kieran, you must remember something."

Grimacing, he shook his head. "We were fighting, and I remember going down. The next memory I have is of Dev in the forest near here."

"You're lying." Tears streaming down her face, Amalie pointed an accusing finger at him. "You used Peter and the others as a shield to escape the English, then hid so you could return as a hero."

Aileen took Amalie into her arms, attempting to comfort her as the hall erupted into chaos. Kieran's heart seized in his chest. How could she think such a thing? He loved Peter, loved them all as if they were his own brothers. He'd wanted to die with them, but some trick of fate had spared him to come home. To this?

Blood boiling with pent-up frustration, he began unfastening the metal points closing his leather jerkin. When he tossed it onto the dais, the crowd gradually quieted, curious gazes fixed on him. He pulled his *léine* over his head and dropped it, as well.

Then he held out his arms, grimly pleased by the gasps he heard. He spun about so they might see the healing slashes on his back and shoulders.

Raking his kinsmen with a disdainful glare, Kieran left his clothes where they'd fallen and stalked from the hall.

"Thank you, Father," Aileen repeated, kneeling before the crucifix that reigned over the altar in the chapel. "For hearing my prayers and bringing Kieran home, thank you."

Tears welled in her eyes as she looked heavenward, knowing Magnus shared her gratitude for their son's safe return. "But I swear to you, husband, if he ever leaves like that again, I'll throttle him myself."

In her mind, she heard a deep rumble of laughter, and she smiled. "Every day, I see more of you in him. The way he handled the doubters this evening must have made you proud."

A shuffling at the door halted her conversation, and Aileen rose, crossing herself as she genuflected before the altar. 'Twas no secret she often conversed with Magnus, but she kept their discussions to herself.

"Good evening, Aileen." Maureen greeted her with a warm hug. "I'm here to give thanks, as well."

"A miracle, to be sure."

Aileen regarded her daughter-in-law cautiously. A fetching lass with auburn hair and blue eyes, her innocent features masked a calculating heart. When Adam died, his brother assumed the responsibility of either finding her a suitable husband or personally ensuring she bore more children. Though Kieran adored Maureen, he exhibited no interest in either wedding or bedding her, a fact that kept the clan gossips well entertained.

"He managed the council deftly, as always," Maureen went on proudly, as if the accomplishment were her own. "I was thinking to visit him this evening and tell him so."

"He's tired from his journey. Leave him be."

"Where did he travel from, do you know?"

Weary of questions she couldn't answer, Aileen shook her head. "I've no idea. If you'll excuse me, I must tend to something before I retire."

"Of course." Maureen embraced her again. "Sleep well."

Walking to the altar, she knelt and bowed her head as the soft phrases of a simple prayer echoed through the small church. Aileen exited the chapel and glanced about the bailey. One of the guards on the wall walk raised a hand to her, then held a finger to his lips. She nodded her thanks and retrieved her bag from behind a water trough before slipping through the postern gate.

She didn't have far to go, but once away from the keep, the darkness pressed down on her with palpable force. Clouds shifted across the new moon, hiding and then revealing it as she hurried along the path she'd trod as a girl, infatuated with the ruddy charm of Magnus MacAuley. The glen where they'd first met was the most enchanted place she knew, and 'twas there that she lowered her pack to the ground and opened it.

She poured fresh milk from a skin into a lovely porcelain cup. On her own pewter trencher she sliced bread still warm from the oven, then drizzled honey over it. As the final touch, she poured wine into one of the crystal goblets Magnus had brought her from Dublin. Her tasks complete, she stood and held her arms wide to embrace the Celtic spirits that inhabited this very special patch of ground.

"Queen Maire, I hope you will accept this humble meal in thanks for your good care of my son, and for guiding him home to those who love him. Should you ever require anything of me, you need only ask, and I shall repay my debt to you."

A quiet breeze sighed through the pine boughs overhead, grazing her cheek with a soft touch. Satisfied, she quit the clearing and left Maire to her repast.

Sitting outside the little cave, Brynna stared through the canopy of trees at a flawless night sky. Her rest had revived both her body and spirit, and she chewed some of the dried meat she'd brought in her pack. On the morrow, she'd search out some early berries, perhaps even find a few of the sweet roots that grew hereabouts. If she kept to the forest and heeded her intuition, she'd be safe enough.

The sliver of a new moon hung just above the horizon. The symbol of promise and new beginnings, she mused with a smile. It pleased her to know Kieran would have both.

She only wished she could have been the one to live out that life with him.

Kieran sat on the sill of his open window, the breeze ruffling his hair as he stared out over the valley. Lights from scattered houses blinked like grounded stars, and the drowsy bleating of sheep reached him on the cool night air. He imagined children saying their prayers, hearing a story before settling under the bedcovers, mothers and fathers bidding them good rest before retiring to their own beds.

Sweet, simple, peaceful. How he envied them.

The large wine goblet he'd filled and refilled several times dangled empty from his fingers, but he made no move to fill it again. Even the dulling effect of aged claret was powerless in the face of what plagued him. A seemingly endless stream of people had found their way to his chambers, entreating his forbearance, begging forgiveness for those who'd been harsh with him.

In truth, he bore them no animosity. They'd lost so much, and he'd returned with naught but a few scars. Nay, 'twas not his kinsmen who vexed him so. 'Twas the voice that seemed caught in his memory like a moth in a web.

I love you, Kieran MacAuley.

Who could have said such a thing to him? And why had he forgotten her?

He rubbed a hand over the relentless ache in his chest, but no amount of attention would ease the strained muscle.

Setting his goblet on the sill, he leaned his head back to consider the stars. Perhaps the voice that haunted him belonged to a woman who also gazed up at the night sky, wondering what had become of him.

"I'm safe now. I pray you are, as well."

A whisper of movement brushed his lips and was gone. As the fledgling moon rose higher, Kieran waited for another touch from her.

But it never came.

Following the sweet melody of a folk song, Kieran paused at a clearing in the trees. Mist hung over a small pool, and he smiled at the sight of a water sprite at play.

Over her shoulder, she looked at him, rosy lips curving with an irresistible invitation.

Without a single thought, Kieran shed his clothes and slipped into the water. After a playful splash, she disappeared beneath the surface, and he chased after her. The length of his strokes surpassed hers, but she was much quicker than he, darting about like a minnow.

Standing motionless in the center, he caught her when she surfaced for air. She laughed merrily, and he joined her. The easy, lighthearted sound of his own laughter startled him, but he had no wish to stop.

He took her mouth in a hungry kiss she returned a hundredfold. She tasted of raspberries and honey, and he sighed as her hands moved over the muscles of his shoulders, down his chest to rest on his waist. Beneath the water, her fingers stroked him as she rolled her hips in a wordless request.

Kieran lifted her, groaning as she settled over him and wrapped her legs around his waist. He teased the budding tip of her warm, wet breast with his tongue. A woman's moan of pleasure met his efforts, and she began riding him, rising and falling as the steaming water undulated about them in sensuous ripples.

Tight as a fist, her body nearly strangled him within its liquid depths. When she tensed, he took her scream into his mouth and plunged to the center of her, shuddering with the force of his release.

Never had a woman evoked such a powerful response from him. Deep in his soul, he knew she was the one made for him. Fiery and passionate, she gave as she took, making him want something he'd never contemplated before.

He wanted to give her everything.

Without warning, she vanished from his arms. His eyes flew open, and he searched the recesses of his bedchamber for some sign of her, berating himself as he eased back into the pillows. The lass hadn't spoken a word to him, hadn't offered her name. Perhaps she didn't even exist, but was a pathetic attempt by his imagination to fill his empty bed.

Briefly, he considered going belowstairs to hunt up a willing maid. But even as he knew in his heart the enchanting nymph was real, he knew no quick tumble with another woman would come close to matching what he'd felt with her. Having known it, he'd never again settle for anything else.

"Och, lass," he whispered into the darkness, "who are ye?"

CHAPTER FIVE

Aileen approached the head table, unable to believe her eyes. At her place sat the pewter and crystal ware she'd left in the faery circle the previous night. But now they were filled with wildflowers that couldn't possibly be growing anywhere nearby. Their fragrance carried across the wide table, evoking images of summertime, although outside the windows a late spring frost dusted the trees.

"An odd thing, to be sure," Maureen commented as she appeared with a large pot of porridge. "Where would anyone find such flowers this time of year?"

"I've no idea," Aileen stammered as she sat down. She considered asking Maureen to take them away, then thought better of it. Clearly, Maire had enjoyed her meal and wished to give her something in return. Faery folk could be quite unpredictable, and she'd no wish to insult the queen's generosity.

"Good morn to you, Kieran," Maureen greeted him as he made his way to the carved oak armchair reserved for the chieftain.

"And to you."

"Are you hungry?" she asked.

"Nay." He slumped into his chair. He felt a twinge of remorse at her disappointed expression, but he was in no mood to soothe her easily ruffled feathers. After she left for the kitchens, he noticed the array of flowers and turned to Aileen with a chuckle. "Is there something ye wish to tell me, Mother?"

"They were here when I arrived."

Despite the black cloud his restless night had left over him, he grinned. "Have ye been conversing with the *sídhe* again?"

She glanced about, then leaned closer. "After I left the chapel, I took some sweets to Maire in thanks for returning you home."

" 'Twould seem she appreciated the gesture." When he stopped to think how she'd accomplished her errand, his fragile good humor vanished. "Ye left the keep after dark?"

"Don't you be starting with me. I'll go where I've a mind to, when I wish it."

"You're a tempting target, and the forest is teeming with spies. I'll not have ye wandering about for the English to get hold of. Promise me ye won't do it again."

"Kieran—"

"Promise me!" He pounded his fist on the table. "There's no quicker way to me than through you, and the English know it. Ye shouldn't take such risks, not for anything."

Her eyes studied him, and he fought the urge to squirm. How was it she could still make him feel like a lad of ten?

" 'Tis not only to me that you speak, is it? You're worried about her."

Leaning back in his chair, he massaged the blinding ache between his eyes. "Who?"

"The one who helped you."

He bolted from his chair and began pacing. "She saved my life and I left her behind. How could I have done such a thing?"

"Your chest pains you?" she asked, concern filling her eyes.

Kieran dropped his hand to his side with a defeated sigh. "Aye, all the time." He waited until the serving girls had scurried off before adding, "And I hear a voice, the most beautiful laughter. Mother, I fear I'm going mad."

She gave him her wise smile. "In a sense, you are. You're in love, Kieran."

"With whom?" He slammed his chair against the table in frustration. "I canna recall her name, yet I see her as clearly as I do you. Then I wake up, and she's gone."

But the feel of her remained. Branded on his hands, his mouth, the length of his body, where those sensuous curves had touched him. Warming his bed though no one lay beside him.

Aileen rose from her seat and rested a hand on his arm. "You've not yet recovered from your injuries. Be patient with yourself, as you are with all of us. Your memory will return, and then you'll go find her. Fretting over it will only make things worse."

"You're right. I just can't rid myself of this feeling."

Her eyes sharpened at the reference to his renowned instincts. "What feeling is that?"

"She's in danger, Mother, and I canna help her because I don't know who she is."

His confession hung in the air like an executioner's ax. Frustrated by his helplessness, he strode from the hall and headed for the stables. Perhaps a ride would settle his mind and allow him to think more clearly.

At the foot of the steps, he stopped as a dozen warhorses trotted through the main gates. The armored knights halted as one, spreading to form a protective ring about the rider in their midst.

"May the Good Lord and all His blessed saints be praised." The imposing man lifted his face reverently toward heaven, then bowed his head and crossed himself. He swung from his mount and crossed the bailey with the powerful stride of a much younger man.

Thomas Fitzgerald, the eighth Earl of Desmond, dressed like a fighting man and spoke like a priest. Well-educated and wealthy beyond measure, he'd served as Lord Deputy of Ireland 'til Edward became suspicious of the Anglo-Irish lord's loyalty. In his place now stood the butchering Earl of Worcester, but Desmond had lost none of the respect he'd garnered during his tenure. With a firm hand, he'd fairly dealt with English and Irish alike, earning the admiration of them all.

His tanned face creased with a smile as he grasped Kieran's shoulders. "'Tis good to see my favorite godson alive and well."

"'Tis good to be seen that way," he quipped, and they both laughed. "What brings ye here?"

Sorrow eclipsed the fond twinkle in Desmond's eyes. "I come to offer my condolences to the clans. I've been in Drogheda and only received the awful news a few days ago. Word has not yet spread of your miraculous escape."

Kieran's mind went to the angel who'd saved him, and he shook off the unsettling images of the night before. "Would you and your men care to rest awhile?"

When Desmond relayed the invitation to his captain, the man shook his head. "Thank you, but no. With your permission, Chief MacAuley, I shall set up a perimeter outside the walls and leave two guards at the gate."

Kieran bristled at the implication that he couldn't protect his exalted guest. "I assure you, the earl is perfectly safe within these walls."

The knight frowned deeply. "The earl is not safe anywhere."

With that, he turned his mount and spoke to his men, who swiftly moved to carry out his orders.

"Ye had trouble while ye were away?" Kieran asked his visitor as they ascended the wide steps into the hall.

Desmond sighed. "We have trouble everywhere. I fear 'twill only get worse."

But when Aileen approached them, his frown lifted into a smile, and he bowed to her. "Good morn to you."

She laughed and kissed his cheek. "You needn't be so formal. It's wonderful to see you again. Would you care for something to eat?"

"Indeed I would. I smelled Grania's biscuits from the crossroads."

As was customary, Kieran offered Desmond his own chair, but the man graciously declined. Though born into the political elite, Magnus had often said that Thomas Fitzgerald's character was even more noble than his birth.

"So, Desmond," Kieran said as he buttered a roll, "how go your plans for the university in Drogheda?"

"Slow, but I'll not abandon the notion just yet. Such an institution would greatly benefit all of Ireland."

He went on to discuss recent events all over the Isle, and several times Kieran was struck by how the man expressed himself, never referring to English and Irish but to the plight of commoners and the duty of those in power to end the wars and improve life for everyone. 'Twas that very trait that had cost him Edward's favor, but Kieran admired him all the more for maintaining his convictions in the face of such opposition.

Desmond finished half a dozen biscuits while they talked, then took a swallow of mead. Sitting back in his chair, he trained a somber look on Kieran. "Tell me what happened at Westmeath."

When he began the same tale he'd told the night

before, Desmond held up a hand. "I know that much. Tell me how such a tragedy came to be."

Kieran hadn't spoken of it to anyone, and he strove to remain calm as he relayed his suspicions. "A raid this early in the year should have come as a complete surprise. But not only was the garrison prepared, their ranks had tripled. None of our scouts noticed the extra horses. Once the cavalry engaged us, we could do little more than take down as many English as we could."

The older man frowned. "Do you remember anything more?"

"Coming home. Everything else is gone."

Desmond's frown deepened. "Never have I heard of such a thing."

"It's as if someone wiped his memory away," Aileen said with a sympathetic hand on his arm.

The earl tapped his chin with his forefinger. "Someone who wanted to be certain you'd not remember her. An Englishwoman, perhaps?"

Kieran could still hear the lilt of her voice, and he shook his head. "Nay, she's Irish."

Desmond traded a bemused look with Aileen, then chuckled. "Do not worry, Kieran. As keen as your instincts are, I'd wager she'll not remain a mystery for long."

Though 'twas nearly dusk, the evening was a warm one. Her ankle throbbed incessantly, making every step a trial. When she came upon a brook, Brynna gratefully sat on a large rock and unwrapped the length of wool she'd tied about her ankle. The bruises had deepened from purple to near black, but dangling her foot in the cool water eased the pain.

She cupped some of it in her hands and drank. Her parched throat begged for more, so she reached in again. The ripples brought to mind the night she'd looked into Kieran's dark eyes and found much more than she'd ever hoped for. A man who loved her simply because she breathed.

"Oh, Kieran," she murmured, trailing her hand through the water. "I pray you'll be happy."

The bite of steel at her throat stopped her heart as a strong arm clamped over her chest.

"Well, now," a cultured English voice chuckled at her ear. "What have we here?"

Again Kieran heard it, the soft inland brogue that had disturbed his sleep since he'd come home. Each night while he wandered the forest of his dreams, he heard it in a different place—beneath a canopy of pine boughs, off in the misty distance. Her laughter seemed to find him in the wee hours, plucking at his heart as one would a harp. Blindly, he followed it, knowing it would lead him to her.

Last eve had been filled with ominous silence.

This morn, his ears echoed with weak sobs. A shiver rattled him though he wasn't chilled, compelling him to leave his warm bed. He pulled on his clothes and drew a heavy cloak over them. As an afterthought, he retrieved a woolen throw from the back of the settee and slung it over his shoulder before leaving his bedchamber.

In the hall below, he found Dev still in the clothes he'd worn the night before.

"And where do ye think you're going?" his cousin demanded.

"To search for a little house in a willow tree."

"You're daft."

"Are ye coming with me or not?"

With a wistful glance down the corridor that led to his bed, Dev sighed and drew on his cloak again. "Aye, if for no other reason than to avoid telling your mother you've gone again."

While they hastened through the misty dawn, Dev grumbled, "Slow down. I'm half dead already."

The words hit Kieran with an impact that stopped him in midstride. Clutching his chest, he searched for the feeling that had forced him from his bed. 'Twas fainter now, as if she were slipping away from him. He didn't know who she was or how he'd find her, but he had to try.

"We must hurry," he said as he swung open the stable door.

"Why?"

"I don't know." Gideon's nickered greeting cheered him. The familiar sound eased his nerves a bit.

While he saddled Boru, Dev groused, "This makes no sense, chasing after a woman ye don't even remember."

Kieran was of no mood to debate that point, so he mounted and headed toward the main gate. As they approached, a guard scrambled to open the portcullis.

"Good morn to ye both," he grunted while he hoisted the heavy iron gate.

"I hope so," Kieran muttered, trying to calm his

restive stallion. He saw the other two exchange puzzled looks, frowning in a mute disapproval he chose to ignore. He hadn't the time to explain things no one would understand.

After they'd been on the road awhile, he took the fork that led westward, perturbed when his companion halted and began wagging his head. "Ye can't be thinking of starting trouble with the English."

"Of course not. I'm looking for a house by a willow tree."

"Are ye certain this is the way?" Dev asked as he blew on his cupped hands.

"If ye plan to do nothing but complain, I'll thank ye to go home and leave me in peace."

"Considering ye don't remember her, she must be some lass."

Kieran cast him a withering look. "She saved my life."

"That she did. To be honest, I'd like to thank her myself."

They rounded a bend in the road and pulled their mounts up short.

"Sweet Mary," Dev breathed, hastily crossing himself.

Transfixed by the awful sight, Kieran dismounted and walked to the center of the crossroads, where an ancient oak marked the intersection of two main paths. A young woman had been brutally beaten and tied to its trunk. Her face was a mass of blood and bruises, her lips swollen and split. Beneath her shabby russet dress, bones had certainly splintered under the merciless blows. Imagining what they'd done to her before that made his blood boil.

Praise God she was dead.

No doubt she'd been lashed to the tree in warning to others who might consider opposing the English. When he stepped closer, he saw the nymph from his dreams. The thong about her neck had been tied around the tree as well. The leather bit into her flesh, and dried blood circled her throat, a sure sign that when they'd left her, she was alive and struggling to get free.

The deep welts left behind caused his temper to spike. What sort of depraved monster could do such a thing to a woman?

He slipped an arm about her and reached to his waist for his dirk.

"What are ye doing?" Dev glanced about nervously. "Have ye forgotten we're on the English side of the line?"

"I can't leave her like this. Help me, would you?"

He supported her while his cousin cut the ropes that bound her to the tree. She didn't crumple as he'd expected, but collapsed into his arms with a mewling whimper.

"God's blood!" Dev's eyes nearly jumped from his head. "She's alive."

"That she is. And no matter how high the fine is, I intend to keep her that way."

Dev held her while Kieran swung up to Gideon's back and opened the woolen throw. When Kieran took her in his arms and folded the blanket about her, she relaxed into his embrace, pillowing her cheek on his shoulder. She felt familiar somehow, her gentle curves melding perfectly with the hard planes of his chest. Her unquestioning trust touched him deeply, and he pressed a kiss to her bruised temple.

"Hold on to me, sweet one. You're safe now."

One of the main doors banged open, and Aileen glanced up to find Kieran striding through the hall with a woolen bundle in his arms. He sank to his knees on the bare hearth and began loosening the blanket as if it concealed some priceless treasure.

She hastened to the fire and knelt beside him. A woman's head lay cradled in the crook of his arm, her face covered with too many wounds to count. When Aileen rested a hand on her forehead, she shifted, grimacing as she moaned.

"She's half frozen," Kieran explained. "We found her tied to a tree at the crossroads."

"How could anyone do such a thing?"

"When I find them," he replied, in a voice that was lethally calm, "they'll not live long enough for you to ask."

He slid the chilled throw from beneath the lass and reached out to take the warm one Devlin handed him. This he wrapped about her, hardly disturbing her before guiding her head back to his chest. Aileen watched him tenderly kiss the girl's brow, whisper something in her ear. Though she made no response, she turned slightly, cuddling against him like a child seeking comfort.

"She seems to know you." Looking into her son's eyes, she saw guilt laden with misery. "But you've no idea who she is, do you?"

"Nay. Mother, she's the one who helped me. Please—"

His choking voice trailed off, and she patted his shoulder in understanding. "We'll do all we can for her. Settle her upstairs while I fetch what I need."

After a heavy sigh, he nodded and walked toward the ascending staircase with Devlin in tow. As she hurried toward the kitchens, Aileen sent up a fervent prayer for aid, as much for Kieran's sake as the girl's.

She wasn't certain he could bear the loss of one more soul entrusted to his care.

Throughout the day, Kieran prowled the corridor outside the most lavish guest chamber he had to offer. Maids bustled in and out bearing linens, hot water, all manner of healing ingredients. The activity told him she lived, but no one stopped to reassure him.

"Why can I not recall her?" he asked again, dragging both hands through his hair in frustration. "She must have risked her life to help me. I should remember her."

"No man's memory is large enough to hold all the women you've known," Dev mumbled around a mouthful of apple.

"This one is different." Kieran braced his hands on either side of the door, rested his forehead on the solid oak. "You saw her. How could that wee lass take such a beating?"

"Perhaps she's not a lass a'tall."

"What are ye blathering about?" Kieran demanded.

"I'm saying she may not be what you think. I've heard tales of *sídhe* living in the forest for one reason or another. A faery can take away memories or give them back, whichever suits her best."

"She's not a faery."

Dev grinned. "And just how many faeries have ye known?"

"None."

"Are ye certain?"

"*Dún do bheal.*"

The fool shut his infernal mouth but didn't stop grinning. He leaned back and folded his massive arms, eyes dancing with merriment while Kieran resumed his pacing.

Brynna awoke in a fog, dimly aware that she was in pain. Everywhere. When she tried to take a deep breath, she felt the cloth binding her ribs. All about her she heard scurrying feet and hushed voices. Soft wool brushed her arm as someone hurried past her. At the sound of a closing door, she registered the warmth of the room and understood she was in a house somewhere. She opened her eyes to assure herself she'd finally found a haven from the English, and the lovely face of a motherly woman swam into view.

'Twas a face she knew all too well.

"Nay," she whispered, unable to believe fate had brought her to the people she'd fought so hard to protect.

The woman smiled and patted her hand. "No need to be frightened, my dear. You're safe now."

"I must go." Brynna struggled to rise from the

bed, but her body retaliated with sharp stabs in a dozen places.

"You'll not be going anywhere very soon. You're in Dunsmere with the MacAuley. No harm will come to you here, I promise you." She paused for another reassuring smile. "I'm Aileen MacAuley."

"I canna stay here. Please, for the sake of your clan, let me go."

"Nonsense. You'll remain with us 'til you're fully recovered."

She stepped away from the bed, then opened the door and spoke to someone in the corridor. Brynna closed her eyes and tried to control her uneven breathing. When she heard a movement at the door, she opened her eyes.

Kieran.

Dressed in mahogany trews and a belted ivory *léine,* he filled the room to near bursting with his masculine presence. She drank in the sight of him, joyous tears filling her eyes as he hastened to her side.

"Mother told me you'd woken. How fare you?"

"Well enough."

"You look much better."

His reserved tone struck her oddly, and then she understood: He didn't remember her. Relief flooded her heart, and she relaxed a bit. If he thought her a stranger, he'd have no cause to keep her in Dunsmere. In a few days, she'd be healed enough to travel, and she could slip away, knowing he and his kinsmen were safe.

'Twould be torturous to leave him behind when she longed to curl up in his arms and give him back the memories she kept cradled in her heart. Though it saddened her to know he no longer shared those feelings, she knew it was for the best.

He whisked her tears away with his thumb. "Sleep now. I'll return when you've rested."

Bending to kiss her forehead, he left her with a smile that carried her into an exhausted sleep.

Hearing a soft knock at her door, Brynna smoothed the sleeves of her gray dressing gown and folded her bandaged hands on the coverlet. Enthroned within the rich tapestries of the tester bed, she felt like a princess. "Aye?"

Kieran opened the door partway but stayed outside, eyes averted. "Are ye presentable?"

"As presentable as I can be."

He glanced up and down the hall before entering and closing the door behind him. "Do ye like sweets?"

She laughed at his mischievous tone. "I adore them."

From behind his back, he brought a lumpy piece of linen hiding something he obviously wasn't meant to have.

The smell was unmistakable, and she pressed her hands together to avoid clapping. "Honey cakes?"

"Aye. Fresh ones." He laid the pilfered treats in her lap and settled on the large bed beside her like an eager boy. "Careful. They're still a bit warm."

She took a cautious bite, sighing as the confection melted on her tongue. "They're delicious. Thank you."

"You're welcome."

"Would you care for one?"

When he selected a cake for himself, she clicked her tongue. " 'Twas the biggest one!"

"I'll leave ye the rest, then, to make it up."

"How generous of you."

While she devoured the treats, he watched her with growing curiosity. How odd that he felt so at ease with a woman he didn't know. Didn't *remember*, he corrected himself. And yet she seemed to recall him, teasing him as few women did while he was clothed.

When she'd finished her cakes, he folded the linen deliberately, taking time to collect his thoughts. He raised his head and looked into eyes the likes of which he'd seen only in his dreams. Glowing like warm emeralds shot through with gold, they appeared to see a great deal more of him than he would willingly share.

"You seem to know me, but I must confess I've no memory of you." She didn't react with dismay as he'd expected, but looked down and began tracing the openwork pattern of the coverlet. Mindful of the tender spots on her face and throat, he slid his knuckle under her chin and lifted her head. "I've a few questions to ask you."

"No doubt you do."

"I'll thank ye to be answering them truthfully."

"Of course, Chief MacAuley."

"Don't be calling me that." Chuckling, he tapped her pert nose. "I've seen how ye look at me. I'd wager my best stallion you've called me by name a time or two."

She acquiesced with a shy smile. "Kieran."

"I see you, hear your voice in my dreams at night. Why is that?"

She didn't respond, but he suspected she well knew why images of her tormented him so relentlessly. "Who are you, lass?"

"Brynna."

As he repeated the unusual name, it felt soft on his tongue. "'Twas you who saved me after the raid."

"Aye."

"Did the English do this to you?" When she nodded, he frowned. "Do ye know why?"

"I refused to give them information about you."

Those words told him a great deal more about his petite guardian than she could ever know. With determination and her delicate body, she'd protected him from his enemies.

Even now, he sensed she was shielding him from something, and he took her hand. "Some injuries canna be seen. Often those are the worst kind."

She wore the unflinching expression of a woman who'd witnessed far too much in her short lifetime. "You're asking if they raped me."

He grimaced in discomfort. "'Tis not an easy thing to ask."

"Especially when you know the answer. They seemed to take particular pleasure in dishonoring me."

"Describe them to me."

"So you can take revenge on them? I'd not allow you to do such a foolish thing. It's over, Kieran. Let it rest."

Her attitude baffled him nearly as much as it angered him. "Do ye not wish for them to suffer for what they did to you?"

"They will."

"The English authorities have little concern for the welfare of an Irish lass. I would deal with them properly."

Smiling, she shook her head. "I'm not speaking of the English. Others will avenge me."

She offered nothing more, and he realized he'd not convince this soft-spoken lass to do something simply because he willed it. Much as he needed more details, he was loath to tax her strength. As she recuperated, he'd gain her trust and the answers he sought.

She glanced around the quarters in which his mother housed her most favored guests. "This is such a wonderful home. You must have loved growing up here."

"I have been to many places, but Dunsmere is my favorite. When you're feeling better, I'll show ye more of it."

Her eyes went to the window, and she frowned. "I'm content in here."

"Spring will be here soon. Perhaps you'll feel different then." When she didn't respond, he asked, "What is it, Brynna?"

" 'Tis safer inside."

Considering what she'd been through, he understood her reluctance to leave the keep. "Unfamiliar things frighten all of us," he told her with an encouraging smile. "But I've no doubt in time you'll enjoy roaming about the valley."

"I canna remain here."

"Can ye tell me why?"

She shook her head, and he pressed a bit. "I remember a willow tree with a little house in its roots. My cousin Devlin and I were searching for it when we found you. Is that where you lived?"

"It was."

"And where have you been since then?" When she didn't answer, he bit back a curse. "You've no place to go, have you?"

" 'Tis not your concern."

At the end of his diplomatic repertoire, Kieran summoned his sternest expression. "I'm chieftain here," he declared, tapping his chest for emphasis, "and I alone decide what happens on MacAuley land. Until you've healed and I'm satisfied you're in no more danger, you'll stay here. Mother loves having guests, and as ye can see, we've plenty of space."

"You don't understand."

"Then explain it to me."

She looked on him with tremendous longing, as if he were something she wanted desperately. Kieran fought the impulse to take her in his arms and coax her secrets into the open, where they could confront them together.

Together.

The word slammed through his mind, evoking murky images from the dreams that plagued him. Silken skin under his hands, a sensuous body offering him all he could ever want. Though he still had no idea who she was, of one thing he was certain.

He couldn't possibly let her go.

CHAPTER SIX

Kieran glanced up when his mother paused before his desk. "You needed something?"

"What is it you're working on?"

"Trading accounts." Tossing down his quill, he rocked back in his chair with a wry grin. "Please distract me."

Closing the heavy door, she crossed his study to stand beside him. She stared out the window a moment, as if something in the distant hills fascinated her. When she met his gaze, he saw uncharacteristic hesitance in her eyes.

"It's about Brynna."

He folded his arms in anticipation of a problem. "What of her?"

"She's healing very quickly."

"That's good, is it not?"

"Kieran, I've tended dozens of people in my lifetime. She's been here only a sennight and already she's up and about. Never have I seen broken bones mend so rapidly. There's something not right about her."

"I agree she's unusual. Unusually brave, considering what she did for me."

"Brave, indeed. She's determined to leave in the morn."

"Is she, now?" he replied, prodded to his feet by the very idea. "We'll see about that."

But Aileen caught his arm. "What is Brynna to you?"

"I swear I don't remember any details. I only know I was dying, and if it weren't for her, I'd not be here now. I'll not allow her to leave while she's in danger from the English."

"I've watched you with her a time or two." She brushed a bit of hay from his sleeve, gave him a knowing woman's smile. "Perhaps you haven't forgotten everything about her."

He laughed. "Mother, when will ye cease throwing prospective wives at me?"

"When you choose one and begin fathering some bairns of your own."

"Children baffle me, and well ye know it."

"Children fascinate you," she corrected him with a fond smile. "Your nieces adore you, and the lads about the keep follow you like pups."

"Because I know how to sneak treats from the kitchen."

Her expression sobered, and she gave him an imploring look. "Kieran, you've so much love inside you. You'd make a fine husband and a wonderful father, if you'd consider it for even a moment."

His chest tightened under the impact of her plea. "What is this truly about?"

"I nearly lost you." Eyes swimming with emotion, she gripped his forearm. "And now Brynna has returned to you. You've been granted another life, Kieran. I beg of you, don't waste it."

"I won't," he promised as he removed her hand. "Meantime, I must talk some sense into our guest before she does something foolish."

He strode down the corridor to the chamber where Brynna was resting. Supposed to be resting, he corrected himself when he opened the door to find her clad in nothing but a linen shift, her mended gown dangling from her hand. 'Twas so ugly, he'd not have lain it under a saddle, yet she seemed perfectly content to defile herself with the accursed thing.

Kieran ripped the offensive dress from her grasp. "What the devil do ye think you're doing?"

"I'm dressing."

"Not in this." He hurled the glorified rag across the chamber, then stalked to the tall wardrobe and surveyed the dresses inside. One of deep blue silk caught his eye, and he removed it. "You can wear this."

She had the temerity to wag her head at him. " 'Tis not mine."

"I'm giving it to you, so it *is* yours." He was behaving like a lunatic, and he strived for a calmer tone. "This gown suits you much better. It would please me greatly to see you in it at dinner this eve."

Her eyes widened as she clutched the elegant dress to her. "You wish for me to join you?"

"Aye, if you feel well enough."

"What of your kinsmen?"

Kieran frowned. "What of them?"

"I've heard the maids talking with your mother. They say I'm healing too quickly." Her eyes went to the embroidered bodice in her hands. "I fear others will notice it as well, and think badly of me."

"Should you wear this"—he lifted the rich folds of the skirt—"they'll think you're the most beautiful woman to grace my table in a very long time."

Her grateful smile tugged at his heart, and he cupped her cheek in his palm. The gesture felt familiar, and before he realized what he was doing, he'd leaned in to kiss her. Her lips yielded to his, and she curved against him with a little sigh. Whatever troubled his mind, his body recognized her instantly, coming to life as he gathered her into his arms.

'Twas nothing like what he felt for women he barely knew, a man's reaction to a lush body or a seductive smile. This was far more than desire. His blood roared with the need to feel Brynna under him, hear her whisper his name as he lost himself inside her.

"Kieran MacAuley."

His mother's sharp tone sliced through his lustful trance. Stepping away from Brynna, he fought to calm his racing heart. The rest of him was beyond hope.

"Please forgive me, lass." Her reddened lips shamed him, even as they tipped into an impish smile.

"Since you put it that way, Chief MacAuley, I should be pleased to join you for dinner."

He took her hand for a more acceptable kiss. "Tell me, Brynna—what did I like best about you?"

She answered with her enchanting laugh. "Everything."

Aileen shooed her into the adjoining sitting room and slammed the door. Then she rounded on him, shaking a stern finger. "And you: Chieftain of one of the richest clans in Ireland, and here you are acting like a bull in rut. Off with you, now. Take a swim."

'Twas what she used to tell Magnus when he cornered her in the kitchen or the corridor, intent on taking whatever she felt inclined to give him at the time. Wed to her most of his life, he didn't stop chasing her until she tearfully laid him in the ground.

Grinning, Kieran strolled across the chamber to kiss her cheek. "I'll go if you'll burn this for me." He retrieved the pile of threadbare brown wool and handed it to her.

"But this is Brynna's dress."

"I wouldn't put it on Gideon. Burn it."

To her credit, she didn't voice the thoughts behind the bemusement in her eyes. "That blue gown was Maureen's. 'Twill need a good bit of work to fit Brynna."

He hadn't considered that when he'd thrust the dress at Brynna. Still, he wanted to see her draped in silk and pearls, looking up at him from her place on his arm.

The vivid image unnerved him, and he brushed it aside. "Another will do as well. But for the love of God, find her something decent to wear."

With that, he turned on his heel and strode off to take his swim.

After a bracing lungful of air, Kieran plunged into the lough. He surfaced near shore, a good deal calmer than when he'd arrived. But the water brought to mind a hazy memory of a moonlit pool and the lass he'd thought a dream until he found her beaten and left for dead.

The mere thought of what she'd endured enraged him, and he dunked under again, this time to cool his temper.

When he came up for air, he found Dev sitting on the bank shaking his head. "Ye need to stay away from her."

"She's living under my roof," Kieran spat as he hauled himself from the water. "How do ye suggest I avoid her?"

"In that pile of rock?" Dev laughed and motioned toward the towering keep. "You evade Maureen easily enough."

As he pulled his *léine* over his wet trews, Kieran glared at his grinning cousin. "And what is it you find so damned amusing?"

"You, trying to drown yourself. Aileen must've sent ye out here."

"Aye." He sighed as he sank to the ground.

"Caught you with your hands where they shouldn't be, did she?"

They exchanged male grins, and Dev laughed

again. "Why don't ye just admit it? You're so taken with that lass, you've gone and lost your senses."

"I swear, it's as if I know her." Dragging his wet hair back from his face, Kieran stared at the shafts of new grass beneath his feet. "I just don't remember her."

"Well now, there's knowing and there's *knowing*." Dev chuckled, then grew quiet. "Tell me something, Kee."

At the sound of his boyhood name, Kieran glanced into a pair of sober blue eyes. "How many women do ye honestly remember?"

"A few." Bonny faces he could recall, though their names escaped him at the moment.

"Would ye care to hear my opinion?"

'Twas one of the man's finest traits. He held a carefully considered opinion on everything around him, yet never offered it unless he was asked. When Kieran nodded, he continued.

"There's something different about Brynna. That difference allowed her to save you, kept her in the back of your memory. No matter if ye met her a month hence or a lifetime, you'd know her when ye saw her again."

"I recognized her at the crossroads," he mused, twirling a bit of moss between his fingers. "And when she said my name, I knew her voice."

A sympathetic paw clapped him on the shoulder. "Och, man, 'tis even worse than I thought."

The chapel bell began tolling, marking the end of the day, and Kieran watched his clan gather for another evening together. Families milled about the bailey, fathers hoisting children onto their shoulders and kissing their wives. Ruddy lads raced in with their dogs, yanked at the braids of their favorite girls.

'Twas this he'd fought for his entire life. The preservation of the Irish way, tied to the land, bound to clan through generations of loyalty and hard work. But of late, he'd started to think of other things. Wedding banns and babes, a quieter existence overseeing the vast territory of the MacAuley while the younger men went off to war.

But if he stepped back, who would lead them? With the planting finished, new divisions would begin training in earnest, anticipating the customary summertime raids. Blaming his healing shoulder, he'd delayed joining them, but before long he'd be forced to choose.

War or home.

In the past, they'd been intrinsically linked in his heart. Kieran fought for Ireland, for the MacAuley clan, to protect what they'd built with their bare hands. 'Twas a rich land, and they husbanded it with loving care. Their linen was coveted the world over, and their wool had no equal. They harvested far more corn and barley than they could use, exporting the surplus from Dublin in sailing ships that brought back silks and spices from the East.

If he retired to the valley, he knew many would assume his near brush with death had weakened his warrior's resolve.

In a way, perhaps it had.

His eyes were drawn to a flutter of movement in an upper chamber. Brynna stood framed by the window, leaning on the sill to peer into the bailey below. Her gaze wandered from the castle environs toward the lough.

She wore a crimson gown, her chestnut hair rippling over her shoulders in loose curls. When her gaze settled on him, she waved and offered him the loveliest smile he'd ever seen. And like a besotted fool, he smiled and lifted his hand in reply.

"You're hopeless," Dev muttered. "Why can't ye just admit it?"

His eyes on Brynna, Kieran shook his head. "Because I don't know why."

"When it comes to women, who knows anything? She ties ye up in knots, ye wed her—simple as that. Ye think too much."

"The chieftain must consider his decisions carefully, for the benefit of everyone."

"Aye, and what of Kieran?"

Puzzled, he looked to his cousin. "What of me?"

"'Tis the man I'm speaking of, not the Fearless One." He pounded his own massive chest. "What is your heart telling you?"

"I'm not like you. My heart doesn't talk to me."

Dev got to his feet, crossing his huge arms while he glared. "If ye feel the need to lie to me, I can understand it. Just be certain you're truthful with yourself."

After the giant of a man stalked off, Kieran turned his attention to the sun as it eased from the sky. The still water reflected the beautiful colors, vibrant reds and golds blending into palest pink. Though he was looking in that direction, Brynna sensed he wasn't admiring the sunset as she'd been doing.

She fought the temptation to look into his mind and discern what troubled him. From the other man's angry stance, she knew they'd argued over something. Now Kieran sat on the bank, arms resting on his bent knees while he stared into the distance.

Framed by the magnificent sunset, he was completely, utterly alone.

Though the main hall bustled with preparations for the evening meal, no one went to fetch him. The air had a decided nip to it, yet he sat on the ground in his damp clothes. Snatching up a woolen throw, she went down the nearest staircase and found a door that led into the bailey.

Dozens of people filed past her, talking and laughing as they trooped into the hall. Fighting her ingrained shyness of strangers, Brynna hastened through the open gates and headed down the sloping bank. Each stride took her farther from the safe confines of the stone walls, and her steps began to falter. Accustomed as she was to the blanketing shadows of the forest, the wide-open expanse made her feel more than small. It made her feel vulnerable.

Another glimpse of Kieran steeled her resolve, and she continued toward him. When she paused beside him, a smile lit his features, and he swiftly gained his feet.

"Brynna, what are ye doing out here?"

"It's growing colder." Remembering the blanket she held, she offered it to him. "I thought you might need this."

"Thank you." He wrapped it about his waist,

tucking one end in to secure it. "I know how being in the open frightens you. 'Twas very brave of you to bring it to me."

The unexpected praise made her smile. "How is it a courageous warrior understands a groundless fear such as mine?"

"No fear is groundless." He looked out over the water. "Do ye know what I'm afraid of, Brynna?"

"Nothing?"

He shook his head at the retreating sun. "I'm afraid of dying alone." Turning to her, he smoothed a lock of hair over her shoulder. "But then, you knew my fear when you came into that glen to comfort me."

'Twas knowledge he shouldn't have, and she wondered what had brought it to the surface. Adoration flooded his dark eyes, and he stepped closer until only the barest space separated them. He lifted his hands to cradle her face, regarding her with desperate intensity.

Kieran saw no fear in her eyes. In them he saw the courageous lass who'd stepped into the pit of hell to rescue him. She'd become the nymph who haunted his nights, bringing hope to a heart withered by a lifetime of war. He cursed the trick of fate that had stripped her from his memory.

And then he kissed her.

Though she seemed cautious at first, she relaxed into his embrace with the same little sigh he'd heard earlier. Captivated by the eerily familiar feel of her body, he drew her closer and deepened the kiss.

When reason asserted itself, he wrenched his

mouth from hers. "By the Devil, you bring out the very worst in me."

"Do I?" she asked a bit breathlessly.

Her cheeks held not the blush of a maiden but the passionate color of a woman who knew what he longed to give her and wouldn't hesitate to take it.

"Brynna, tell me true: Were ye in love with me?"

After a moment she nodded, and tears welled in her eyes. Though he was fair certain he understood what brought her so near to weeping, he asked, "Are ye still?"

The tears streaming down her face answered him more eloquently than any words. He released her, and she backed away before fleeing as if he were a demon intent on swallowing her whole.

He could still feel her in his arms, how perfectly she fit against him. There was no denying it. Some part of him knew her, and his memories were strengthening by the day. Throughout the keep, he'd heard the mutterings of his kinsmen, seen the worry etched on the elders' faces.

Many thought he'd been enchanted by her and was slowly going mad. Others surmised that Brynna had struck him with a faery bolt and he would regain his senses when she left him. Only Dev and his mother suspected the true cause of his distress and, hard as he'd fought the notion, Kieran could no longer ignore the truth of it.

He was in love with a woman he didn't remember.

Dev filled his cup with mead and drained it almost as quickly.

Carrick laughed and refilled it for him. "Thirsty, are ye?"

"Arguing with Kieran always leaves me parched."

His lighthearted cousin grinned. "Rock stubborn, that one. What were ye tussling over this time?"

"Her."

Dev nodded toward the archway where Kieran had appeared with his mysterious guest. Carrick followed the motion and let out a soft whistle of appreciation. "And who might that be?"

"Brynna."

Carrick choked on his mead and gaped at Dev. "Brynna? The lass ye found in the forest?"

"Aye. She mends quickly."

"You mend quickly. That"—Carrick motioned with his cup—"is a blessed miracle."

Dev had no argument for that. Or for the effect Brynna had on Kieran. Always wary of the gossips, their chieftain entertained few women within sight of the clan. But this one he held close to his side, his hand resting over hers while he made introductions. For all his hard-headed blustering earlier, he seemed quite content with Brynna on his arm.

Despite the bruises lingering on her face, she was a vision to behold. Delicate but by no means fragile, she moved with regal grace, nodding and smiling at each person presented to her. She traded pleasantries with Elizabeth, one of Kieran's lovely sisters-in-law, then knelt before Sarah and Lynette, listening as intently to the girls as she had to their mother.

When the younger one produced a kitten,

Brynna took the wee thing and cuddled it to her cheek. She held it gently, rubbed noses with it while she said something that made the girl laugh. Kieran crouched beside her, rubbing a finger over the little beastie's forehead as he embraced Lynette with his other arm.

'Twas easy to see a family in the affectionate circle, Kieran with his own wife and child. In his heart, Dev knew the disastrous raid at Westmeath had been their chieftain's last. His cousin just didn't realize it yet.

Kieran looked toward the hearth and smiled. After handing the kitten to his niece, he stood and offered Brynna his arm. They strolled across the crowded great hall, their steps in rhythm while he pointed out various things to her.

As they drew closer, Carrick murmured, "By the saints, have ye ever seen such a lass?"

She's no lass, Dev longed to say, but he held his tongue. Kieran looked like a man who'd been granted his heart's greatest desire. Whatever Brynna's pedigree, she made him happy. God knew no one else ever had.

"There y'are," Kieran said as they paused before the fire. "I've been looking for you. Brynna, this is my cousin Carrick."

He bowed and took her hand for a kiss. "*Fáilte.* Welcome to Dunsmere."

"Thank you." She smiled and tipped her head back to look up at Dev. "And you must be Devlin, my rescuer. I owe you more than I can ever repay."

She laid a bandaged hand on his arm in a show

of gratitude that stunned him. Her touch reached through the linen sleeve, warmer even than her smile. Little wonder she'd turned Kieran's head so completely.

Customarily wary of strangers, he found himself grinning down at her. "In truth, I went only to keep Kieran from more trouble."

"He's fortunate to have you watching over him."

"And when I wasn't, you took my place." Dev lifted the dainty hand from his arm and kissed a spot free of wrapping. " 'Tis the MacAuley who are indebted to you."

Trouble flitted through her lovely eyes, and he released her hand, thinking he'd caused her distress.

Kieran seemed to notice it as well. "Are ye hungry?" he asked her.

"A bit."

The clipped answer was at odds with the warmth she'd shown only moments before, and she crossed her arms before her in a defensive gesture. Dev traded a worried look with Kieran, who shook his head slightly.

He gave Brynna an easy smile. "We should get you something to eat."

She hesitated, then took his arm and followed him to the head table. Dev had known his share of unpredictable women, but never had he seen such a display. He'd wager his considerable weight in gold that Brynna returned Kieran's feelings in kind. But at the mention of his clan's debt to her, she acted like a woman presented with something distasteful.

"What do ye make of that?" Carrick asked, eyes

fixed on the couple weaving their way through the benches.

"Ye know how women are. One moment they smile, the next they frown."

"She seemed frightened of something."

Eyes narrowed, Dev looked toward the front of the hall, where Kieran had settled with Brynna beside him. "Aye."

"The English?"

"After what they did to her, 'twould be understandable. But I don't think she worries for herself." Turning, he met Carrick's grim look with one of his own. "She fears for the MacAuley."

"Why?"

"That I don't know. I pray Kieran does."

It seemed their earlier conversation had dislodged a significant block in Kieran's memory. While they ate, his gaze followed her every move as if he couldn't bear to let her out of his sight. To test him, Brynna peppered their discussion with references to their time together in the forest. Some he clearly had no memory of, but many elicited a spark of recognition from his dark eyes.

Unschooled as she was, still her magick had never failed this way. None of the other men she'd tended had returned to find her. She had no doubt that should her father appear outside the gates of MacAuley keep, Kieran would fight rather than relinquish her.

Her mother's warning was still ringing in her ears when a pretty young woman dressed in black appeared at his side. He gained his feet, and she put a hand on his arm, giving him a dimpled smile. "Kieran, I've not met your guest. Would you care to introduce us?"

"Brynna, this is my brother Adam's wife, Maureen."

Even as they smiled at one another, Brynna sensed the other woman's flash of resentment. Before she could wonder about its cause, it was gone.

"In truth, I'm Adam's widow, and near the end of my mourning, thank God." She gave Kieran a meaningful look and tucked her hand into the crook of his arm. Then she turned her attention to Brynna. "Will you be staying with us long?"

"I've not yet decided," she hedged.

"I suppose home is calling you, as it does all of us."

Brynna thought it best not to join this particular fray. Unaccustomed as she was to such strategies, still she recognized the artful attempt to belittle her. No doubt every member of the clan, from wizened crone to smallest child, was well acquainted with her sparse history.

Maureen turned to Kieran with a smile. "Might I speak with you a moment?"

"Of course."

A pretty blush swept her cheeks, and she lowered her eyes before lifting them to his face. "In private."

When he glanced at her, Brynna gave what she hoped was a polite smile. "Don't concern yourself, Chief MacAuley. I know the way back to my chamber."

He'd scarce opened his mouth to respond when

Maureen began tugging him between the crowded tables toward the far archway. Over his shoulder, he flashed an apologetic smile that Brynna acknowledged with one of her own.

Once he'd gone, she left the bustling hall with as much dignity as she could muster.

"So you understand my point." Maureen folded her hands in her skirts with an expectant look.

Seated opposite her in a damask chair, Kieran had no idea what she'd been blathering on about—worn tapestries or some such thing. Once he'd ascertained that her sole intent had been to divert his attention from Brynna, his interest in her problem had waned.

"I defer to your judgment in this. Do what you think best."

Hoping to end their pointless conversation, he stood and held his arm out to her. When her gaze dropped to her hands, he swallowed a sigh. How had Adam done it? She was little more than a beautiful child packaged in a woman's body, leaving Kieran at a loss as to how she should be managed.

Responsible for dozens of people, old and young, forthright and bashful, he'd grown adept at handling the myriad personalities of his kinsmen. But Maureen's shifting nature baffled him, tested his patience as no one else's did. He sat on the stool beside the settee and rested a hand on her shoulder.

"Maureen, look at me." After a moment she complied, and he frowned at the tears staining her fair skin. "What is it?"

"My mourning is nearly done."

How could he forget? She reminded him of it at every opportunity. Wiping her cheeks, he summoned the reassuring tone he'd use with a frightened child. "I know that, sweeting. Already, several men have spoken with me about you."

Her chin trembled in a smile, and she sniffled. "Truly?"

"Truly. When the time comes, you'll have a host of husbands to choose from."

"Who?"

Custom dictated she not know their names 'til she was free to wed. Then again, he'd never been a slave to etiquette. "Do ye promise not to tell Mother?"

That got him the laugh he sought, and he rattled off the names of several who'd expressed genuine interest in her.

"Which will you choose?" she asked.

" 'Tis not for me to decide."

She tilted her head with a confused expression. "But with Adam and my da gone, you're the man responsible for me."

"Do ye not wish to choose your own husband?"

A smile lit her troubled features. "Aye."

"And do any of those men appeal to you?" When she shook her head, he chuckled. "Have ye someone else in mind, then?"

"Aye." She nodded, eyes shining like sapphires in the firelight. "You."

Sweet bloody hell.

His first impulse was to jump from his seat and put as much distance between them as possible. Then reason kicked him hard, reminding him that his mother had told him many a time of Maureen's great regard for him. Consumed with drilling his men for their ongoing battles, he'd conveniently ignored her warnings.

Maureen's eyes brimmed with fresh tears, and he searched for words to fill the awkward silence. " 'Tis an honor to know you feel this way."

"But you've no wish to marry me," she added in a miserable whisper.

'Twas the truth of it, but he hadn't the heart to tell her so. "My wishes have naught to do with it. I canna marry now, with things as they are."

"Adam continued to fight after he wed me, as do many others."

How could he explain it to her? For him, war and marriage simply didn't mix. He didn't understand why he felt so strongly, but in matters as grave as this, he followed his instincts without question.

Feeling twice his age, he stood and offered his hand to bring her to her feet. "I promise to provide for you 'til you wed, and I shall always care for you. But I'll not widow you again."

She said nothing as he escorted her back to the hall. He wasn't certain what to make of her reticence, but he forgot his anxiety while he searched the gathering for Brynna. Shy as she was, he hadn't expected her to remain belowstairs for long without him.

Before someone else could snare him in conversation, Kieran ascended the winding staircase. At Brynna's door, he raised his hand to knock, then thought better of it. She was still mending and needed her rest. In the morn, he'd seek her out and make another attempt to discover who she was and what she was hiding.

CHAPTER SEVEN

Glancing back at the keep rising from the morning mist, Brynna breathed a sigh of relief that no one had commented on her leaving. Then again, so many people entered and left the extensive compound, one small figure wasn't likely to cause much concern. Except for Kieran.

Tears threatened, and she blinked them away. She didn't need to read his thoughts to recognize his growing feelings for her. The path he'd chosen could only lead where it had gone before, and that she couldn't allow. She hadn't saved his life only to destroy it with selfishness.

Once in the shelter of a ring of birch trees, she paused to catch her breath, bracing herself against a nearby trunk as she felt her balance waver. Pressing a hand to her sore ribs, she closed her eyes and swallowed a whimper of pain.

A hand clapped over her mouth, cutting off her startled scream. Pulled against a chest as hard as stone, she fought back with all her might, kicking and clawing anything she could reach.

" 'Tis dangerous wandering about the forest alone."

Overcome with relief, she collapsed into Kieran's arms.

He swept her up as if she weighed nothing and gave her one of his maddening grins. "Now, will ye be telling me what possessed ye to sneak off, or shall I guess?"

"I wasn't sneaking. I was walking."

"Trust me, lass, I've done my share of sneaking, and that's precisely what ye were doing."

His long strides carried them back toward the keep, and she sighed. "I told you I cannot stay here."

"And I told you I won't allow you to leave. Must I assign a man to guard your lovely hide?"

She smiled at the deft compliment. At the moment, her mending hide was anything but lovely. "I suppose that man would be you."

"Excellent idea. If only I'd thought of it myself."

Her laugh was cut short by a stab in her side, and this time she did whimper. Kieran shifted her, and she dropped her head on his shoulder as the pain eased a bit.

"Better?" he asked.

"A little."

"I've broken a few ribs myself, and it's quite painful. They'll mend quicker if you rest."

Brynna cuddled against him, savoring the protected feeling he gave her. Wrapped in his strong, capable arms, she could so easily forget everything but him.

Curious stares followed them through the bailey and into the keep, but no one spoke to them as he carried her to her room and laid her in the generous bed.

"Rest now," he entreated with a gentle kiss for her lips. "We'll discuss your escape later."

"I'd have no need to escape if you'd only let me leave."

"Are ye daft?" His dark eyes snapped with fury. "Have ye forgotten the men who beat you for helping me? You're a fugitive from the English now, Brynna. They'd be within their laws to execute you on sight."

He regretted the harsh words, but he was desperate to make her understand the danger she was in. Consternation showed in her eyes, quickly chased off by determination.

"I'll be cautious."

"You were cautious before."

"But your clan—"

"Has survived much in its history," he told her in his most soothing tone. "We'd do better if you'd tell me what enemy we face."

She didn't answer, and the last thread of his patience snapped.

"As you wish." Rising to his full height, he folded his arms across his chest and scowled down at her. "But should you attempt to leave again, the guards have orders to stop you."

"You wouldn't dare keep me here against my will," she told him in the haughtiest voice he'd ever had the displeasure of hearing.

"You're in my territory now, lass." Kieran added

the wry grin that drove his mother to distraction. "You'll find I'm quite daring when it suits me."

"Holding me prisoner suits you, then?"

"For now."

"And when you grow tired of guarding me?"

"I'll inform you at once." With an exaggerated bow, he lifted her unbound hand to his lips. "Meantime, you should rest. You'll need your strength for this running battle with me."

He sauntered out the door, chuckling at the frustrated scream that trailed after him.

Donovan Ryan stared through a window at the distant hills of Tara. All his life, he'd lived in Ferndon Castle, within sight of the sacred place from which the high kings of Ireland drew their power. The throne had stood empty for centuries, but the crumbling walls rose from the evening fog, waiting.

"What news have you for me, Major Hawlings?"

"We found no trace of her, Lord Ryan," the man told him in the clipped accent of the native English. "On the morrow, we begin a wider search of the area surrounding the crossroads. If the woman was indeed Lady Brynna, we'll find her."

"How is it my daughter came to be questioned in such a vicious manner?"

"I'm not yet convinced it was she. The prisoner refused to give any information, including her name. Regrettably, her defiance made a difficult situation untenable."

"Should this woman prove to be my Brynna"— Donovan waved the report that listed the men who had interrogated her—"I shall deal with the bastards who debased her as if she were a common whore. As a courtesy to you, I give you fair warning."

Hawlings scowled. "I must warn, you such actions will not go well with my king. His forces are spread quite thinly in this region. He'll not appreciate your depleting their number."

"Point made and taken, Major."

The man nodded and strolled from the spacious sitting room, leaving Donovan alone with his thoughts.

Kieran paused in the corridor outside Brynna's room, wondering at the open door. As he peered into the cozy bedchamber, he saw no sign of her and smiled. Apparently, she felt well enough to join them for dinner.

Encouraged, he swiftly descended the stairs and looked about the crowded hall for her. Laughter reached him from the far table, where she sat amid a throng of male admirers. Young and old, they sat transfixed, listening to what seemed to be a most entertaining yarn. As Kieran approached, he heard more laughter.

"A fine tale, to be sure." Carrick chuckled. "Is it true?"

She merely smiled at him, and he grinned back like the fool he was. When her gaze fell on Kieran, her smile vanished. "Good eve to you, Chief MacAuley."

The formality was most unlike her, and he nodded just as stiffly. "And to you."

"Did you want something?"

The fire in her eyes belied the demure tone of her voice, and he strove for calm as his own temper flared. "Dinner will be served shortly," he replied, offering his arm to her.

"Thank you, but I'd prefer to eat here."

The men blinked as one, but none dared even a glance at him. The lads met her announcement with great enthusiasm and begged for another story. Ignoring him completely, she launched into a tale about a wizened crone who conjured fortune from the waters of a magical stream.

Kieran stood there a few moments to avoid the impression that she'd run him off. As he slipped from the merry circle, no one seemed to notice his leaving. He made his way to the head table, seething over the unpredictable nature of women.

What the devil was wrong with her? Was he to allow her to walk into harm's reach simply because she wished to do so? Beyond any history they might have together, Brynna was in need of his protection, and protect her he would. Whether she wanted it or not.

Throwing himself into his seat, he drained his tankard in a few swallows. Attentive as always, Maureen hurried over with a pitcher of mead.

"More, Kieran?"

"Aye, much more."

She smiled as she refilled his cup. "Your guest seems to have grown tired of your hospitality."

" 'Twould appear so," he grumbled, his eyes fixed on the distant table where Brynna sat.

"Perhaps it would be wise to let her go."

Kieran rubbed at the pain between his eyes. "I canna do that, Maureen. I don't know what sort of danger she's in."

"She seems to be capable of fending for herself."

Unable to believe what he'd heard, he stared between his fingers at her. "Have ye forgotten how she nearly died at the hands of those soldiers?"

"Of course not, but she needn't stay here. You could send her to Gallimore."

He considered the suggestion, then shook his head. "I want her here."

"With you?"

The mild accusation irked him, and he glared at her. "So I know she's safe."

Maureen lifted a careless shoulder and moved down the table to fill the waiting cups.

Brynna could feel Kieran's anger from across the room, ebbing and flowing like the tide. Several times she found him watching her, his expression shifting from bewilderment to outright fury. She'd wounded his pride, which she'd not intended, but she'd run short of options. If he refused to let her leave, she must force him to throw her out.

The man who had shyly introduced himself as Conor produced a shepherd's pipe from his belt bag, and others shoved the tables and benches toward the walls to clear space for a swirling reel. Conor wielded his instrument with great skill, and another man brought out a sheepskin drum to keep pace for the dancers.

She was watching them when Carrick left the

dancing and took her hand to bring her to her feet.

" 'Tis not for looking at," he teased, dark eyes flashing much like Kieran's. " 'Tis for doing."

"But I don't know how," she protested as he swept her into the pattern.

"Neither do I."

She laughed, and he grinned down at her. "Ye have the most beautiful laugh I've ever heard."

"Enough of that, ye mindless whelp," Devlin thundered from behind him. "Turn her over, now."

Carrick hesitated, but a scowl from his towering cousin sent him off in search of someone else to pair with.

"What's in that head of yours?" Devlin asked her in a muted voice. "Can ye not see how you're hurting him?"

Her gaze went to Kieran, who seemed perfectly content with his fourth partner of the evening. Not that she'd been counting them. "Aye, he looks miserable."

"'Tis his way, nothing more. Not many see what's hidden beneath it. Those that do would never use his feelings against him."

How could he possibly know that she saw what Kieran hid from everyone else? Shaking off a question she had no answer for, Brynna sighed. "I don't mean him harm, but he must let me go."

"Why?"

She longed to tell him, nearly as much as she wanted to confide in Kieran, but trust was a luxury she'd forfeited long ago. "I cannot explain it to you."

Those keen blue eyes studied her for a long moment. "Rather, ye will not, I'd wager, but I'll offer a bit of advice: Kieran is beyond stubborn, and if he deems it best for you to stay, then you'd do well to go along and be done with it. Fighting him only makes him more determined."

Bristling at his comment, she drew herself up to her full height. "I'm quite determined myself."

"That I can see," he muttered with a shake of his head. "Of all the lasses in Ireland—"

He left off abruptly, and Brynna glared at him. "What?"

"Nothing."

With a heavy sigh and a kiss for her hand, he left her staring after him.

After an interminable evening of dancing and frivolous conversation, Kieran gratefully closed the door to his private chamber. Leaning back against it, he closed his eyes to blot out the image of Brynna moving through his enamored kinsmen, laughing while she charmed every last one of them.

As he stirred up the fire, he reasoned that she'd been living alone and was merely enjoying the company of other people. In his heart, he recognized his grousing for what it was: envy.

For the first time, he'd coveted what another man held in his arms, and the feeling shamed him. He possessed more riches than most men even dreamed of—wealth, land, power—and yet he'd surrender it all for one thing.

Brynna.

In his bed this night, by his side in the morn. Though his yearning still baffled him, 'twas pointless to deny it. His longing made her contempt nearly unbearable, but there was little he could do. If he yielded to her wishes and allowed her to leave, God only knew what would become of her.

As he stared into the flames, the image of her battered body lashed to that tree filled his memory. He would keep her from further harm, he vowed as he shed his clothes. She might despise him for it, but she'd be alive and well. Perhaps one day she'd allow him back into her heart.

Grumbling at his foolishness, he parted the heavy drapes about his bed and slid beneath the covers. Exhausted from a long and trying day, he fell asleep quickly, swept into the realm where his nymph awaited him.

But this night she was far from playful. Urgency rippled the air about them, and her demanding kisses left him weak. As her body settled over his, he realized something was wrong.

He was awake.

"Maureen!"

He shoved her onto her back and bolted from his bed before he lost his senses and finished what she'd begun. He cursed as he tripped over his boots, again while he gingerly donned his trews. After several deep breaths to cool his raging blood, he took a throw from the back of the settee.

Keeping his gaze averted, he handed it through the curtains to her. "Put this on."

"Kieran—"

When he repeated his command, he heard a sigh, followed by the whisper of wool over bare skin. He gave her a moment to compose herself, then pulled the brocade aside. "Come out now, sweeting. 'Tis no place for you."

Her eyes went a misty blue. "But I want to be with you."

If she knew what he'd nearly done, she'd feel differently. With a firm grip on his lust, he offered his hand to her. After glaring at him for several moments, at last she relented and left his bed.

Beneath the bedcovers he found her dressing gown. Not black, as tradition dictated, but a soft lavender embroidered with wildflowers.

"Callie made it for me." She snatched it away as if she feared he'd confiscate the illicit robe.

He smiled to soothe her easily riled temper. "It suits ye well. I should like to see you in it."

She gave him an incredulous look, then a knowing woman's smile. "Lead us not into temptation?"

"You would tempt a dead man." Chuckling, he nodded to the gown. "Put that on so I can talk to you."

He strolled toward the fire to allow her to dress. No doubt, half the keep knew she was in his room. By mid-morn, the other half would know it, as well. On an ordinary day, such a problem would gain his full attention 'til it was resolved.

But since Brynna had arrived, his days had been far from ordinary.

As Maureen approached the hearth, he pushed aside his errant thoughts and focused on her. "I think 'tis time to end your mourning."

She blinked, tilting her head in confusion. "It's not yet been a year."

"It's been long enough. A woman deserves a husband who loves her. I'll bring it before the council at our next meeting, if you approve."

"I do." Her eager expression quickly dimmed. "You don't want me, do you?"

Despite her trickery, he couldn't bring himself to hurt her with the truth. "I canna have you. I've told ye that."

She clasped her hands and looked down at them. "I thought if you made love to me, you'd feel differently."

He wouldn't have loved her. Frustrated and angry, he'd have taken her, and roughly at that. There was no gentle way to explain that to her, so he said, "My feelings for you will always be as they are now. Ye may trust in that."

When she lifted her head, he watched as the last bit of hope left her eyes and trailed down her cheeks. God save him from a woman's tears. Though his impulse was to gather her into his arms and comfort her, he took one of her hands for the sort of kiss he'd given her many a time. "Shall I escort you back to your room?"

A delighted smile shone through her tears. "You would do that?"

"Of course."

He offered his arm, and as he opened the door, he angled a look down at her. "No more of this, Maureen. Promise me."

She wrinkled her nose like a little girl who'd been denied her favorite treat, but she nodded. "I promise."

"Now, then." He gave her shoulders a quick hug

as they entered the corridor. "About that list of husbands . . ."

Tired and dusty from a patrol of the broad valley, Kieran thought his boots felt leaden as he dragged them up the steps and into the hall. He could avoid it no longer. He must begin training before his body went completely to rot.

"Here y'are, Kieran." Dev offered him a tankard filled with mead. " 'Twill wash the dust from your throat."

"Many thanks." He drained it and set it on the table before turning toward the stairs.

"Won't ye be joining us?" Carrick asked, his serious tone at odds with his barely suppressed grin.

"Nay. Enjoy yourselves, and I shall see you at dinner."

"Methinks our chieftain has trouble we might help him with." Cavan grinned, patting the bench beside him. "Sit a while and tell us about it."

Folding his arms, Kieran glared at his father's cousin. "Amused, are ye?"

The man laughed outright. "Tell me, when did ye go from devising ways to rid yourself of women to chasing after one?"

"I'd not tweak him," Dev advised with a chuckle. "Ever since Brynna arrived, he's been edgy as a starved wolf."

"And what would ye have me do?" Kieran demanded.

"Ye know my thoughts," Dev reminded him.

"Aye. You'd have me wed a woman who drives me mad."

" 'Tis the best sort to marry," Cavan replied. "Keeps life interesting."

Despite his foul mood, Kieran laughed. "My life is interesting enough with all of you."

The older man's look grew sober. "The lot of us canna replace a wife and children who adore you. Then again, you could always wed one of your lovely sisters-in-law."

Biting back a caustic reply, Kieran wheeled about and stalked from the hall, doing his best to ignore the merriment he left behind.

At the head of the stairs, he turned toward his chambers. Before he'd gone half a dozen steps, he heard his mother's voice.

"Brynna, please let me in."

Alerted by her wheedling tone, he reversed direction and strode down the corridor that housed the guest chambers. "What the devil is going on?"

"She's eaten nothing all day. And now she's bolted the door and refuses to answer me."

"Where's the key?"

Her eyes snapped with volatile O'Connell temper. "If I could find it, would I be begging her to open the blessed door?"

Unleashing a curse that pinkened even Aileen's cheeks, Kieran pounded his fist against the door. "Brynna, open this at once!"

"Will you let me leave?"

"Nay."

"Then I'll not open it."

Her icy tone did nothing to cool his ire, and he swore again, casting about for a solution. He found it in a pair of battle-axes crossed on the far wall above a much-mended banner. In two quick strides, he crossed the hallway and ripped one of the massive blades from its cradle.

Aileen's eyes widened in alarm. "Kieran, what—"

"Brynna, stand back," he ordered.

"Why?"

He replied with a blow from the ax, cleaving through the solid oak to send the bolt clattering to the floor.

As the door swung open, he saw Brynna, hands on her hips as she glowered unmercifully at him. "What in the name of Brigid do you think you're doing?"

In no mood to spar with her, he dropped the ax and entered her chamber. With an exaggerated bow, he held out his hand. "I wish to speak with you. Come with me."

Tossing her head, she tilted a defiant chin at him. "I will not."

"You may walk, or I shall carry you." He forced a smile. "Your choice."

" 'Tis no choice, and well you know it."

Keenly aware of their gathering audience, he retreated a bit. "Please, Brynna."

"Do you cede?"

"I propose a temporary truce," he countered, offering his hand again. This time she accepted it, strolling through the mess as if it didn't exist. While he escorted her down the corridor, he heard the excited whispers and swift feet of gossips at work, but was far too tired to care.

Brynna expected him to march her straight to his

private study and finally have it out with her. Throughout the day, she'd plotted what she would say and do to anger him enough to release her.

When he strolled past his chamber toward the backstairs, she realized her carefully laid strategy was for naught. "Where are you taking me?"

As they descended the stairs, he continued staring straight ahead. "If you'd indulge me, I've something to show you."

Skirting the bustling courtyard, he led her behind the chapel to a fresh grave. On a stone marker chiseled into the shape of a Celtic cross, she read the inscription.

Kieran MacAuley. The Fearless One.

Beneath the first two lines were carved the clan's symbolic oak leaf and the years of his birth and death. A chill of foreboding stole over her before he grasped her arms and turned her from the morbid sight.

"If not for you, I'd be in there." He nodded to his empty grave. "My clan would be without their chieftain, and my mother would be mourning her last son. Never will I be able to repay my debt to you, but at the very least I can keep you safe."

"Kieran, you don't understand."

"No, I don't." The warmth left his eyes, and they went nearly black. "I canna fathom why an intelligent woman would put herself in such danger."

"I've no choice."

"I have given you one."

His commanding tone rankled in her ears, and she narrowed her eyes with displeasure. "To stay here. As your guest or your prisoner?"

"That choice is also yours."

"And if I should choose to leave?"

His grip on her tightened, and he glowered down at her. "I'll find you and drag you back here, where I can protect you from your own foolishness."

"First I'm intelligent and now I'm foolish? I do wish you'd decide."

Anger flared in his eyes, and through clenched teeth he muttered, " 'Tis not enough you haunt my nights—must you bedevil my waking hours, as well?"

His revelation startled her, and she firmly tamped down the excited flutter in her heart. "Apparently so. Unless you'd care to reverse your position and allow me to leave."

"If you'd only tell me why, I might consider it."

"No, you won't. You'll placate me by listening, then refuse."

" 'Tis for your own good, lass." His harsh look had softened, as had his tone.

"I did well enough looking after myself before—" She sank her teeth into her lower lip to stem the angry words.

"Before ye met me," he finished for her. With a gentle touch, he traced the scar about her throat. "Ye saved me from the English, Brynna. I want only to do the same for you."

A beguiling combination of arrogance and tenderness, Kieran MacAuley was the sort of man no woman could resist. When he opposed her, she could fight him easily enough.

But as he drew her into his arms for a leisurely kiss, her defenses fell away.

"Since you put it that way"—she gave a little grin— "I suppose I could stay a while longer."

Kieran waited in the corridor outside Brynna's chambers. After his temperamental display with the ax, Aileen had threatened him with dire consequences if he dared cross the open threshold. Hands clasped behind his back, he studied a new tapestry in a show of carelessness he didn't truly feel.

Untamed as the land that had birthed her, Brynna fascinated him in a way he'd never known. He'd enjoyed his fair share of women, letting them go when they expressed their need for more than he could give. Ireland was a jealous mistress, he told them, and she left him with little time for another. Could it be he'd found the one to replace her?

When Brynna appeared in the doorway, he thought perhaps he had.

Dressed in the blue silk, a pearl circlet nestled in her hair, she looked as if she'd stepped out of a faery tale. The gown had been hemmed and cleverly pleated to accent the graceful frame beneath it.

She stopped abruptly and leveled an icy glare at him. "Come to admire your handiwork?"

Though he tried to return her contemptuous look, his traitorous mouth lifted in a half-grin. There was no denying the magic she aroused in him. Perhaps 'twas time she knew of it, as well.

"Actually, I've come to admire my mother's handiwork."

"What are you talking about?"

"You look exquisite."

As she studied him, her eyes gradually shifted

from suspicious moss to glowing emerald. "Thank you."

"You're welcome."

She stumbled on the threshold, and he reached out to steady her.

"Thank you again," she murmured, blushing furiously as she retrieved the slipper she'd lost. "These shoes are a bit too big."

"Then why are you wearing them?"

"They match the gown."

When he ceased laughing, he found her glaring at him. "Forgive me, Brynna, but I'm most relieved to discover you're like other women, after all."

With a haughty toss of her head, she made to shove past him, but he recognized her intent and blocked her. An odd notion struck him, and he tested it by thinking he would move to his left.

When she darted to his right, he grabbed her and held her fast. "You can sense my thoughts."

Her eyes widened, bringing a dormant memory to life. Following his instincts, he brushed a finger over her cheek and nearly choked on the adoration that flooded her eyes. His body raged to have her, and he pushed her to arm's length as he fought to tether the possessive beast inside him. It chanted in a low growl, matched by the heavy thudding of his heart.

Mine. Mine. Mine.

The force of desire hit him like a physical blow, all the more troubling because the woman he coveted harbored so many secrets.

"Kieran?"

Her concerned tone broke through, and he held

up a hand as she stepped toward him. "No. I canna think when you touch me."

Heedless of the warning, she pressed closer. "Must you always think?"

"I'm the chieftain."

"The chieftain is not allowed the feelings of a man? What sort of life is that?"

" 'Tis my life, Brynna." Even to his own ears, he sounded bitter.

"And are you happy being alone?"

The last came in a whisper laced with empathy. In that moment, he knew what must have drawn him to her, what enticed him even now.

She understood.

He framed her face in his hands. Nearly free of bruises, 'twas by far the sweetest he'd ever seen. When her lips curved invitingly, he tasted their softness. Her heart raced in rhythm with his own, and he buried his face in the curve of her shoulder, inhaling the wondrous scent of a summer garden.

His hands glided over the warm blue silk while his mind stripped it away. As he had each time he touched her, he imagined her beneath him, the heat of her kisses, the welcoming embrace of her body.

She made him yearn for things he'd once thought he would never have.

Allowing himself one last kiss, he took her hands and stepped away from her. Such a vision was she, he paused a moment to savor the picture she made.

"What are you doing blocking the way?" Aileen demanded as she bustled down the hall. She paused for an approving look at Brynna. "Lovely, is she not?"

"That she is."

"I'd wager she's quite hungry." In the subtle way she had, his mother prodded him back a step. "Off with you, now. If you can't be trusted to escort her properly, I'll summon Devlin."

"No need to roust him, Mother. I promise to behave." He extended his arm to Brynna. "At least 'til dessert."

Laughing, they strolled down the hallway together. Their voices mingled pleasantly, trailing off as they descended the stairs that led to the main hall.

Aileen watched them go, marveling at the change in her son. His troubled brooding had given way to the lightheartedness she cherished, but she'd noticed something else, as well: a hopeful look in his eyes she'd not seen in a very long time.

"Please, God," she whispered with a quick look up, "let her love him."

CHAPTER EIGHT

Kieran kept his word and behaved perfectly, well-mannered as any nobleman she'd ever known. But several times, Brynna found him considering her with a ravenous gleam in his eyes, as if his mind had slipped the elegant gown from her body and was pleased with the result.

He shared his pewter trencher with her, leaving the most tender venison for her to eat. After she'd finished her spiced apple compote, he offered his to her, as well. Leaning back, he rested his chin on his hand as the chieftain's ring glowed in the candle-light. An aura of careless power surrounded him, resting easily on his strong shoulders.

Nowhere could there exist a man as magnificent as Kieran MacAuley.

"Brynna, if you've any heart at all, ye must cease with that spoon."

Smiling, she dipped it back into the bowl to scrape the sides. " 'Tis delicious."

"Aye."

Savoring his rapt attention, she offered him the last bite. He leaned over to take it, swirling his tongue suggestively over the empty spoon.

"Do you like sweets, Chief MacAuley?"

"Very much."

His regard wandered to her lips, and they opened of their own accord. He reached for his napkin and dabbed at the corner of her mouth. Grinning, he grazed her lower lip with his thumb. "I canna kiss you here."

"Of course not," she stammered, feeling utterly foolish. She knew how to behave at table. What was wrong with her?

"Then again," he continued, rising from his seat to extend an arm to her, " 'tis a fair night for a walk."

Brynna glanced about to find several curious looks aimed at them. "Now?"

"Now."

There was no resisting the playful glint in his eyes. She stood, and he tucked her hand into the crook of his arm.

"Where are you going?"

They turned toward the sound of Aileen's voice, and Kieran smiled. "To show Brynna your gardens."

" 'Tis a lovely night for it."

"My thoughts, as well," he agreed before steering Brynna from the crowded hall.

They strolled through a rear door and turned toward a line of neatly trimmed hedges. The waxing moon glowed overhead, its light muted by a thin sheen of mist. Through the air flowed a current of expectation, as if changes were in the offing. She prayed the MacAuley would weather them well.

Running her hand over the soft boughs, she inhaled the crisp scent of evergreen. "It smells like the forest."

"I thought ye might enjoy finding something familiar here. Besides me, that is."

She returned his smile, and he gathered her into his arms for a long kiss. His lips wandered along the line of her jaw, and he murmured, "Why were ye trying to leave?"

"You called a truce, Kieran," she reminded him as she pushed him away. "When will you let things be?"

"When you trust me."

Though he said nothing more, she heard the hurt in his voice, saw more of it in the pained lines of his face. Her evasiveness had begun to do him harm, and she could bear it no longer. "I do trust you."

"Then tell me the truth. All of it."

A slender doe stepped from the shadow of a tall hedge. She nibbled a bit of grass, then lifted her head to consider them with all-knowing eyes.

"By the saints," he murmured. "Have ye ever seen a deer with green eyes?"

"Once or twice."

Glowering at it, Brynna issued a command in some language he'd never heard. Tossing her head, the doe trotted off and vanished into the twilight.

Awestruck, Kieran turned his attention back to the woman in his arms. "What did you tell her?"

"That I'd be handling this my own way."

"Dev's right. You *are* a faery."

Though her teeth worried her lower lip, her eyes never left his. "A bit."

"Come now, Brynna." He chuckled. "Either you're fae or you're not."

"My mother is *sídhe* and my father is mortal."

"Was that your mother?" He nodded in the direction in which the doe had gone.

"Aye, come to remind me the truth must be given when demanded."

He smoothed a lock of hair back over her shoulder. "And why would ye need such a reminder?"

"Often, the truth is not easily given. Or taken."

"Did you conceal it before," he asked, "or have I merely forgotten?"

"Yes."

"To both?" Her hesitant nod made him frown. "Why would ye do such a thing?"

"I felt I had no choice."

Before he could question her further, over her shoulder he saw a grim-faced Carrick hurrying toward them.

"What is it?" he asked.

"English cavalry coming this way."

"How many?"

"Ten. They carry a banner of truce, but ye know the English."

Kieran saw the look of dread in Brynna's eyes but had no time to ask about it. Instead, he took her hand, and they followed Carrick back into the hall.

After relaying the worrisome news to Dev, he turned to Carrick. "I'll discover what they're about. No one leaves the keep."

"I fear they've come because of me," Brynna countered in a hushed voice. "I'll go with you."

"Nay. You'll remain here, out of sight."

With a quick kiss on her cheek, he strode out the main doors into the bailey.

Kieran waited for a guard to lift the portcullis so he could pass through the main gate. Outside the bars that guarded the opposite end of the barbican, he saw a mounted English soldier. When he emerged, nine more came into view. He swept the area with an assessing glance but saw nothing to alert him to danger. Though Dev and Carrick had protested, he'd insisted on meeting the soldiers outside.

If the English desired entry to MacAuley Keep, they'd have to tear down the walls stone by bleeding stone.

Their leader nudged his horse forward several paces and nodded in greeting. "Chief MacAuley, I'm Major Frederick Hawlings, commander of the British garrison at Westmeath."

"I know who y'are, Major Hawlings," Kieran responded in a conversational tone. "What brings you this side of the line?"

Tension hung thick in the air, heightened by the deadly whisper of a dozen archers on the wall walk notching their arrows. To the major's credit, he didn't so much as flinch, nor did his eyes leave Kieran's. It took a brave man to stand inside his enemy's territory with nothing but the chieftain's honor to protect him.

"My inquiries about the area tell me you have a guest. An English guest."

"You're mistaken, Major. My visitor is as Irish as I am."

"As a resident of English Westmeath, the young lady is a subject of King Edward, and he seeks after her welfare."

Kieran had purposely not admitted he was harboring a woman, and silently he cursed the wagging tongues of his kin. "She fares well enough, considering what was done to her."

Frowning, the man shifted in his finely tooled saddle. Apparently, he had no wish to discuss the torture of a woman whose only crime was possessing a generous heart.

"Chief MacAuley, I shall be blunt: His Majesty is concerned she's being held against her will."

What could Edward find so fascinating about an outcast Irish lass? Crossing his arms, Kieran spread his feet in the seemingly casual stance that alerted his men to possible trouble. "Are ye suggesting I need take a woman prisoner to make her stay with me?"

The guards laughed heartily, and Hawlings's mouth quivered with humor. "Of course not. I'm merely carrying out the orders I was given. Once I'm confident she remains here of her own volition, I shall report such to my king and leave you in peace."

The man already knew Brynna was there, so what harm could it do? Without taking his eyes from the English officer, he called out for Dev.

"Aye?"

"Fetch the lass, if she'll come. Assure her I'll not allow her to be harmed."

"As you wish," his cousin replied before hurrying back to the hall.

"Not a move from you or any of your men," Kieran warned, pointing above his head to the archers still poised for attack. "Or they'll kill every last one of you."

"I'd not even consider such a thing, I assure you."

Kieran approached the officer's chestnut stallion, held a hand out for the horse to sniff before stroking the broad forehead. "'Tis an impressive mount you have."

Hawlings smiled and patted the destrier's massive neck. "Indeed. I acquired him in Connacht. They raise fine horses there."

Kieran grinned up at his visitor. "Irish horses."

"Some of the best in the world. Samson is by far the bravest horse I've ever had the privilege of owning."

"'Tis a shame to risk our loyal friends in battle, is it not?"

"Yes, it is."

The metallic screech of the portcullis opening broke into their conversation, and Kieran glanced back to find Brynna walking toward him.

He held his arm out for her, and she took it before granting him a lovely smile. "You sent for me, Chief MacAuley?"

"These men came to ensure you're not my prisoner."

"Did they, now?" She laughed, as if the idea were absurdity itself.

"I'm pleased to see she's faring so well under your care," Hawlings said, nodding politely. "Does she wish to remain?"

"She does."

Though Brynna's tone was sweet, Kieran noticed the pleading in her eyes, the cool response in the Englishman's. "You're satisfied, then?"

"I am. I shall note your cooperation in my next report."

"I'd prefer you didn't."

"Of course." Hawlings nodded. "I'm grateful for your assistance, all the same."

He circled his mount and motioned to his men, cantering off with them in tow.

After they'd gone, Kieran looked up to the wall walk. "Well done. They'll think more carefully next time they consider interrupting my dinner."

The men laughed, lowering their weapons while they discussed the unusual events. Wondering at the odd exchange, Kieran walked Brynna back through the main gate. At the foot of the wide steps, she halted and turned to him. "Kieran, there's something I must tell you."

"Ye know Major Hawlings." When she nodded, he swore under his breath. "Please tell me you're not English."

"Of course not," she snapped. "I merely chose to live in a house on the wrong side of a line no one can see."

Her show of temper made him smile. "Then how is it you're acquainted with an English officer?"

"He's one of my father's men."

Foreboding prickled just under his skin, warning him. "He's the commander at Westmeath."

" 'Tis his official post, but he has other interests

as well." She fixed him with a beseeching look that told him he'd not like what she had to say. "Donovan Ryan is my father."

Torchlight flickered in Kieran's dark eyes, lending him the look of an avenging angel.

"Never mention that traitorous bastard's name in my presence again." His even tone was at odds with the fury in his gaze, as was his gentleness when he cupped her chin. "Ryan's daughter. God help me, what have I done?"

"I know he betrayed the clans at the Battle of Kildare, but I swear to you, I knew nothing of it. I left when I learned what he did."

He yanked his hand away as if he could no longer bear to touch her, and his eyes filled with memories. "Have you any idea how many men died in that battle?"

Fists at his sides, he began pacing. "Ryan brought us horses and trained soldiers, as did his allies. We had a fighting chance at Kildare, with so much cavalry at our disposal. They withdrew so quietly, we weren't aware of it 'til they were nearly gone."

He halted, pinning her with an agonized look. "They left us there to die."

The words twisted in her heart, and she fought to contain a rush of tears. "I know."

"Did ye also know this clan swore vengeance on him and all associated with him?"

The only sound was the crackling of torches as a breeze swept through the bailey. Tension circled them like a stalking wolf.

The dull roar emanating from the gathering hall swelled, and she knew he must address the concerns of his kinsmen. A visit from the English was no small matter.

"What will you tell them?"

"I'm not certain."

She could feel the conflict raging within him as reason warred with emotion. Renowned for his keen instincts, he tempered them with an agile mind and uncompromising loyalty.

"There y'are." Carrick hailed him from the entryway, and Kieran looked up the steps. "Everyone is waiting to hear what happened. Shall I tell them while you finish with Brynna?"

Kieran glanced back at her, steeled himself against the tears welling in her beautiful eyes. "I'm finished with her. Escort her to her chamber and post yourself outside."

Ignoring her pleading look, he watched Carrick walk her up the front stairs to the upper floor. After a deep breath to settle his nerves, he mounted the steps and entered the hall. Once inside, he surveyed the assembly and grinned. "I'm told you'd like a report of our encounter with the English."

Laughter rippled through the crowd, dispelling much of the apprehension he'd sensed when he'd first rejoined them. After relaying the brief discussion, he asked, "Have you any questions for me?"

"What possessed ye to bring an English wench here?" a lanky farmer demanded.

"I brought an Irish lass in need to those I thought had sympathy enough to help her. Are ye telling me I was wrong, Daniel?"

Cowed by the scolding, Daniel relented a bit. "If she's not English, why was Hawlings sent?"

"I canna say. Being a Gaelic barbarian, the workings of the cultured mind escape me," he added with another grin that made them all laugh.

A pang of guilt hit him squarely, but he reasoned it away. He'd not been truthful, but neither had he lied. Brynna needed his protection. From the English, her own father and his own kin when they learned her true identity. Pushing aside the worry gnawing at him, he parried several more pointed queries, reassuring his people as best he could.

At last, everyone seemed satisfied and filed from the hall. Kieran called to Dev, motioning him close enough so they could talk without being overheard. "The soldiers have truly gone?"

"Near as we can tell."

"On the morrow, I'll take a patrol out to ensure they've left no spies about the valley."

Dev's face broke into a grin. "Or you might enjoy the day with your lovely guest while I beat the bushes for English dogs."

"I think not."

The smile faded, replaced by a quizzical look. "What's happened?"

"Nothing I care to discuss."

Dev gave a single nod of understanding. "I'll meet you at the gates after breakfast, then."

What was he telling them?

Shivering in her woolen dressing gown, Brynna paced before the fire. What had she been thinking, remaining in Dunsmere? If she'd gone when she was first able, none of this would have happened. Kieran might miss her, but his clan would be safe, his life going on as it was meant to.

When she turned to begin another circuit, her eyes went to the gaping doorway, and she smiled. She'd not gone because he'd chased after her and carried her back to the only safe place she'd known since leaving Ferndon.

By morning, her father would receive word of her whereabouts and send an escort for her, if he didn't come himself. More than two years she'd been gone, staying ahead of his searchers by dint of raw intuition. She loathed hiding like a frightened mouse, cold and hungry and alone. But truly, she saw no other way.

For a brief moment, she considered removing herself from Kieran's thoughts before leaving Dunsmere, then discarded the notion. Altering memory wasn't an exact thing, and she could destroy knowledge he needed to guide his clan through the labyrinth she'd inadvertently created. She paused and looked into the crackling flames.

Her heart wept for her lost chance at happiness, a loving husband, children to cherish. Perhaps Kieran felt the same and, despite the obstacles they faced, they could devise a way to be together.

Brightening at the sunny thought, she hastened from her bedchamber, only to be stopped by Carrick.

"And where might ye be going, Mistress Brynna?"

"I must speak with Kieran."

"I was told to bring ye here and stand guard, not allow ye to go traipsing about the keep."

"I'll not be traipsing, I'll be going straight to his

chamber." She drew herself up in imitation of her mother's regal stance. "You may accompany me if you like, but I will speak with him."

After a moment, he relented with a sigh. "Very well, but if he orders ye out, you'll go. Agreed?"

"Agreed."

Grinning, he offered her his arm. "Now I understand why he's so twisted up over you. You're a difficult woman to refuse."

"Some men prefer a challenge."

"That'd be Kieran. Never the easy road for that one."

He was in love with the daughter of his sworn enemy.

In ancient times, Kieran would have been honor bound to take the *scian* from his waist and slit Brynna's delicate throat. Even now, at the very least he should turn her out and forget she'd ever existed. Unfortunately, he'd already discovered he was incapable of doing that.

He'd followed his heart into this bog, and look where it had led him. Led them.

At a loss for what else to do, he filled a carved wooden tankard with wine. If Brynna stayed, Donovan Ryan would descend on the MacAuley and punish them for daring to hide his daughter from him. They would fight, and he'd eventually tire of harassing them and go. But at what cost?

And what of the cost to Brynna? He owed her his life. If he relinquished her to her father, she'd flee into the forest as she'd done before, and he'd never see her again. The warmth of her smile, the contagious peal of her laughter would exist only in his memory, growing dimmer by the day 'til they vanished forever.

Gazing into the fire, he swallowed half the wine, barely felt it sliding down his throat. Frustrated beyond anything he'd ever known, he hurled the cup into the fireplace and fisted his hands on the oaken mantel. When the flames hissed at him, he growled back. Morgan's ring shone in the firelight, capturing his waning attention.

So often, the sight of it had comforted him, reassuring him in troubled times, filling him with pride when his clan triumphed. This night, it made him feel unworthy. Like an all-knowing eye, the golden oak leaf seemed to stare at him, imploring him to do something. Anything.

A knock at the door jolted him from his black musings. "Aye?"

"Kieran, it's Carrick."

What the devil was he doing away from his post? In half a dozen furious strides, Kieran crossed the chamber and flung open the door. The reprimand died in his throat when he saw Brynna, dressed in MacAuley wool fashioned for a lady.

So beautiful, she made him ache with wanting. He longed to lose himself in her, forget everything, if only for one night. Instead, he crossed his arms and scowled at her. "You needed something?"

Apparently unimpressed by his brusque manner, she regarded him without a hint of fear. "To speak with you."

"I've retired for the evening. I thought I told you to do the same."

"You did, but—"

"You assumed I meant otherwise?" he interrupted, desire setting his temper aflame. "Have ye not learned I choose my words carefully, Brynna? If I say something to you, I expect you to listen."

"Why?"

"Because I'm chieftain here!"

She tossed her head in the challenging gesture he'd come to know well. "I'm not MacAuley. You have no power over me."

"That's plain enough," he snarled. "Now leave me in peace."

"Not until you've heard me out."

"For the love of—" 'Twas a waste of breath, arguing with her, so he stepped aside to allow her in. "Carrick, you may go. I'll see Brynna back to her chamber."

"A pleasant evening to ye, then."

Carrick sauntered off, whistling carelessly on his way down the corridor. Wishing to avoid any further scandal within his walls, Kieran left the door open and turned to face the loveliest—and thorniest—problem he'd ever encountered. "Bewitching my men, are ye, lass?"

"There was no need. Carrick likes me."

Though his expression revealed nothing, his eyes sparked with anger. "You wished to speak with me?"

"Kieran, I had no control over my father's actions." He didn't respond, and she went on. "When I realized the danger your clan would be in because of our association, I did my best to protect them."

"By stealing my memories of you."

His accusing tone fanned her temper, and Brynna glared at him. "What would you have had me do?"

"Ye might have told me the truth. I care for scores of people. Did ye not trust me to do the same for the woman I love?"

As quickly as he'd spiked her anger, he swept every shred of it away. "After all I've told you, still you love me?"

"I canna help loving you," he confessed, misery flooding his dark eyes.

"And I love you. Were your father here, do you honestly believe he'd cast me out?"

They stood only paces from one another, yet he felt very far away. Closed off and reserved, carefully guarding his emotions.

He stepped away from her and resumed his staring into the fire. "It matters not. I'm chieftain now, and the decision is mine."

"So you'll remain loyal to the MacAuley, to Ireland. But in doing so, you'll betray your own heart."

With all the dignity she could muster, she stalked from his rooms and slammed the door behind her.

"You're absolutely certain it was Brynna?"

"There could be no doubt, Lord Ryan," Hawlings replied.

"And she's well?"

"Remarkably so, considering the reports we received. I posted your men around Dunsmere, as you requested."

"Excellent." Donovan retrieved a sheaf of papers from his desk. "Before your arrival, I was looking through your report of the raid. I've a question for you."

"By all means."

Coming 'round his imposing mahogany desk, he stared straight into the Englishman's eyes. "How is it a man as shrewd as MacAuley has taken it upon himself to shelter a woman he must know very little about?"

"I've no idea."

"Think on it a moment."

In less time than it took him to blink, Hawlings's face drained of every last tinge of color. "The widow in the glen."

" 'Twas my Brynna, come to aid those she could. The man she was keening over was no one's dead husband, but MacAuley himself."

To his credit, Hawlings offered no excuse for his lapse in judgment that night. "They seemed quite well acquainted when I saw them in Dunsmere. Are you certain she'd not met him before the raid?"

"How could I know? She's been gone so long." Donovan heard the anguish in his voice and strove to regain his composure. Then the Englishman's observation registered more clearly. "How well acquainted?"

"They appeared at ease with one another. She seemed to trust him, and he kept a hand on her at all times, as if to reassure her."

Taking in the new information, Donovan strolled to the window and gazed in the direction of Tara. "What know you of Irish legends?"

"Very little."

"Have the English a concept of a singular mate? One whose soul was fashioned with the same characteristics as your own?"

"A few men I know have such marriages," Hawlings replied. "They are quite rare."

"Long ago, men of war kept themselves free of emotional distractions. When presented with the maid who matched him, the warrior plunged his sword into the soil and devoted himself to propagating his fierce blood in the next generation of his race." Donovan turned to find the major watching him with an expression of polite forbearance. "MacAuley carries a warrior's blood in him."

"We all do. My men and I are no less skilled than he."

"A soldier is not a warrior. Kieran fights because he must." Donovan fisted his hand. "Ireland commands him, drives his past and his present. He is the cornerstone of the Gaelic resistance. Remove him, and the rest will tumble to your king." In emphasis, he opened his hand and swept it through the air.

"Lord Ryan, while I respect your knowledge of the Gael chiefs, I must oppose you on this. Formidable as Kieran is in battle, he hasn't the stature you attribute to him."

"Have you ever built a castle, Major?"

The man smiled. "No, I haven't. I've taken many of them down, however."

"Then you understand the concept of the cornerstone. Its strength relies not on its size but rather on the hardness of the stone. Kieran MacAuley was quarried from solid granite. He holds this uneasy alliance together with grit and his bare hands. Until you find a way to nullify his influence, Gaelic resistance in this region will continue."

"The Irish of Meath are your problem to solve."

Donovan laughed. "In a sense, perhaps I have. His fated bride controls his future and the destiny of this entire island."

"Surely you're joking. No woman has such power."

"This one does. Beyond that, she has the means to continue the warrior line. Even a great leader requires a mother to birth and nurture him 'til he reaches manhood."

"You speak of Brynna."

Donovan nodded. "At first light, withdraw the men from around Dunsmere. I think it wise to leave MacAuley alone for a time, allow him to become attached to his enchanting guest. If I've surmised correctly, she'll be of as much use to your king now as if she'd actually joined our cause."

"By your command, Lord Ryan."

The English officer bowed and took his leave, closing the door behind him.

He'd wasted his breath, Donovan grumbled silently while he stared into the gathering darkness. How could a privileged whelp from Surrey comprehend ancient Irish lore? If it couldn't be drawn on a map or traded for wares, the English had no use for it.

Descended from Celtic legend and *sidhe* royalty, together Kieran and Brynna possessed some of the most potent magick in all Ireland. How to harness it? That was the question.

"You cannot."

Startled, he turned to find the Queen of Meath glaring at him from his hearth. Maire's crackling eyes shamed the firelight, and though she stood far smaller than he, her regal air made her seem much larger than she was. A lesser man might have blanched at the fury emanating from the powerful *sídhe,* but Donovan strolled to a table to pour her a glass of the sweet wine she fancied. He held out the glass to her, but she made no move to take it.

Chuckling, he sipped it himself. "It's been ages. What brings you to me?"

"You know I come because of Brynna. Have you not done enough? Now you seek to destroy her single chance at happiness?"

"A chance you created, no doubt. I never could comprehend your fondness for that impudent MacAuley."

She raked him with a haughty sneer. "A queen need not explain her actions to one such as you."

Maire had always known just how to anger him, taunting him beyond endurance. Though she was the most exquisite creature he'd laid eyes on, in truth 'twas her remarkable spirit that had entranced him all those years ago. A time when they weren't queen and noble but equal in all things.

When she loved him.

"Maire, you knew I was searching for Brynna. How could you leave me wondering whether my only child were alive or dead?"

Her eyes blazed hotter, but she repelled his effort to engage her and remained where she'd first appeared. "She was well enough until the hounds of your English master got hold of her."

"Why did she not defend herself?"

"She did as much as she was capable of. Her powers are wild and uncontrollable."

"And where were you while your precious child was raped and beaten near to death?"

Sadness consumed the fire in her eyes. "A distraction elsewhere kept me away until it was too late to help her."

"Your consort, no doubt."

Maire shook her head. "Ronan would not dare do such a thing."

But she was far from certain of it, he noticed as he sipped his wine. "And MacAuley? Did you send her to him?"

"Nay. Of her own accord, she found and healed him."

"I had a vision the night before. I saw him die. Morgan's sword appeared in my collection." He pointed to the long table that held the blades of rebellious chieftains he'd dispatched in his pursuit of the throne.

"Your sight has always been quite unreliable," she told him airily, shaking out a glimmering sleeve as though bored with their argument.

"Why?"

She seemed put off by his question, and he quelled a satisfied smile. For years, he'd enjoyed nothing more than riling his quixotic lover into confrontations that ended in his bed. No mortal woman had ever come close to matching her fiery passion.

But now, she regarded him with a pitying expression. "You've no understanding of true courage."

"Think you I reclaimed my birthright"—extending his arms, he indicated his vast holdings—"by being a coward?"

She quieted his rage with a sad smile. "Courage does not always wield a sword. Often, 'tis found in the tender heart of a woman who does not leave a man to die alone in the forest."

"The Ryans were destined to rule Ireland," Donovan reminded her.

"One's destiny can change."

Her sage tone made him uneasy, and he parried with arrogance. "Not mine."

"Pursue it then, if you must. But leave Kieran and Brynna to their own."

"And should I choose otherwise?"

She vanished without giving him an answer.

CHAPTER NINE

"Irish," Dev spat, pointing to the tracks he'd found on the ridge. "Unshod horses, flat boots. They've sent our own to spy on us."

Ryan.

The name sprang into Kieran's mind, but he dared not voice his suspicions, even to Dev. He looked across the valley to MacAuley Keep. In the misty dawn light, it appeared serene and confident, trusting in its location and the wits of its chieftain to protect it from harm. Inside the sheltering walls, the bailey teemed with people who desired nothing more than to live their lives in peace. Raise children and livestock, plant crops that bore plentiful harvests.

God, he wanted that. A simpler life with fewer cares. A wife and children, as Cavan had phrased it, who adored him.

"I'm so tired of fighting."

The words clogged his throat as he sank onto the fallen limb behind him. After a quick glance around, Dev plunked his huge frame down as well.

GET UP TO
4 FREE BOOKS!

You can have the best romance delivered to your door for less than what you'd pay in a bookstore or online. Sign up for one of our book clubs today, and we'll send you **FREE* BOOKS** just for trying it out...**with no obligation to buy, ever!**

HISTORICAL ROMANCE BOOK CLUB

Travel from the Scottish Highlands to the American West, the decadent ballrooms of Regency England to Viking ships. Your shipments will include authors such as CONNIE MASON, CASSIE EDWARDS, LYNSAY SANDS, LEIGH GREENWOOD, and many, many more.

LOVE SPELL BOOK CLUB

Bring a little magic into your life with the romances of Love Spell—fun contemporaries, paranormals, time-travels, futuristics, and more. Your shipments will include authors such as KATIE MACALISTER, SUSAN GRANT, NINA BANGS, SANDRA HILL, and more.

As a book club member you also receive the following special benefits:

- **30% OFF all orders through our website & telecenter!**
  (Plus, you still get 1 book FREE for every 5 books you buy!)
- **Exclusive access to special discounts!**
- **Convenient home delivery and 10 days to return any books you don't want to keep.**

There is no minimum number of books to buy, and you may cancel membership at any time. See back to sign up!

*Please include $2.00 for shipping and handling.

YES! ☐

Sign me up for the **Historical Romance Book Club** and send my TWO FREE BOOKS! If I choose to stay in the club, I will pay only $8.50* each month, a savings of $5.48!

YES! ☐

Sign me up for the **Love Spell Book Club** and send my TWO FREE BOOKS! If I choose to stay in the club, I will pay only $8.50* each month, a savings of $5.48!

NAME: _____

ADDRESS: _____

_____

TELEPHONE: _____

E-MAIL: _____

☐ **I WANT TO PAY BY CREDIT CARD.**

☐ VISA ☐ MasterCard ☐ DISCOVER

ACCOUNT #: _____

EXPIRATION DATE: _____

SIGNATURE: _____

Send this card along with $2.00 shipping & handling for each club you wish to join, to:

Romance Book Clubs
1 Mechanic Street
Norwalk, CT 06850-3431

Or fax (must include credit card information!) to: 610.995.9274. You can also sign up online at www.dorchesterpub.com.

JOIN NOW!

They sat without speaking for several moments until Dev broke the silence.

"And what do ye intend to do about it?"

"What are my choices?"

"Step down as commander. Train the men rather than lead them." His cousin gave a knowing grin. "Run off with Brynna."

"What would *you* do?"

"Go with her. Never have I seen you so happy as when you're with her. She makes ye forget everything else."

"That she does." He chuckled. "I still don't understand why."

"Does it matter?"

"Not as much as it did yestreen."

"Does she know that?" When Kieran shook his head, Dev pushed him to his feet and gave him a hearty shove. "Then go and tell her now, ye bleeding fool. I can manage one patrol alone."

Brynna was perusing the books in Aileen's library when a movement in the doorway caught her attention. Before she could react, Kieran had crossed the floor and pulled her into a fierce embrace.

"Kieran, what—"

He kissed her hard, wrapping his arms about her as if he feared she might vanish. Her body gave way to his, every vestige of anger forgotten. In that moment she'd have granted him anything he asked for. When he drew back, his eyes shone with a heady mix of desire and desperation.

"Forgive me, lass. When I found your chamber empty, I thought I'd missed you."

Running a finger over her lips, she smiled up at him. "Actually, your aim is impeccable."

Laughing, he swept her into his arms, spinning several times before kissing her again. "If I set ye down, will ye promise to stay?"

Baffled by his turnaround, she frowned. "Have you forgotten I'm Donovan Ryan's daughter?"

"I care not if you're the Devil's own. I canna go on with my heart in pieces at your feet." He heaved a long, resigned sigh. "When we're together, ye drive me mad. When we're apart, I can think of nothing but you."

Her own heart was dancing, and she fought off a delighted smile. "It sounds miserable." When he raised a brow, she laughed. "Would it help to know that when you're not trying my patience, you make me very happy?"

Cocking his dark head, he grinned. "It might."

She framed his face in her hands and stood on tiptoe to kiss him. "I love you, Kieran MacAuley. Every stubborn, magnificent bit of you."

"And I, you," he murmured, returning the kiss. "Apparently, nothing can change that."

A knock on the open door cut him short.

"Pardon me, Mistress Brynna." The sturdy-looking lad standing outside nodded to her. "Kieran, the council's waiting for you."

Closing his eyes, he hung his head and shook it. "I'd forgotten, Samuel. Thank you for coming to fetch me."

The boy checked over each shoulder and whispered, "Just so you know, Eamon's half a measure short on patience this morn."

"Is he, now?" Kieran chuckled. "And why is that?"

"I've no idea. I'm just passing the message along."

"There are spies deployed throughout the valley," Eamon announced, as if he were the first to know of them.

"There are always spies about," Cavan reminded him curtly. "What's your point?"

"Given the volatile political situation in Meath, harboring an English detainee is unwise. We'd do well to turn her over and let them deal with her."

"Deal with her?" Kieran echoed disdainfully. "Ye mean kill her."

Eamon raised his hands in a motion obviously intended to placate. "Their laws are different from ours, but not that different. Surely Brynna's previous encounter with them was a misunderstanding."

"I owe my life to Brynna," Kieran said in the calmest tone he could muster. "I'll not turn her out for them to hunt down and tear apart. Next topic."

After a long, assessing look at him, the leader of the council referred to the precise script that filled his scroll. "Very well, then. We'll move on to the matter of betrothing Maureen. As is tradition, our chieftain has first right to wed her."

Quelling a smile, Kieran shook his head. "There are men among the clan far better suited to her than I."

Cavan chuckled, as did a few others. No doubt their wives would know of Maureen's future husband before she did.

" 'Tis an impressive list," Eamon remarked. "Which match do you think would be best?"

"Daniel," Kieran answered, mentioning a well-to-do farmer who lived some distance from the keep. "They've been friends since childhood, and he has a gentle way with her. Beyond that, he has the means to provide for her and a host of children."

"His cottage is quite small. They would need a larger home."

"I'll build them one."

He was sincere, but the council members laughed, and after a moment he joined them. There was no point in denying it: Wedding Maureen to Daniel would rid him of a vexing problem.

Eamon raised his hand for quiet. "To a vote, then. Those in favor of this match?"

A resounding chorus of agreement met his query, and he recorded the unanimous decision in his journal.

'Twas past noontime when they finished, and Kieran thanked God he'd survived the harrowing meeting without killing anyone.

Brynna sensed someone watching her and glanced up to find Kieran standing in the doorway of her room. He looked absolutely miserable.

"Your meeting went well?"

"Well enough, I suppose. I'd hoped you might spare some time for me."

For his sake alone, she managed a smile. "Of course."

Curious looks followed them as they strolled down the corridor to his study, a comfortable room filled with books and portraits of his ancestors. Tall windows looked out on a day rapidly growing brighter as sunshine burned away the fog.

"Please sit." He motioned to the wide settee.

Feeling tiny in the masculine room, she sat and folded her hands while she waited for him to speak.

His expression bespoke supreme patience. Clearly, he expected their conversation would be a trying one. "Why did ye not tell me of your father before?"

"I saw no need to trouble you with that knowledge."

"Because ye meant to leave."

"Aye."

Frowning, he crossed his arms. "Trouble me with it now."

"What do you wish to know?"

"Everything. Start with why he betrayed us."

Brynna allowed herself a deep breath. "With King Edward's help, he intends to take for himself the throne of Ireland."

Kieran snorted his opinion of that. "None but the O'Neill will sit as High King."

"My father is more amenable to the goals of the English. 'Tis why Edward supports his campaigns. Noble dissension causes great strife among the clans, and faltering alliances will smooth the path for imperial interests here."

"You know far too much of all this. No man would entrust such information to his daughter."

"I was part of his plan."

His dark, assessing stare seemed to last an eternity.

"How so?"

"He hoped to use my powers against his enemies."

"And did you?"

"Never would I do such a thing. I told him as much, but he felt that in time I'd yield to his demands." Gathering her courage, she met his suspicious gaze. "Major Hawlings was involved in the raid at Westmeath, leading a company of English soldiers. I suspect my father helped them devise their strategy."

He responded with a violent oath she'd never heard before. "I knew 'twas an Irish trick."

While he absorbed what she'd told him, she fought the urge to continue talking, to assure him he'd not brought a traitor to the heart of his clan. She resisted the temptation to steal into his thoughts. He must find his own way through this maze.

"Brynna, did ye somehow take a span of time from my memory?"

His swift change of direction startled her, and she struggled to appear calm. "I did."

He paced away from her, casting about the room as if trying to piece together some sort of explanation. When he turned back to her, his expression wasn't a pleasant one. "What possessed you to do such a thing?"

"I did it so you could return to your life and I to mine."

"Did ye not consider that I might need those memories? That perhaps I'd object to your taking them from me?"

"I had no idea some of them would return," she explained. "I didn't anticipate seeing you again."

"And that made it acceptable?"

There was no sense in arguing over it. He would never understand. Shrugging, she laced her fingers together and looked down at them. "I did what I felt best."

The plush cushion shifted as he sat beside her. "One more question and I shall leave off."

Calling on every bit of her courage, she raised her eyes to his and nodded.

"Is it possible for you to give me back what I'm missing?"

No one had ever made such a request. Then again, she'd not seen any of the men she'd tended once they left her. Reversing what she'd done was simple enough, but the aftermath could be devastating for him. "If I were to agree, you'd be flooded with the bad as well as the good."

"I'd remember all that happened?"

"Yes. But 'twas a difficult time for you." She prayed her reluctance would sway him from the course he seemed so intent upon following.

"I'd not be wounded now."

"Not physically. But much of your battle took place here." She rested a hand on his chest, just over his heart.

He covered it with his own, granted her a look filled with trust. "You nursed me through those days. Will ye do it again?"

In her mind, she recalled the way he'd looked after the raid. She couldn't bear the thought of his suffering through it all again, but if he did, she'd stay by his side to help him as much as she could. "If this is what you truly want, I'll stay with you."

" 'Tis what I truly want."

When she leaned forward to kiss him, he stayed her with a hand on her shoulder. "Will doing this harm you?"

Knowing how crucial it was for him to have his past intact, she was touched deeply by his concern. Smiling, she shook her head and gave him the kiss that would restore the time missing from his memory.

Almost immediately, he sagged against her. Brynna drew his head to her shoulder, held him while he shook with battle-induced rage, his hands balled into fists on either side of her. Behind tightly closed eyes, he saw battered bodies strewn about a glen cloaked in the morbid silence of death.

His legs ached, chest and arms burning with wounds he knew weren't real. As the strength fled his body, from a great distance he heard someone calling his name.

When he pried his eyes open, he found himself on the floor, looking at the hewn beams in the ceiling. Brynna lay across his chest, grasping his shoulders. He understood she was trying to shield him from the force of whatever gripped him, but he couldn't summon the words to reassure her.

Instead, his arms wrapped about her, and her head flew up from his chest. Tears streaked her delicate face, and he lifted a shaky hand to smooth them away.

"Kieran?" He tried to smile, but only managed to lift the corner of his mouth; his entire body began shivering. Then he remembered she could divine his thoughts.

What happened?

"I don't know." She pillowed his head in her skirts and settled a throw over him. "One moment I was holding you and the next you pitched from the settee as though someone had struck you. You rolled to your back and stopped breathing. Never have I been so frightened."

Kieran reached for her hand, brought her damp palm to his lips in apology.

The movement sapped his remaining reserve of strength, and he fought for one last coherent thought.

Thank you, Brynna.

Brynna awoke encircled by Kieran's arms. Outside the windows flanking his desk, she saw the waning afternoon light and wondered how long she'd been asleep. Tilting her head back, she took in the view of him at rest, peaceful and without worry. 'Twas a rare sight, and she drank in the picture he made, tucking it into a corner of her heart.

When she tried to slip from his arms, they tightened about her. Without opening his eyes, he asked, "Where do ye think you're going?"

"If someone finds us together this way, you'll not hear the end of it."

He chuckled and drew her closer. "Since ye first arrived, I've heard of nothing else. Half of them think I should marry you and be done with it."

"And the others?"

Stretching, he raised his left arm above his head and rubbed his cheek against her hair. "They think I should wait 'til the crops are planted."

His teasing made her laugh, but she quickly sobered. "They don't know who I am."

"Aye." He yawned, apparently unconcerned. "That could pose a problem."

"Kieran, be serious. Your clan wouldn't accept a Ryan as a scullery maid, much less wife to their chieftain."

He made no response, and she bolted from the lulling comfort of his embrace. "I'll not allow you to give up your position for me."

"The damage is done. If ye were to leave this moment, I'd still be forced to tell them your history, warn them your father may retaliate." He seemed to be carefully weighing his words. "Each morn I expect to open the gates and find him outside. There's evidence of spies about the valley, and the tracks are quite fresh. He knows you're here. Why does he not come for you?"

"I've no idea."

Again he hesitated, and her trepidation grew with the lengthening silence. "Can ye divine the answer for me?"

Even as she nodded, the light left her eyes, leaving them a dull green. She closed them, but not before he saw them cloud with tears.

"Wait." Cupping her chin, he lifted her head so her gaze met his. "I canna ask this of you. Were I to use your sight that way, I'd be no better than he."

"Your cause is a just one." She seemed not to notice the tears slipping down her cheeks, but each one tore at his heart, and he brushed them away with the pad of his thumb.

"It matters not. Some things are wrong, no matter the purpose."

"If the gift were yours, you'd use it without a second thought."

"That I would," he agreed.

"Perhaps if I aid the MacAuley, they'll view me more kindly when they learn the truth."

"Very well, then." He sat in a large chair and held his arm out to her. Once she'd settled in his lap, he said, "Tell me why he's holding back."

She closed her eyes without hesitation, and he marveled at her willingness to help him. Such a charming maze was she. He'd gladly spend the rest of his days solving the puzzle of her.

Her laughter brought him from his musing, and he smiled. "You've learned something?"

"Apparently, he hopes that if he leaves me here awhile, you'll fall in love with me."

Kieran grinned, kissing her. "He knows me better than I thought."

"He thinks I'm the fated bride from the old warrior's tale."

The words struck a resounding chord within him. "He may be right. 'Twould explain why you couldn't remove all my memories of you."

"My magick is unpredictable."

"Has it failed before?"

"No, but I was cast in your path again."

"I was searching for that willow tree when Dev and I found you," he reminded her. "Each day I remembered a bit more of you. In time, I'd have pieced you together on my own. When I want something, I find a way to have it."

"Do you, now?"

"Aye," he murmured at her throat. With his lips, he followed the corded edge of her bodice, smiling as he mouthed the upper curve of her breast. "Sweet Brynna. What shall I do with you?"

"No doubt you'll think of something."

Laughter scattered the last of the tension hanging between them, and he kissed her soundly. Slipping beneath her skirts, his hand smoothed over her leg.

He lifted her bare foot to his lips. "Where are your shoes?"

"In my room, perhaps. Shall I go find them?"

"Nay." Reaching for her other foot, he pulled her legs around his waist. "I like them this way."

Their playful exchange was cut short by a soft knock at the door.

"Is the chieftain to find no privacy anywhere in his own keep?" he bellowed, grinning before he claimed her mouth.

"Kieran, I'd like a word."

"Take any you like, Mother," he retorted between kisses. "But I beg of you, leave me in peace 'til dinner."

Brynna stayed him with a hand on his shoulder. "You should talk with her now, before you tell the others."

He considered for a moment, then nodded. "One moment, Mother."

Lifting Brynna from his lap, he strolled across

the room to open the door. With a kiss for Aileen's cheek, he stepped back to allow her inside.

Beaming, she hastened to where Brynna stood and embraced her. " 'Tis glad I am to see you here. Does this mean you've decided to stay?"

"If the MacAuley will have me."

"Which leads to what we must discuss with you." Kieran motioned her to a comfortable chair. Watching a variety of expressions move over her features, he relayed what he now knew of Brynna's past and their uncertain future.

"Did I not tell you there was something different about her?" She turned a fond gaze on Brynna. "Don't look so worried, dear one. The MacAuley have been well favored by the *sídhe* for generations. Once your identity is explained, they'll not think of it again." Then she frowned. "Your father, however, is another matter."

"So it has been wherever I've gone. 'Tis why I began living alone."

Aileen gave a sad shake of her head. "Outcast through no fault of your own. Such is the consequence of endless war, I suppose. We come to mistrust everyone and everything."

The tolling of the chapel bell ended their conversation on a somber note, and Aileen smoothed her skirts as she stood. Walking toward Kieran, she took his hands in hers.

"Whatever you decide, I shall support it. My only wish is for your happiness. So much have you given Ireland; surely she owes you something in return."

* * *

"You couldn't conjure a bit of luck, could ye, lass?" Kieran murmured that evening as they dined together in the hall.

With a nervous laugh, she shook her head. Cursing the hesitance he saw in her eyes, he took her chilled hand for a kiss. "I love you."

She granted him a courageous smile, her grip tightening for a moment before she released his hand. With customary bravado, Kieran kicked his chair back from the table and leapt onto the sturdy seat. He spread his arms and waited for quiet.

" 'Tis glad I am to see so many of you this night, for I've a story to tell."

He recounted the events since Brynna's arrival, filling the previously blank spaces with the details he'd learned. When he finished, chaos swept through the assembly like a firestorm as people shouted to be heard over those around them.

Kieran jumped down from his perch and pulled Brynna to his side, as much in reassurance as protection. Silently, he thanked Morgan for instituting the rule that no blade larger than an eating knife be brought to the MacAuley table. A few of the men appeared riled enough to slit his throat without a second thought.

"You should have brought this before the council," Eamon scolded him, shaking with rage. "We could have avoided this scene."

"Sheltering her is far too dangerous," Daniel added in a reasonable tone. "She's the daughter of a man with no conscience."

"And of a *sídhe*," Kieran reminded him loudly

enough for those around them to hear. "Or do ye object to that, as well?"

Daniel glanced about uneasily, as if he expected a wood sprite to appear and cast a wicked spell over him. "The faery folk are welcome in Dunsmere, as always. We're indebted to them for their good care of us."

Many nodded concurrence, and Kieran seized upon a strategy that just might shift the situation to Brynna's advantage. "If I were to turn out one of their children, how do ye think they might react?"

His goading prompted more argument, and he allowed it to continue, praying the advice of the wiser ones would overcome the opinions of those most inclined to throw Brynna out into the night.

"Brynna—" His mother's voice floated up from somewhere deep in the throng. "Tell them why you left Ferndon Castle to live in the forest."

The rustling of skirts and shuffling of boots followed her request, and Brynna gave Kieran a quizzical look.

" 'Tis a question for you," he told her. "Answer it or not, as you wish."

After a deep breath, she nodded, and he helped her climb onto the chair. She glanced about the hall, and he thought she might decide against answering. But a fiery look drove the uncertainty from her eyes, and she drew herself up to her full height, straight and true.

"My father's obsession with the throne drove away any honor he once had. Many times he asked for my help in his cause, and I refused him.

When I learned of his role in the battle at Kildare, I left."

"Living all alone," one of the women commented. "How did you manage it?"

"When I sensed his men drawing too close, I would move on."

She answered several more questions with the same composure, and Kieran knew her quiet explanations did more to sway his kinsmen than he could have done in hours of shouting. Anger gave way to sympathetic muttering, though many of the graybeards vowed they'd discuss this later around the hearth. The debate was far from over, but he breathed a bit easier, knowing the first step was behind them.

Then a meaty fist caught him unawares, and he landed hard on the unforgiving stone floor.

"Why did ye not tell me about Ryan?" Dev demanded. "On the ridge this morning, how could ye sit there and not tell me?"

His cousin took one step closer, but no more. Something rooted him where he stood, though he tried mightily to move his enormous feet. When he glared at Brynna, she returned the look with one that crackled with her own fine temper.

"Let me loose," he snarled. "He deserves a thrashing, and by God, he'll get one."

Without blinking, she stepped into his range. "You wish to deliver a thrashing? Perhaps you should direct it at the one you're truly angry with."

"Don't tempt me."

As Kieran dragged himself from the floor, he noted the change in Dev's eyes. His initial rush of fury had dissipated with that crushing blow, and he only continued sparring with Brynna because he couldn't retreat. Wishing to spare his stalwart cousin any further humiliation, Kieran silently asked her to release him.

Once he was free, the others scrambled to clear a path as Dev stormed from the hall.

With a wry grin, Kieran rubbed his throbbing jaw. "That went well, I think."

Cavan laughed, clapping him on the back before giving him a broad wink. "A wise man would leave plenty of mead about the keep this eve."

" 'Tis done." Kieran accepted the hand offered him. "I think it best if I retire. You'll be at the hearth?"

"Indeed, I will." He leaned closer and quietly added, "Anything beyond boasting, you'll hear about."

Kieran had long relied on Cavan to relay any malcontentment voiced out of the chieftain's hearing. Days such as this were rare, but he found them easier to navigate with the information his well-respected kinsman provided him.

"What of Devlin?" the older man asked.

"I'll give him time to stew, then speak with him in the morn. He'd not listen now, no matter what I said."

"Ye have the right of it, to be sure." Cavan turned to Brynna and smiled. "Not to worry, lass. The MacAuley are stubborn but fair. You've done nothing wrong, and we'll not turn ye out to be made a prisoner."

Bowing to her, he patted Kieran's shoulder and

melted into the milling crowd. Kieran made one last sweep of the hall, hoping to find that Dev had returned, he was nowhere to be seen.

Putting that concern from his mind, he forced a smile and offered his arm to Brynna. "Shall I escort you to your chamber?"

The worry in her expression mirrored his true feelings, and he knew she'd not been lulled by his display of carelessness.

"You should go and find Devlin."

"So he can separate my head from my shoulders?" He laughed as they ascended the winding staircase. "I think not."

"He's more than furious, Kieran, he's hurt. He thinks you don't trust him."

"He knows better. A night with Callie will heal his wounds, and we'll work through the rest of it on the morrow."

She paused on the step above him and turned to face him. "Callie left with Stephen. You didn't see them?"

"Apparently not." He chuckled, sobering when she frowned at him. "What?"

"Don't you listen to the gossip within your own keep?"

"I try not to. 'Tis a foolish distraction I don't need."

"The women of this clan know a good deal more than you think. For instance, did you know Cavan is romancing your mother?"

Kieran stared at her, unable to imagine his mother in the arms of anyone but his father. Yet he'd seen her with Cavan many a time, and there was no denying they enjoyed one another's company. The burly smith had a way of making her laugh, and she doted on him shamelessly.

Resting a hand on his cheek, Brynna smiled. "Did you expect her to remain alone forever?"

"In truth, I gave it no more thought than whom Callie might be setting a trap for these days."

"You'd do well to be more attentive to what happens here." With a graceful motion, she indicated the walls that surrounded them. "These people are as important as your infantry."

"More so. 'Tis for them that we fight."

"If you continue to distance yourself from them, when the fighting ends, you'll return to a valley filled with strangers."

Her perceptiveness unnerved him, and he could think of nothing to say.

"You're doing it now, retreating from me."

She grasped his hands to hold him, her gentle tug traveling down his arms and through his entire body. In the forest with her, he'd followed his heart without question because it had led him to what he'd long ago given up wanting.

Entranced by those twinkling emerald eyes, he lowered his mouth to hers for a thorough kiss. Even the wildest part of him craved the tenderness of her touch, yearning for something that would carry him beyond the morn and through the rest of his life.

As soon as he possibly could, he'd make her his wife. Then, he thought with a grin, he'd take her to his bed and not leave it for at least a sennight.

She laughed. "And what might that wicked smile be about?"

"A strategy I'm devising."

Glowering, she pulled herself out of his arms and continued up the stairs. "Must you always speak in battle terms?"

"I'm a man of war, Brynna," he reminded her as he followed. " 'Tis how I speak."

"You're a man first and a warrior second."

"Some days." Though he longed to hold her again, he sensed she'd not accept it just then. He clasped his hands behind his back and continued walking as she glanced up at him.

"The man in you might care to know I much prefer seduction to conquest."

Her light tone chased back the clouds descending on him, and he chuckled. "Do ye, now? I must remember that."

When he stopped, she turned to him with a confused expression. "This isn't my room."

"It is 'til your door can be repaired."

"Who is it you mistrust?"

"No one." He reached past her to open the door. She tilted her head with a knowing look, and he cradled her cheek in his hand. "Everyone. While tempers are running so high, I wish for you to sleep behind a door with a sturdy lock."

Even so he felt uneasy, but her grateful smile soothed him a bit. She covered his hand with hers and fixed him with an adoring gaze. "Thank you, Kieran."

"For what?"

"For caring about me, protecting me. I've not felt safe in a very long time."

Tempted to leave her with an unforgettable kiss for her dreams, he dared not test his fleeting patience. Instead, he brushed his lips over her forehead and stepped away.

"Sleep sweet, Brynna."

CHAPTER TEN

In the wardrobe, Brynna found several of the dresses tailored for her, each as finely made as the one hanging beside it. They made a rainbow of colors from pale blue to deepest wine, embroidered with graceful swirls and flowers. She changed into a nightgown, then hung the elegant silk with the others. Smoothing her hands over the full skirts, she closed the door carefully to avoid crushing them.

She fell asleep the moment she snuggled under the bedcovers. She'd not been sleeping long when she felt a tapping at the back of her mind and rolled over, hoping it would cease.

It returned with more force, and she grudgingly tuned her senses to her dark surroundings. Hushed voices reached her from the corridor. Though she couldn't hear the conversation, the tones sounded amiable enough as they drifted away.

But instinct sent her from the bed, casting about for someplace to hide. The wardrobe was the only thing at hand, so she stepped inside, pulling the door closed just as the lock turned and someone entered the chamber.

She heard the rustling of bedcovers as the intruder searched for her, and she shrank into the darkness of her terribly obvious hiding place.

Running footsteps sounded in the hallway, and her would-be attacker fled without a sound.

"Brynna, are ye here?"

Overcome with relief, she opened the wardrobe door and fell into Kieran's arms. "Thank God, you're here. He was just about to find me."

"You're shaking." Tossing his deadly *scian* on the writing desk, he brought her head to his bare chest. "Do ye know who it was?"

"Nay."

"Was he short or tall?"

She looked up at him. "I don't know."

"Did he say anything?"

When she shook her head, he frowned. "You locked the door after I left?"

"Of course." Foreboding shivered through her, and she fought down the chill it left behind.

Perceptive as always, Kieran tightened his grasp and gently kissed her. "You're overwrought from a trying day. Come with me and get some rest."

"With you?"

"Aye. That way, I'll know you're safe."

His words struck her oddly, and it occurred to her that he'd come to her rescue without hearing a single call for help. "How is it you knew I was in danger?"

"You were frightened." At her baffled look, he realized he'd not answered her question. Offering his arm, he said, "We'd do well to discuss this someplace more private."

As they made their way down the corridor, heads bobbed out of several doors, followed by excited whispers and hushed replies. By morning, everyone in the keep would know he'd taken Brynna to his chamber in the middle of the night. Despite the dire circumstances, he couldn't help smiling.

He escorted her through the door he'd left open in his haste to reach her. After settling her in a chair, he bolted all the outer doors, then tossed several logs onto the dwindling fire. He poured a small glass of wine and handed it to her before pouring a larger one for himself.

"Thank you." As she sipped, she studied him over the rim of the crystal glass. "How could you know I was frightened?"

"In truth, I'm not certain." Kieran sat on a stool at her side and took a long swallow of his wine. "When I returned here after the raid, I was sadly out of sorts. I'd lost something but couldn't recall what, or who, it might have been. Now and then, I'd get a chill up my back, the way I do when someone is behind me in battle. But I was always alone and nearly drove myself mad trying to reason it through."

" 'Tis the warrior's sense. A valuable gift for a fighting man."

"I've always thought so. But with no threat, I couldn't imagine what prompted my unease." Grimacing, he paused for another sip of wine. "One day, I woke to the sound of your weeping in my ears. I set out to find you, praying I'd be in time."

She rewarded him with a grateful smile. "Which you were, and again this night."

He took her hand, circling his thumb over her palm as he lifted his gaze to hers. " 'Twould seem my sense now protects you, as well as myself, but I canna think who among the MacAuley wishes to harm you. Can ye help me discover who it is?"

"I haven't that sort of skill," she confessed with a frown. "I must know someone or be nearby to divine their thoughts."

He dredged up a smile of encouragement. "Your evening has been long enough. Get some rest, and we'll discuss this in the morn."

Hauling himself to his feet, he made for his study.

"Kieran?"

He paused in the connecting doorway to look back at her.

She rose from her chair and walked toward him. Snowy linen followed the graceful curves of her body as she moved, her hair a fall of riotous curls over her shoulders. As she stepped into his arms, she gave him the playful smile he adored.

"Would you care to stay?"

"Very much." Settling his arms about her waist, he kissed her forehead. "But I fear you'd not get much rest if I did. No man could resist such a temptation."

She lowered her lashes. "I'm not a maiden, so what does it matter?"

"It matters to me," he told her with a light kiss for her lips. "What's done is done, and I canna change it, but never would I dishonor you as the English did."

She gazed up at him, eyes misty with emotion. "Thank you, Kieran."

The corner of his mouth lifting in a wry grin, he released her and stepped back. "I canna recall a woman ever thanking me for not bedding her."

As he retreated to the doorway, she gave him a sly smile. "Imagine how grateful I'll be when you do."

"Trust me, lass—you'll be nowhere near as grateful as I."

Her hand tucked in the crook of Kieran's arm, Brynna stepped from the hall into the bright sunshine the following morning. Dozens of eyes watched the top of the steps, and she fought the urge to duck her head. They were looking at Kieran, she assured her nervous heart. 'Twas only natural for them to be interested in their chieftain.

As they descended the steps, a lad appeared at the edge of the bailey, leading two horses. The chestnut stallion hailed Kieran in a deep-throated whinny, then turned to the palfrey at his side with a reassuring nicker.

"Gideon is the bay, Faylinn the dapple." Kieran stopped at the bottom of the steps and canted his head toward her. "I forgot to ask if you ride."

Brynna pressed her hands together to contain her excitement. "Of course I do. I've not seen such beautiful horses since—in a very long time," she finished in a rush as she held out a hand for each mount to sniff.

"Faylinn has a taste for these." Reaching into his pocket, he handed Brynna a few chunks of sugar and ran a hand over the mare's silky forelock. "She belongs to my mother, and she's quite thoroughly spoiled."

"Are you, now?" Brynna kissed the horse's velvety nose while she nibbled at the sugar. "You're certain Aileen approves of my riding her?"

" 'Twas her suggestion," he replied as Gideon ate an apple from his hand. "Faylinn is the gentlest horse in the stable, and she'll follow Gideon anywhere."

Once the horses had finished their treats, Kieran lifted Brynna into the finely tooled lady's saddle. He mounted Gideon in an impressive leap and urged him into a trot. He seemed not to notice the curious stares that followed them through the bailey and out the main gate. Inspired by his confidence, Brynna adopted the same careless mien, smiling down on those who glanced at her.

A few responded in kind, but most either looked away or gazed straight through her as if she weren't even there. She stifled a sigh. Kieran might have put her background aside, but his kinsmen weren't so forgiving.

Some of them might never accept her.

The thought dimmed the beautiful day as surely as dark thunderclouds. Others came close on its heels, and before long she was well and truly discouraged.

"Brynna?" She whirled to find Kieran at her side, his brow lined with concern. "Forgive me for startling you, but you've said nothing since we left the keep. Would ye prefer we go back?"

"Nay."

He swung from his saddle and came to stand beside her. Looking up at her, he smiled and held out his arms to her.

Once she was on the ground, he gathered her close. "Tell me what troubles you."

As her worries tumbled out, he regarded her soberly, nodding here and there to show he understood. And with one kiss, he swept all her worry away.

"I know the MacAuley, Brynna. Unbending as they seem, their hearts canna remain hardened against one such as you. They're angry now, and more than a bit fearful of your father. When it becomes clear he doesn't mean to invade Dunsmere to reclaim you, their fear will ease, and in time they'll come to trust you."

"And until then?"

"I suppose I should keep you close at hand."

As he wrapped his arms more securely about her, she nestled into his embrace. His heart beat steadily beneath her hand as she rested her cheek on his chest.

Then she noticed the mammoth pile of stones nearby. Raising her head, she looked about the hillock. "What is this place?"

"This," he replied with a proud sweep of his arm, "was the first English castle Morgan claimed for Ireland. He and his men took it apart with their bare hands, stone by stone, to show the English what would happen if they continued sending armies to Ireland. Then he built his own keep in sight of this one, to remind us all of what we've accomplished."

"I've heard so many stories about Morgan," she commented as they climbed the gentle slope. "He must have been a remarkable man."

"That he was. Some of the elders claim part of

him was reborn in me. Quietly, of course," he added with a wink.

She smiled. "Of course."

" 'Tis said his wife Gwynn was of Welsh faery blood." He stopped at the apex of the hill and looked across the valley toward MacAuley Keep. "She bore him three sons and four daughters and loved him 'til the day he died in her arms. The next morn, his body was gone and Gwynn nowhere to be found. Some think she took him away to bury him, or to the faery realm to restore his life. Others say they're both still here and that if the moon is right, you'll find them walking the old paths together."

He drew her backward into his arms, and Brynna cuddled against him with a contented sigh. "I like picturing them here, watching over their children."

"I favor that ending, as well." He nuzzled her shoulder, kissed along her neck to her ear. "What say you, Brynna? Would ye give up the pleasures of heaven to stay with me?"

Settling her arms over his, she tipped her head back to smile at him. "I'd give up anything to stay with you."

"A promise easily made but difficult to keep." It was a stranger's voice.

Startled by the unexpected response, Kieran wheeled to find a gray-whiskered man strolling toward them as if he'd emerged from the stones themselves. Kieran snatched the dirk from his boot, placing himself between Brynna and the intruder.

"You will not be needing that," the man said, holding both hands with palms forward. "You and your kin are safe from me, Kieran MacAuley. I am neither scout nor renegade. I wish only to speak with you."

He offered no reassurance of Brynna's safety, however. Uneasy, Kieran dredged up a bit of civility. "Very well. I hope you'll forgive me for not recalling your name."

"My name is of no consequence, but the message I convey to you is of the utmost importance." His gaze went to Brynna, and his eyes brightened to an eerie silver. "Had you left as you'd planned, there would have been no need for this."

"You should know I consider her a member of this clan." Kieran put a hand on her shoulder. "Any threat you make to her includes me."

Their visitor's eyes shifted to a deadly slate. "Trust in this, Chief MacAuley: You do not wish to risk your life for her."

Brynna faced him, her expression one of annoyance. "Why are you here?"

"I came because your mother cannot be trusted to deal with you properly."

Alerted by a spark in the stranger's steely eyes, Kieran pushed Brynna behind him and prepared to fight. Before he could blink, a slender woman appeared between him and his opponent, hands raised to keep them apart.

"Enough." The single word was laden with authority. She looked at Kieran with warmth in her emerald eyes, at the other with a glare icy enough to freeze the entire Irish Sea. "You will leave now."

He regarded her with such affection, Kieran could

scarce believe it was the same man. "I know how dearly you love them, but this has gone too far."

"What the devil are you talking about?" Kieran demanded.

The old man turned to him with a bemused expression. "Your work is not finished, warrior. You must lead your men into battle."

"I've done as much as any and more than most. I shall gladly serve Ireland in other ways."

"The decision is not yours."

"It must be his!" the woman protested. "You cannot dictate the path of his life."

"The future of Ireland rests on the outcome of his actions, my love."

"I have not forgotten that."

"Then I take my leave of you." Raising her hand to his lips, the man frowned, as if his heart were breaking. "You know what must be done."

She gave a curt nod, and he kissed her cheek before dropping her hand.

Then he disappeared.

Slowly, Kieran turned to Brynna. "I pray you can explain this."

"I can." Indicating the mysterious woman who'd come from nowhere, she said, "This is my mother, Maire."

He waited for her to continue. Then he realized that was not merely her mother's name. "Maire? Queen Maire?"

"Such a clever lad," the slender woman replied, patting his cheek with a motherly touch. Her skin felt like running water, yet her fingers seemed solid as she brushed the hair from the star at his temple.

"Was it Ronan I challenged with naught but a dirk?"

"It was."

"Your consort?"

Maire raised a graceful brow and gave him a slight smile. "Indeed."

Kieran wrested his gaze from her and looked at Brynna. Because of her mother's ethereal appearance, their likeness wasn't readily apparent until he considered their eyes. Deep, verdant green, like an untouched meadow in summer.

"The Queen of Meath is your mother," he ventured, testing the unbelievable words. Once spoken, they seemed slightly more tenable. "The Queen of Meath is your mother. Of course."

Catching up a dainty faery hand, he bowed and brought it to his lips. "Welcome to Dunsmere, Your Majesty. Would you care to sit awhile?"

She smiled, and he escorted her to a makeshift stone bench.

She held out her arm for Brynna, hugging her as she sat. "My precious one. How are you?"

"Much better."

" 'Tis my fault you are in such danger."

"You shouldn't blame yourself, Mother. Men do what they will."

Considering what she'd suffered, Kieran thought her exceptionally forgiving. He, however, was not.

"You should have helped her when she was attacked by the English," he told Maire flatly. "Why didn't you?"

Tears shimmered in the queen's eyes, but the next moment they were gone. "When I discovered what had happened, she was already with you."

"You could have come to her here."

"There was no need."

Her haughty tone enraged him, and he scowled at her. "You could have eased her pain, mended her more quickly. You might have come to tell her you cared whether she lived or died."

"Kieran," Brynna chided him, "you mustn't judge what you don't understand. There's only so much Mother can do for me."

"Which is why you fight me at every turn. You've grown so accustomed to fending for yourself, you push away anyone who tries to help you."

"Kieran is right." Maire's adoring gaze went to her daughter. "I never should have allowed you to become involved in this."

"Why did she?" he asked.

"To save you, of course. Her heart is far too soft for this world."

Her words took the heat out of his temper, and he decided 'twas best to let the matter drop. He sat on the ground before them, leaning back as he braced himself on his hands. "Forgive me if I offended you, Your Majesty."

She swept away his apology with an understanding smile. "You have done nothing to forgive. To prove it, I shall allow you one question, and I promise to answer it truthfully."

He sifted through all the things he'd always wanted to know. Past history he didn't understand, what the future held for his extensive family. At last, he settled on a single request.

"Will Ireland ever be free?" At her sage nod, he asked, "Will I live to see it?"

"That is two questions."

"Mother."

"Very well. No, you will not live to see it."

"But your descendants will," Brynna added.

His heart swelled protectively for the bairns he'd not yet held. Children he'd not have known if Brynna hadn't risked her life to save him.

"I've one more question." Maire set her lips in a firm line, but he flashed his most charming smile. "Please?"

Narrowing her luminous eyes, she unleashed a murderous scowl. He waited for her anger to subside. So much had she done for him already, surely she'd not refuse to answer another question.

"One more," she snapped.

"Will you be the grandmother of my children?"

Her cool expression melted into one so endearing, he thought she might weep.

"A sly one you are, Kieran MacAuley, asking me that way."

So emotional was she, he felt great sympathy for her. Brynna was all but lost to her. How many others were kept from her? "Have you other grandchildren?"

"A few, but they are not allowed to know me. Many of my children feel I have failed them by not granting their every whim. Brynna has only ever asked me for one thing." She looked fondly at the lass by her side, then turned back to Kieran. "To spare you."

"Then I owe my life to you as well. What would you have me do with it?"

"That is for you to determine. I ask only that you not ignore emotion while you make your decisions."

With Brynna in his life, 'twas unlikely he'd ever again neglect his heart. He gained his feet and bowed grandly to her. " 'Twould honor the MacAuley if you were to stay and dine with us this eve."

"Join you?" she squeaked, her composure fleeing in the face of a simple act of hospitality. "You wish to introduce me to your people?"

"Aye. Though I've a feeling you're well acquainted with my mother."

"Never have I heard of such a thing." Clearly flustered, she smoothed her hands over the shimmering skirt of her gown.

"I'd be proud to entertain you at my table."

"Such a man. I should scare the wits straight out of your head."

He deflected her petulance with a grin. "I'm difficult to frighten."

"Kieran, thank you for the invitation. I'm certain once Mother thinks on it, she'll view your gracious gesture as you intended."

"I intended for her to visit with us."

After a few tense moments, the capricious faery ceased her glowering and granted him a regal nod. "I would be pleased to join you and yours, Chief MacAuley."

"Excellent."

Eyes shining in gratitude, Brynna went up on tiptoe to kiss his cheek. "Thank you."

"You're welcome."

He brushed his lips over her forehead, then took up Gideon's reins as Faylinn followed behind him.

During their leisurely stroll back to the keep, Kieran took his turn answering questions for the legendary Queen of Meath.

"Stand, dear lady," Maire commanded, taking Aileen's hands to bring her to her feet. "You have no cause to kneel before me."

"I'd never thought to have you in my home, Your Majesty," Aileen whispered, eyes glowing with wonder. "Now I can thank you properly for returning Kieran to us."

"You expressed your gratitude quite deliciously, Aileen. I enjoyed it very much."

Standing with Brynna circled in his arms, Kieran chuckled. "I think they like each other."

"They're very much alike."

"And you," Aileen broke in, pointing a stern finger at him. "What is this about your opposing Ronan?"

"I'd no idea it was he, Mother, I swear it."

He couldn't quite douse a grin, and she heaved the long-suffering sigh of a woman who'd witnessed more than her share of masculine pride. "Would it have mattered?"

"Nay. He threatened Brynna."

"Your son would wrestle Balor himself to protect my daughter," Maire stated proudly. "Surely you've come to understand they were fashioned as one. With the special bond they share, not even Ronan is capable of separating them."

"Except if he manages to kill her," Kieran added, tightening his protective hold.

"He'd not dare such a thing. 'Tis against our laws."

"But he can send someone else."

"Enough of this," Aileen decided in her usual brisk way. "We have an important guest. I trust you'll take no offense if I suggest we find you something else to wear, Your Majesty."

"Of course not. Any of Brynna's gowns will do. And perhaps while I am here, you should simply call me Maire."

Chatting pleasantly, the two women walked down the corridor toward Aileen's rooms.

After they'd gone, Kieran spun Brynna to face him, his hands resting lightly at her waist. "Remarkable."

With a fond smile, Brynna looked after her mother. "That she is."

"I was speaking of you."

She turned to him and laughed. "You've met the Queen of Meath and you find me remarkable?"

"Ever since the moment I laid eyes on you." He paused with a slight grin. "Have you any more secrets to share with me?"

Casting her eyes toward the beamed ceiling, she wrinkled her nose, as if deep in thought. When her gaze returned to him, she gave him the impish grin he'd come to adore. "Nay. You have them all."

* * *

"And these are my nieces, Sarah and Lynette." Kieran finished the introductions with a smile for each of them.

Lynette stared wide-eyed from behind her older sister, but Sarah greeted Maire with a charming curtsy. "Pleased to meet you."

"And you, Mistress Sarah."

"Are you truly the Queen of Meath?" Maire nodded, and Sarah looked at Brynna with admiring eyes. "That makes you a faery princess."

"Not entirely." She laughed. "I'm the same Brynna I was yestreen."

"Not entirely," a voice echoed from her left as Maureen joined them. "We know a great deal more about you now."

Ignoring the barb, Brynna rested a hand on Maire's shoulder. "Mother, I'd like you to meet—"

"This one I know."

Though she said nothing more, disapproval flared in her eyes. Maureen appeared taken aback, and she bobbed her head in a rare show of humility. "A pleasure, Your Majesty."

A furious look met her comment, and Maureen wisely continued on her way.

"Mother, that was very rude."

Maire continued to glare after the young widow. "With one such as her, 'tis difficult to be polite."

Brynna cast a troubled look at Kieran, who deflected it with one of his seemingly careless grins. She'd come to understand that he often used them to mask his own concern in an attempt to keep life within his walls on a more or less even keel.

"There's Grania," he said, offering his arm to

Maire. "She's the most gifted cook in Ireland, not to mention she'd thrash me if I didn't present her to you."

"A warrior and a diplomat," she commended him. "Morgan would be proud."

His eyes lit at the mention of the man he so admired. "You knew him?"

"Of course. Such a man was he. Handsome and strong. As cunning in negotiations as in battle." Pausing, she tilted her head with a little smile. "Out of respect for Gwynn, I never bedded him, but I wanted to."

Brynna clicked her tongue in dismay, but he laughed. "I must remember to guard my thoughts when you're about."

The two of them strolled toward Grania, and Brynna heard more laughter, not all of it Kieran's. It greatly pleased her to see her mother enjoying herself. She often seemed unhappy with the life she led, turning to the mortal realm for moments of joy.

Years ago, that loneliness had led her to the arms of Donovan Ryan. Brynna often wondered if, given the opportunity, Maire would choose contented mortality over endless longing.

As Brynna walked toward the head table, she overheard a most interesting conversation.

"Not just the daughter of a *sidhe*," one of the weavers said to her companion, "but of Queen Maire herself."

" 'Tis a great favor we've done her, sheltering Brynna here," the other added in a proud voice. "The fae will be heaping good fortune on us, they will."

"Do you think Kieran will marry her?"

"Have you seen how he looks at her?" The spindly one added a romantic smile. "The most beautiful maids in Ireland couldn't turn his head, and now he has eyes for none but her. 'Twon't be long before he's wed and siring a dozen more just like him."

They went on to debate how many sons and daughters Kieran might father, wondering if any would possess their mother's unusual gifts. Wondering, as well, if Brynna might ply her magick for the benefit of her husband's kin.

Though she'd expected such talk, still it saddened her. She wished Kieran's family could accept her on her own merits and consider her faery ties a boon. Mindful of the delicate balance of politics in and around Meath, many times she'd resisted the temptation to alter events in fear of changing things she couldn't foresee.

Until she'd walked into that blood-soaked glen and felt the agony of Kieran's dying. That night she'd convinced herself she was saving the Hope of Ireland, but in truth 'twas the man, not his legend, that had compelled her to interfere.

His laughter reached her over the din of the crowded hall. She looked toward where he stood with a niece in each arm while he and Maire talked with several people. Strong beyond measure, kind and wise, he embodied the finest traits she could imagine. Moreover, he evoked the best in others, convincing them to set aside their differences and unite against their formidable enemy.

As if he sensed her gaze on him, he looked across

the hall and granted her a smile that made her flush from head to toe. 'Twas not the leer of a warrior, but the sort of intimate look a man bestowed upon the woman he loved.

This was the man she'd saved. And no matter the consequences, she would do it again.

CHAPTER ELEVEN

"You're a late one this morn." Kieran opened the
bed curtains and sat beside her. "Are ye not feeling
well?"

Brynna smiled. "Only tired. Have you talked
with Devlin?"

"He hasn't come back. Carrick promised to send
word to me when he returns."

"He's been gone four days now."

"In the past, he's been gone longer," Kieran assured her with more confidence than he felt. "He's
a man grown, and he does as he pleases."

Reaching a hand to his face, she brushed her
thumb beneath his eye. "Still, you're worried. I see
it."

And he saw the weariness in her. Deep circles
shadowed her eyes, testament to the difficult days
and nights she'd endured since the failed attempt to
abduct her. Uncertain if the enemy they faced were
mortal or fae, Kieran wouldn't risk letting her out
of his sight after dark. His sword within easy

reach, he slept on the long settee in his study, alert to any unusual sound within the keep.

Swallowing a yawn, he asked, "Might I bring you something?"

"No, thank you."

"I'll leave you to your rest, then. Should you need me, I'll be on the training field."

"Mind your shoulder," she cautioned him. "It's not been fully tested since you injured it."

Kieran stood to pull a padded doublet over his tunic. "Ye sound like my mother."

"Perhaps if you heeded her advice, I'd not add mine."

"I think the two of you are in league against me," he complained as he buckled his scabbard about his waist.

"We prefer you in one piece. Is that so terrible?"

Folding his arms, he grinned through the looped curtains at her. "I stand a better chance of staying that way if I train properly."

She dismissed him with a wave of her hand. "Go, then. I'll roll some bandages for when you return."

Laughing, he gave her a quick kiss and strode from the room.

Brynna awoke some time later, better rested but famished. With the morning meal long over, she had two choices: She could either search out Aileen, who'd certainly find her something to eat, or she could brave the kitchens on her own. If she were to remain in Dunsmere, she must be able to move about the keep and fend for herself.

"Get on with it, Brynna," she muttered. "You can't hide forever."

She shook off her trepidation along with the bedcovers and opened Kieran's large wardrobe to search out something to wear. His own clothes he'd shoved into a narrow space to make room for her ever-growing collection of gowns. The shoes he'd had made for her looked tiny next to his boots, the ribbons on her dresses at odds with the sturdy leather and wool he chose for himself.

Lifting the hem of a studded jerkin, she inhaled his unique scent: leather and horses, mingled with an earthy smell even her well-trained nose couldn't identify. The scent of Ireland, she mused with a little smile. How fitting that it should belong to him.

Bolstered by thoughts of Kieran, she dressed and left his chambers before she could think better of her plan.

When she entered the enormous central kitchen, everyone stopped working to stare at her. Pausing, she forced herself to return the curious looks with a smile. "Good morn to you all."

Grania dusted her flour-covered hands on her apron and crossed the wide stone floor to greet her. "And to you, Brynna. What can we be doing for you this fine day?"

"I realize it's late, but I was hoping for a biscuit and some tea."

"I have plenty of the first," Grania told her in a cheery voice. "I'll steep some tea for you and send up a tray with one of the maids."

"You needn't trouble yourself. I can make it."

After studying her for a moment, the golden eyes crinkled in a smile. "Can you, now?"

Brynna moved to the cauldron hanging above the fire and dipped some of the boiling water into a wooden cup. "I've not had servants to fetch for me in quite some time."

"Forgive me, lass." Grania placed a few biscuits on a trencher and handed it to her. "I meant no offense."

"You haven't offended me. Perhaps I shouldn't have spoken as I did."

The kind woman sat on a wooden bench and patted the place beside her. "Plain talk is best, to be sure. It allows less chance for misunderstanding."

Relief washed over her as she sat down. "Thank you."

"For what?"

"For making me feel welcome," Brynna replied as she nibbled the light pastry. "I fear many of your kin don't share your opinion of me."

"I keep good thoughts for all I meet, 'less they prove unworthy." Her eyes narrowed, and Brynna silently vowed never to disappoint her.

"Did you teach that to Kieran, as well?"

"Oh, that lad." She laughed. "The other five together weren't half the challenge he was. Dropped feet first into this world and started running."

While her lively companion regaled her with one tale after another, Brynna sipped her tea.

"Here you are." Aileen smiled as she kissed Brynna's cheek. "I was looking for you."

"Did you have need of me?"

"No, but I thought with Kieran gone you might wish for some company. I should have known you'd find your way to Grania. We all do."

" 'Twas our mother's role, as well," Grania said with a fond smile. "Her kitchen doled out hearty food and sound advice."

"You're sisters?" She looked from one to the other, but saw no resemblance.

"Aye," both answered at once, then laughed.

"When she married Magnus," Grania explained, "I came along to be her maid."

Aileen's eyes sparkled. "Then she met Thomas, and her maiden days were done."

They laughed again, and Brynna joined them. Pleased to be included in their bantering, she listened while they reminisced and argued over the details.

"Come, now," Aileen chided her sister. "No man is that large."

"Was it you who took him or I? I swear he could drive a spike with it."

They shared another round of laughter; then Aileen shook her head with a sad smile. "A good man he was."

"Like Magnus. Thomas died as he lived, guarding his brother's back."

How many of the MacAuley women cherished similar memories? Filled with humor and sadness, devotion and loss. Shielded from such hardship by her father, Brynna realized she'd missed the most important lesson one could learn.

How sweet it was to love and be loved, through life and beyond into the realm no mortal could begin to understand. 'Twas the desire she'd glimpsed in Kieran when he'd asked her to come home with him, the priceless gift he offered her now despite the misgivings of his clan.

She prayed he'd not come to regret his generosity.

Stephen advanced, and Kieran parried with a twisting motion.

"Not bad." Kieran grinned as they continued. "Not as good as the strategy you use on the lasses, but not bad."

The cooper laughed. "I learned by watching you."

"Fencing or courting?"

"Both."

A shriek echoed through the surrounding hills, and Stephen lowered his sword to glance into the sky. A lone hawk circled in the distance, and he shook his head with a chuckle. "A bird."

"Aye." Kieran tapped his sword against Stephen's. "A soldier puts such things from his mind lest they distract him from his task."

He allowed his student a moment to regroup, then began pressing a bit harder. As he strove for balance, his right shoulder protested, but the only cure for weakened muscles was to use them. He decided to continue, trusting his instincts to tell him when to cease.

The warning came, and he pulled back just as Stephen's blade skittered up the length of his and barely missed his throat. When he lifted a hand to the underside of his jaw, it came away streaked with red. He'd bled much in his lifetime, and it had never concerned him overmuch. But this was the blood of a man with a great deal to live for, and the sight of it sickened him.

"God Almighty." Stephen dropped his sword and held up his hands. "Kieran, forgive me. I'd no idea I was so close."

Lifting his gaze from his bloody palm, Kieran regarded his young kinsman intently, searching for guilt in the eyes so like his own. All he found was remorse and a will strong enough to meet his suspicion without flinching. When had he begun seeing traitors among his own kin?

Suddenly, he felt weary to the bone. " 'Tis enough for today. I'll see you at noontime."

Ignoring Stephen's baffled look, Kieran sheathed his sword and began walking toward the keep. He'd just turned a bend in the path when a whirl of dust before him solidified into trouble.

"Ronan, what brings you out in broad daylight?"

The *sídhe* king chuckled. "Fearless, they call you. I see why."

Not so fearless anymore. "What is it you want? I'm not of a mood to spar with you."

"You have sparred enough this morn?"

Kieran stopped and glared. "Speak your piece and be gone."

"How is it to see the blood of a woman's beloved on your hand?"

Before he could think, his fists closed around Ronan's silken collar. "How do you think it is? To know that if I die, Brynna will be at the mercy of two heartless bastards like you and Ryan?"

"You forget the English."

"Damn the English," Kieran spat, throwing him back a step. "Damn all of you."

Taking up his sword, he raised it above his head to plunge it into the ground, forswearing the life of a warrior.

"No!"

The desperate plea stayed his hand, and Kieran paused to admire the effect his threat had wrought. "Tell me why."

When he got no response, he lowered his blade a hand span. "Do it or I swear, I'll end this now."

"You've inherited Morgan's talent for negotiating, I see." Ronan sighed. "Very well, then. Your final task is to safeguard Ireland from the false liege."

"Every nobleman on this island wishes to rule it. I'd need another lifetime to kill them all."

Ronan beamed, as if Kieran were his own son. "Such a fine warrior you are, but that is not what I meant. I speak of only one man: Ryan."

"I canna get near a man who sleeps with guards at the foot of his bed."

"Perhaps his daughter will help you."

Kieran pressed the tip of his sword over the king's empty heart, pleased to see uncertainty flicker in his eyes.

"As you wish," Ronan acquiesced with a nod. "Always the hard road with you."

Satisfied, Kieran put up his sword, and they resumed their walk. Ronan held his hands behind his back while he surveyed the broad valley before them.

"You're an uncommon man, Kieran MacAuley."

He glanced over to find respect showing plainly in the king's features. "Thank you."

"Some opponents are best fought from a distance," the king continued in the tone of a teacher instructing a student. "Some can only be defeated at close quarters. You must decide which approach to follow with Ryan. Aside from that, I can give you no advice for your last battle."

"I'll wed Brynna first, then deal with Ryan."

Ronan stopped abruptly in the middle of the road. "That is not the warrior's way."

" 'Tis *my* way," Kieran persisted, tapping a finger on his chest. "I'll not sacrifice a single day with her to suit some dusty old legend."

"You shall lose a great deal more should you challenge me."

Something in the way he said it set off a spark in Kieran's mind, and he took a menacing step closer to Ronan. "You sent the English after Brynna."

"I did no such thing."

The *sídhe*'s eyes flashed with indignation, but Kieran refused to back down. "If I'm to be your sword arm, you owe me the truth."

"I owe you nothing." They locked glares for several moments until Ronan finally relented. "I may have told an English officer where to find the woman he was seeking."

The cool explanation only fanned Kieran's temper. "To kill her."

"Not precisely, though it would have made things simpler."

"Maire would never forgive the murder of her daughter."

"Which is why I sent the soldiers." He brushed a bit of dust from his sleeve and let out a bored sigh. "I suspected they would fail to kill her but could still serve my purpose. I assumed you would not want a ruined woman."

"Nothing could ruin Brynna for me," Kieran informed him in a deadly calm voice. "Was it you who tried to abduct her from my keep?"

Ronan drew himself up haughtily. "Of course not. Had I come myself, she would be gone."

Infuriated beyond words, Kieran turned on his heel and stalked away.

"Kieran, are you listening?"

Eamon's irritated voice broke into his thoughts, and he answered, "Of course. The north road needs repair, and you wish to ask the farmers for help with it. Go on."

Hard as he tried, he couldn't focus on the council session. Endless matters about the valley required his attention, but his mind kept returning to the same thing.

Why did Ronan want him to kill Donovan Ryan?

Even with Edward's support, Brynna's father had little chance of becoming High King of Ireland. The clans would never accept him, and though ambitious to the point of treason, he hadn't the resources to take the throne by force. All afternoon, Kieran had rolled the problem about in his mind but kept coming back to the same conclusion.

Ronan wanted Ryan dead out of spite, most likely for his dalliance with Maire. They ruled Meath together, but the legends told of her refusal to wed Ronan, preferring to remain his consort and mother to many of his children. As a boy, Kieran had often wondered at her obstinance. Now, having met Ronan, he could easily understand.

The sound of Eamon clearing his throat ended his musings.

"I have a matter I wish to discuss," he continued with a pointed look down the table at Kieran. "Brynna Ryan."

Startled by the unexpected topic, he affected a mildly interested expression. "What of her?"

"It's come to my attention that you've offered her lodging within your own chambers."

"Since the attempt to take her, I wish to ensure her safety."

Eamon sat back in his chair with a knowing look. "In truth, I'm more concerned with you taking her."

The other members muttered at the insolent comment, but Kieran was far from shocked. The old bull never missed an opportunity to needle him. Humor did little to mask the ill-advised ploy to undermine the chieftain's authority.

Kieran frowned, as if considering the situation seriously. "Perhaps you'd prefer that I marry her."

"Good God, no! I think everyone would prefer she slept in her own bed, under guard if need be. Continuing in this fashion only diminishes people's confidence in your judgment," he added in his fatherly tone.

Kieran considered telling them Brynna lay untouched in his bed while he slept with his sword. Then again, before she'd arrived, he'd not have believed himself capable of such a thing. He suspected they would not believe it, either.

"I'll consider it, then." Weary from the exhausting day, he stood. "Will ye need me for anything else?"

"Go and rest," Cavan advised, hazel eyes twinkling merrily. "And have Brynna see to that cut."

Kieran bade them a pleasant afternoon and left the hall. He had one staunch ally among the council members.

In truth, 'twas one more than he'd anticipated.

Kieran said nothing while Brynna tended the fresh cut on his jaw. There was little she could do other than clean it and rub yarrow salve over it. The wound was far from serious, yet he was uncharacteristically quiet.

"Kieran, what's wrong?"

He stood and paced toward the window of his study. As he looked out over the valley, she thought he might not answer. When he turned back to her, he wore a bemused expression.

"I had a visit from Ronan this morn."

Just the mention of his name set her blood simmering, and she turned her attention to replacing the herbs in the chest Aileen had given her. 'Twas one thing to taunt and threaten her, quite another to involve Kieran. "What is it he wanted?"

He took in a deep breath before answering. "He wants me to kill your father."

Kieran waited an eternity for her to respond, but she didn't even lift her head. Focused on her task, she seemed not to have heard him. But he knew better.

He crossed the room and knelt before her. Stilling her busy hands, he kissed one and then the other as he sought her gaze. "I will not murder your father."

"But Ronan—"

"Doesn't command me." He cradled her cheek in his hand and gently kissed her. "Trust me, Brynna."

With a tepid smile, she nodded and rested her cheek on his shoulder. Again, he was stunned by her faith in him. And again, he vowed to be worthy of it.

When he was certain Brynna slept soundly, Kieran donned a hooded mantle and stepped into his massive wardrobe. Once inside, he pulled the door closed and felt along the back wall for the mechanism some long-ago craftsman had designed for Morgan's safety. He kept the hinges well greased, and the panel opened with only a whisper of sound.

Beyond it, a narrow set of stairs descended into darkness. Arms spread, Kieran braced his hands on the walls and counted to fifty. Then the steps ascended, and at one hundred his foot landed in soft earth. Four paces ahead was a door with no handle. He removed his ring and with his finger found the depression that matched the face of it. Placing the carved oak leaf in the lock, he gave a quarter turn.

Once the door was unlocked, he nudged it open to peer out into a small cave. Satisfied that no one was about, he stepped from the passageway and closed the door.

"By the saints, Morgan," he muttered as he replaced his ring, "ye were a clever one."

Using the bright moonlight to guide him, he moved quietly through the sparse trees to the grouping of birch his mother insisted was a faery circle. 'Twas where she often left gifts to Maire, so he thought it likeliest for the queen to come to him there. He hadn't considered what he might do if she didn't appear.

Now wasn't the time for negative thoughts.

When he reached the little glen, he stood in the middle of it, arms folded while he debated. How exactly did one reach the *sídhe*? Should he call out and alert every bandit within a league, or simply wait for her? In light of recent events, he had no doubt she was watching both him and Brynna. But would she agree to help him?

"If I can."

He spun to find her standing behind him.

She granted him a regal nod. "You wish to speak with me?"

"I need your help."

"I cannot betray Ronan. His tactics differ from mine, but we both seek to protect Ireland and her people from irrevocable harm."

"I'm not asking you to betray him." He paused with a wry grin. "I'm asking you to bed him."

Her lovely eyes widened, her mouth falling open as she blinked. If a faery could blush, he thought she might be doing it now. "Bed him?"

"Tomorrow evening. Even he can be in only one place at a time."

"What possible use could that be to you?"

He shook his head. " 'Tis better for you not to know. But I swear to you, my reasons are honorable."

"Never would I think anything else." After a long pause, she gave him a sliver of a smile. "Such a task is pleasant enough to manage. I trust you will tell me the rest when you can."

"I will."

"I shall look forward to it."

With a dainty laugh, she vanished.

CHAPTER TWELVE

It was late the following night when Brynna awoke to a barrage of feather-soft kisses.

"Come with me, lass," Kieran whispered, his face eager. "I've something for you."

Looking out the window, she saw the full moon shrouded in clouds. "Now?"

"Now."

Standing back to let her up, he wrapped her in her warmest dressing gown and then her gray cloak. Excitement traveled through him to her, speeding her heart with a jolt of anticipation. "Where are you taking me?"

"You'll see."

Stepping into the wardrobe, he helped her inside before closing the door. He pressed on a seemingly solid panel, and it opened noiselessly to reveal a set of stairs. After a long descent in pitch blackness, she felt the shift in direction as they began moving upward.

Standing outside the small cave, Kieran took

both her hands, and in the dim light she saw him grin. "I suppose I should have asked before we left the keep. Will ye marry me?"

She sensed no unwelcome presence nearby, yet she glanced about to be certain. "We've come out here to be married?"

"Aye, but only if you agree to it."

"How could I not? But your mother—"

"Will understand."

He grasped her hand and led her through the underbrush to a weathered standing cross. From the shadows emerged a tall figure dressed in the brown homespun of a cleric.

Kieran greeted him with a single nod. "Father William."

"Kieran."

When the slender man bowed to her, she saw the glint of steel in the folds of his cloak. "A pleasure to meet you at last, Lady Brynna."

"And you."

"Due to the unusual circumstances"—he glanced about the rustic setting with a bemused expression—"in good conscience I must ask if you come to this marriage willingly."

"I do. If Kieran feels such measures are necessary, I trust his judgment."

"Very well, then." He grinned as he opened his Bible. "Gaelic or Latin?"

Kieran returned the grin as he placed a ring on the illuminated page. "Latin."

The priest laughed quietly. As the clouds shifted overhead, moonlight fell on his aristocratic features. He conducted their ceremony in flawless

Latin, and she wondered who he might be and how Kieran had come to know him.

Apparently, her new husband held secrets of his own.

Father William blessed her wedding band and handed it to Kieran. 'Twas studded with gems that glittered even in the subdued light. Holding her left hand, he slid the ring onto her forefinger, then the next while reciting the solemn words that would bind them.

"In the name of the Father, and of the Son, and of the Holy Ghost, with this ring, I thee wed."

The circlet came to rest on her third finger, and he dropped a kiss over it.

"Well done, I'd say," Father William pronounced with his hands on their shoulders. When Kieran removed a small money pouch from his belt bag, the mysterious priest waved it away. " 'Tis reward enough to see you wed with my own eyes."

"For your orphans, then."

His teeth flashed in a broad smile as he tucked the payment into his robes. "For them, I take it. Bless you."

"You know the way back?"

"Indeed I do." He lifted Brynna's hand for a kiss. "A pleasant eve to ye both."

They hadn't gone far when she looked back to find he'd melted into the misty shadows. "What sort of monk is he?"

Kieran chuckled and lightly squeezed her hand. "The sort to marry us in the dead of night without asking questions."

"Kieran."

He laughed again, kissing the top of her head. "I couldn't very well ask Dunsmere's priest to preside over our vows. He's a good man, and I trust him, but he'd be hard-pressed to keep such a secret. William's parish is nearby but far enough away to avoid any problems."

They made the rest of their short journey in silence, not speaking until they stood before the fireplace in his bedchamber. *Their* bedchamber, she corrected herself as he tossed several logs onto the dying fire.

She held her hand before her to see her wedding band more clearly. The circlet of emeralds glowed in the firelight, and she smiled. " 'Tis a beautiful ring, Kieran."

"That it is," he agreed as he poked at the coals. "I bought it long ago in Dublin, though I had no one to give it to. Even Mother knows nothing of it."

"If you weren't betrothed, why would you buy such a ring?"

He set the poker aside and turned to face her. "When I saw it, I envisioned a woman with eyes to match the stones." Cupping her cheek in his hand, he kissed her. "I canna help thinking I bought it for you."

He slipped the cloak from her shoulders and tossed it on a chair. Only when she took off her dressing gown did Brynna recall what she was wearing.

"I wed you in this?" She held the skirt of her nightgown wide.

"MacAuley linen. A fitting outfit for the wife of their chieftain."

"And less to shed later on," she added with a laugh.

Taking her hands in his, he kissed one and then the other before granting her a tender look. "Thank ye for trusting me. I know 'twasn't the wedding you'd have liked."

Though she was no longer a virgin, out of love he'd left her untouched, as a bride should be on her wedding night. So much had he given her, asking for only her love in return.

"It matters not to me." She wrapped her arms about him in a warm embrace. "That we're wed is what's most important."

"I couldn't agree more." Grinning, he toyed with the ribbons that closed her bodice. As he loosened them, the gown fell from her shoulders.

"You're a wicked, wicked man."

"Ye might enjoy knowing just how wicked I can be."

Her retort was lost to a kiss so commanding, it shot the length of her entire body to her toes. Sliding his hands under her skirt, he lifted her and settled her bare thighs about his waist.

"This is how I wanted you, that night at the pool," he whispered at her ear. "Every last bit of you wrapped around me, taking me 'til I had nothing left to give you."

Inspired by the seductive note in his voice, she reached to the laces closing his trews and untied them. She pushed the leather down his hips and ran her hand over the growing length of him. "Is this what you wanted to give me?"

"Aye, lass. That and more."

Bracing her hands on his shoulders, she lowered herself until she'd taken him fully inside her. He filled the narrow confines of her body, and she reveled in the sensation of being part of him.

He kissed along her neck to the underside of her jaw. "How is it ye always smell like wildflowers?"

"I do?"

"Aye. That first night, I smelled it when ye came into the glen."

He took her mouth for a searing kiss, and she forgot everything else as his lips glided to the wild beat in her throat. She tipped back her head, and the bodice of her gown slipped away to bare her breasts.

Taking one of them in his mouth, he circled the tip with his tongue while she tangled her fingers in his dark hair. Her breath came in gasps as he trailed kisses across her skin to her other breast. Slowly, he began to move, and she moaned as he swelled inside her.

Hard and throbbing, he went deeper with every thrust, growling her name as he kissed her again. The tempest inside her met its match in Kieran, unleashing its full fury when he reached the center of her with a ragged groan. She fell against him, feeling somehow weak and strong all at once.

Covering her neck and shoulders with kisses, he let her slide the length of his body until her feet rested on the soft woolen rug. He lifted the linen gown over her head and dropped it on the floor. She reached for the ties on his *léine,* then hesitated and glanced up into his lazy smile.

"I'm yours, Brynna. Do as ye like."

While she divested him of the fine linen tunic, she noticed him stepping out of his boots. "You're far too good at that," she teased, nodding to the boots and trews lying atop her gown.

He slipped his arms about her and lowered his mouth to her ear. Rimming the contour of it with his tongue, he murmured, "We're all given talents."

"I think perhaps you got more than your share."

Chuckling, he swept her into his arms and headed for their bed.

"Before this night is done, my sweet wife, you'll know it for certain."

Kieran dropped kisses along her forehead, down to the tip of her nose, over her cheeks, before the tender assault settled on her mouth. Gently at first, then more insistently, he coaxed her from hazy dreams of their wedding night.

Stretching, Brynna smiled and murmured a reply. Pressed against his powerful body, she felt its rousings as surely as she had only hours before.

She shook her head with a little laugh. "You've barely slept."

"I canna have enough of you, lass," he answered in a low growl, then set about proving it to her.

Suddenly, a maelstrom filled their bedchamber, sending books and maps whirling, even upending a small chair. Kieran threw himself over Brynna to shield her as chess pieces and carved boxes pelted his back.

When the tempest ceased, he peered over his shoulder into Ronan's outraged face.

"What in the name of creation have you done, warrior?"

"Have ye no sense? I'm making love to my wife."

"Do not say it!" The king scowled at Brynna. "You have no regard for the chaos that will come of your deviltry."

"The deviltry was mine alone, Ronan. Should you wish to discuss it further, you may wait for me in there." Kieran nodded toward the open door of his study.

The regal jaw went slack. "What did you say?"

"I conduct no business in my bedchamber. I'll join you when I've dressed."

Ronan blustered for several moments in some unrecognizable tongue, then marched through the door and slammed it shut.

"Arrogant faery," Kieran muttered, looking about him in disgust. "Must he always make such a dramatic entrance?"

"He can hear you," Brynna warned, eyes dancing with merriment.

"I know it. I expected him at some point." He paused for a yawn. "But not so early."

"You're truly not afraid of him, are you?"

"Nay." Kieran grinned. "Are you?"

She gave a most unladylike snort, and he laughed as he pushed her back into the jumbled mound of pillows.

"My very own fearless one," he murmured against her lips before claiming them for a promising kiss. "Don't trouble to leave this bed. I'll not be gone long."

After another kiss, he rolled over and stood. He retrieved his trews from the hearth and pulled them on. When he moved toward his study, she laughed.

"Aren't you going to tie them?"

"Why? I'll only be untying them when I come back."

Her laughter followed him through the door, and he met the *sídhe*'s irritated look with the smile of a well-pleased new husband. "What help may I be to you this fine morn?"

"To plot against me was not insult enough? You enlisted Maire to help you?"

"She knew nothing of my plan." Kieran poured himself a cup of water. After swallowing a mouthful, he grinned. "Did ye not enjoy your evening?"

Something akin to amusement tugged at the corner of the king's down-turned mouth, and 'twas all Kieran could do to contain a chuckle. "I saw no harm in wedding the woman I love."

"She's no maiden. There was no need for such rash action."

"I wed her honestly and claimed her with honor. 'Tis not for you to gainsay me."

"She's not worthy of you. A pretty mongrel, defiled by the touch of other men."

The lofty tone enraged him, but reason tempered his anger with disgust. "You sent them to ruin her. So I'd not take her as my wife and be free to fight your battles."

Ronan seemed startled, but he quickly recovered his composure. "Your instincts serve you well, warrior."

"I wish you'd cease calling me that. My name is Kieran."

He was granted a reluctant smile. "Kieran."

"Even then ye knew she was the one fated for me. Ye knew if I saw her again, I'd not let her go."

Ronan inclined his head with a sigh. "You have baffled me at every turn. I gravely underestimated both your intelligence and your resolve. I shall not do so again."

"One more thing before you vanish." Kieran folded his arms with a somber look. "In the future, stay out of my bedchamber. Should you wish to consult with me, I'll meet you in here."

"You insolent whelp. I hold your fate in my hands and you dare challenge me?"

"My fate rests in this hand alone." Balling his fist, he turned it to show his chieftain's ring. "Beyond that, I ask the same courtesy of you I would of anyone else. I'm not of a mind to waken to a windstorm in my private chambers."

"Perhaps I should find another more amenable to following orders."

"Could it be done, you'd have found him already."

Eyes flashing, Ronan seemed on the verge of apoplexy. "Vexatious mortal."

"Pompous *sídhe*."

The king opened and closed his mouth like a landed fish, and with a flourish of his hand, he disappeared.

Kieran returned to find Brynna sound asleep. He was pleased to see every scrap of paper and book in its original place, each item resting back on its shelf.

That explained the last flick of Ronan's hand, he mused as he pulled on his *léine* and boots. While he properly fastened his clothes, he decided 'twas an opportune moment to visit his mother.

"Married?" Aileen echoed in disbelief, dropping her well-worn psalter into her lap. "In the forest?"

Kieran nodded, his expression solemn, though his eyes twinkled with merriment. "Last night."

"Who married you?"

"Father William."

"Oh, for heaven's sake. The man's more a mercenary than a priest." She let out an exasperated sigh. "You couldn't announce your betrothal and be wed properly?"

He tilted his head in a chiding gesture, and she sighed. "No, you couldn't, with opinions so unsettled. But you could have waited 'til things were resolved, then married with the blessings of your kin."

"If I'd done that, 'twould have been much longer."

While he explained the sacrifice Ronan had demanded of him, Aileen's temper began to boil. "That's absurd."

"Donovan Ryan canna be allowed to become High King. According to Ronan, I'm the one to stop him."

"How do you propose to accomplish that?" she asked.

"Truly, I've no idea, and I had no intention of postponing my marriage to Brynna while I reasoned it through." He knelt beside her chair and took her hand. "I know you're disappointed,

Mother. If I'd seen another way, I'd gladly have taken it."

"What does Brynna think of marrying in such a manner?"

"You can ask her when she wakes."

Grinning shamelessly, he kissed her cheek and strode from her solar with enough swagger to carry an entire army across the River Boyne.

Leaning back her head, she looked up at the portrait that guarded the fireplace. "Your son, Magnus. I hope you're proud."

A rumble of laughter drifted through her heart, and she smiled.

When Kieran entered the great hall, he paused a moment in the archway for a heartfelt prayer of gratitude.

In his usual place at the head table sat Devlin, talking with Carrick while two fawning maids filled their bowls with porridge.

His jaw still stung from the blow he'd taken nearly a sennight ago, and Kieran approached them with a healthy measure of caution. Their conversation ceased abruptly, and Carrick made a hasty retreat.

Kieran tried to appear unconcerned as he took his seat. He wanted to ask Dev where he'd been, why he'd stayed away so long. But as the brute seemed none the worse for wear, he decided to let things rest.

"Good morn to you, Dev."

"And to you. Biscuit?" His cousin passed a

wooden platter heaped with steaming rolls, then the honey.

"Thank you. 'Tis a fair morning, is it not?"

"Fairer for some than others, I'd wager." Dev grinned as Brynna crossed the hall, standing when she joined them. "Shall I guess what's put that devilish gleam in your eye?"

With an arm about her waist, Kieran smiled as he drew her onto his lap. "My wife, of course."

Dev's blue eyes twinkled their approval. "Thank God. All that brooding was becoming tiresome."

Brynna turned to him with her warmest smile. "Welcome home, Devlin."

"Thank you, Brynna. Milady." He gave her a puzzled look. "What shall I call you?"

"Just Brynna."

"Not one for airs, are ye?" When she shook her head, he grimaced. "My apologies for upsetting you."

" 'Twas far worse worrying about you these past few days," she told him, reaching out to touch his shoulder.

Dev's expression warmed with admiration, and he patted her small hand. " 'Tis kind of ye to say such a thing."

"Where have you been?"

Kieran suspected if it had been he doing the asking, he'd have been sternly told to keep his curiosity to himself. But to Brynna, Dev gave a halfhearted smile. "I've been about, thinking." He looked over her head at Kieran, and his smile faded. "I hope ye can forgive me."

"Of course I can, and I pray you'll forgive me. It's not that I didn't trust you. I simply couldn't tell anyone about Brynna's connection to Ryan just then."

"I came to that, while I was gone." His sober look grew even darker. "Carrick told me there was trouble later on."

While they described what had happened, he looked from one to the other with disbelief in his eyes. "Well, then, that explains the rest."

"The rest?" Brynna asked.

"Some think 'twas me who broke into your room."

"That's absurd! Who thinks that?"

"A few have mentioned it to me, as well," Kieran said as he took her hand. "I saw no need to concern you with it."

"Devlin would never do such a thing. Surely you know that."

Her fierce defense of his cousin made him smile. "Aye, but there are those who find sport in stirring up trouble. You've forgotten that, living on your own for so long."

"I suppose I have." She gave Dev a look filled with trust. "I know you'd never harm me."

"I'm grateful to you." He smiled. "What is this I hear about a wedding?"

She laughed, and as Kieran listened to her account of their evening, he realized it was a tale worthy of the bards. Generations from now, few would believe it was true.

Once she'd finished, Dev chuckled. "The council will choke on this, to be sure."

"I'd imagine so," Kieran agreed. "I'll tell them after they've eaten."

"A wise plan. And then?"

Shrugging, he drizzled honey over a biscuit and offered it to his enchanting wife. " 'Tis the MacAuleys' decision, not mine. If they prefer I step down, I'll abide by their wishes."

Dev lounged in his chair and folded his arms across his chest. "And what will ye do if you're no longer chieftain?"

In answer, Kieran grinned at the woman perched on his knee.

She promptly rolled her eyes heavenward. "What am I to do with you?"

Pushing back his chair, he stood with her in his arms. "If you'd care to come with me, I'll show you."

She laughed and kicked her feet. "Have I a choice?"

"Not really."

"But Devlin—"

"Off with ye." He motioned them away with a wave of his hand. "Keep him happy, lass. God knows, no one else can."

"Let me be certain I understand the situation." Eamon drew out his words in a cautious tone. "You brought a woman you barely knew here for us to harbor. When you discovered she was the daughter of Donovan Ryan, you did not turn her out as you should have. In fact, you took her into your room and later snuck into the forest to be married by a priest of dubious credentials."

"I took her into my room to protect her after she

was attacked," Kieran countered. "And I wed her to preserve her honor and mine."

The elder pressed his lips together, clearly unwilling to follow that path any further. "That leaves the matter of her parentage."

"The Queen of Meath is grateful to us for sheltering her daughter. To my mind, her goodwill cancels the ill of Ryan."

"She is the more powerful of the two," Eamon agreed as he tapped his chin. "But your wife's father is still a danger to us."

"If you found that Mary was not whom you thought, could you turn her away?"

Kieran's bold strategy failed miserably. Eamon glared down at him from the dais. "My wife is not under judgment here; yours is. Along with your judgment, ever since you returned from Westmeath."

In truth, his judgment had never been sounder, but Kieran recognized the futility of arguing any further. He'd pushed the conservative members of the council as far as he dared. They conferred briefly, and Eamon stood to announce their conclusion.

"Very well, then. As this is a matter of the utmost importance, we'll take it before the clan. Their decision shall be binding on us all. Is that agreed?"

"I'd have it no other way."

Brynna paced before the fire, anxiously awaiting Kieran's return. For two hours now, the swell of voices in the hall below had grown louder and softer but seldom died completely. Her stomach in knots, she'd tried to read, only to set her book aside in frustration. Her attempts to bridge into Kieran's mind were gently rebuffed, as if he sensed her presence and sought to protect her.

'Twas this she'd feared above everything else. The chieftain's power was of no consequence to Kieran, but his kinsmen's faith in him meant everything. If he felt he'd lost it, he might not wish to remain in Dunsmere. Then what of his mother, his sisters-in-law, his nieces? They depended on him in so many ways, she doubted he could bring himself to leave them.

But could he bear to stay?

By the time the door swung open, she'd worked herself into such a state that she pounced on him like a cat on a hapless mouse. "What happened?"

The grueling evening had chiseled new lines into his face, but somehow he smiled. "Split even. The council members will cast their votes in the morning."

"In the morning? Whose ludicrous suggestion was that?"

"Mine." Still smiling, he gathered her into his arms and kissed her. "Everyone is exhausted, and no good comes of that."

"How can you be so calm?"

"If they wish for me to continue as chieftain, I will. If they wish for me to step down, I will." He passed a hand over the length of her hair to rest on her back. "Whatever comes, I'll provide for you and our children. Ye have my word on that."

"I'd not even considered otherwise." She smiled as she led him toward the fire. "Now sit, and I'll fetch you some wine."

He sat but caught her hand when she turned to go. "I don't need any wine, but I very much need you."

Touched by the simple plea, she curled up in his lap and rested her head on his shoulder. "I wanted to be with you, so you'd not face this alone."

"I know, but I felt 'twas wiser to keep you abovestairs."

"You didn't want me to hear what they said about me."

"Ye might wish to know many had kind things to say. I daresay Dev's account was most effective."

Curious, she lifted her head from his shoulder. "What did he say?"

"That ye saved my life in Westmeath, then again by preventing the English from finding me. That ye tried to leave to keep your father from Dunsmere, but I wouldn't let ye go." He paused for a tender kiss. "That ye love me and would do nothing against my kin."

"He truly said all that?"

"That and more, but I'd not repeat it in the presence of a lady."

His boyish grin made her laugh, but she quickly grew sober. "Do people still think he tried to hurt me?"

"Some do, but there's little I can say to convince them otherwise."

"Which you know because you tried." When he sighed, she folded her hands in her lap and looked down at them. "Forgive me, Kieran. I know I'm difficult to manage."

With his knuckle he lifted her head, and his

frown deepened to a scowl. "Those aren't your words. Who would tell you such a thing?"

She shrugged and cast her eyes away, but he gently grasped her chin. "Look at me, Brynna."

When she did as he bade her, he granted her the adoring smile she loved. "You're a beautiful woman with a keen mind and a boundless spirit. Your father simply didn't understand you."

"I suppose." She sensed something in his thoughts beyond the confrontation with his clan. "Is something else troubling you?"

He hesitated, then gave a tight smile. "Ronan came to talk with me the day before we wed. He admitted to sending those soldiers after you, knowing full well what they'd do. I'm convinced he also sent whoever tried to take you from here."

" 'Tis the most logical explanation for his visit the next day."

He flashed her a roguish grin. "I bested him that round."

"By marrying me in the dead of night." She laughed. "Little wonder he was so furious. All his plans were for naught."

"Never underestimate an opponent." He gave her nose a cautionary tap. "Especially one as clever as Ronan. He's not through yet, and his next attack may be far more difficult to parry."

CHAPTER THIRTEEN

The mood within the keep was so oppressive, Kieran considered staging a tirade just to shatter the tension. Men and women alike tiptoed about, muttering and whispering as if someone had died. He had no way of knowing who had voted for or against him, and in truth he didn't care.

He only wanted the council to make its decision so life could resume its customary pace.

Just before noontime, a lad appeared in the doorway of his study. "Eamon sent me to fetch you."

Finally. "Many thanks, Samuel. Tell the council I'll be down directly."

The boy gave him a baffled look. "He said I should bring you with me."

"No doubt he did."

Quelling a grin, Kieran began another line of numbers in his ledger. Never had he jumped simply because someone told him to. He had no intention of starting now.

After a few moments, Samuel shrugged and went back the way he'd come. Only then did Kieran set down his pen and fold his hands on the desk before him. Scarred and strong, they were the hands of a warrior, not a farmer. Then again, he'd birthed a lamb or two in his time, and when pressed into service, he could wield a plow or scythe as well as any.

He thought of Brynna.

She'd brought joy and love into his life, and the promise of a family of his own. Whether their home be castle or cottage, with her as its mistress, he'd be content.

Bolstered by fresh confidence, he descended the stairs and strode to the foot of the dais, where the council awaited him.

"You sent for me, Eamon?"

"Some time ago."

"For the love of God," Cavan rumbled. "Tell him what we've decided."

Eamon sent him a dark glare, but the smith's was darker still, and the older man relented with a sigh. Turning to Kieran, he said, "Very well. In light of the circumstances surrounding your questionable actions, the council has agreed to continue supporting you as chieftain. Any more such transgressions, however, and we shall be forced to withdraw that support. Do you understand?"

"Aye."

"And you will abide by our decision?"

"As I always have." Though he tried mightily, he couldn't keep back a grin.

Cavan chortled, and a few of the others smiled.

Eamon considered him for a long moment, then shook his head with a bemused expression. "That will be all, then."

"Kieran, what are you doing?"

"Decorating."

His mother laughed as she joined him in the center of his study. "Are you? Odd how much it looks like staring."

Actually, he was imagining Brynna within these rooms, bathed in sunshine, lit by an evening fire. Sharing his nights with her, waking each morning to her breathtaking smile.

"Wait here," Aileen said. "I may be able to help you."

Arms crossed, he strolled into their bedchamber, considering what he wished to keep and what should be replaced.

And what might his new wife want?

While he considered that, he realized the urge to claim the room as his own had begun after he returned from Westmeath. Bereft of something he couldn't recall, he'd prowled his chamber in search of tangible reassurance that he'd not gone mad.

Now he understood that something inside him had been altered so completely, he'd never again be the man he was before. Loving Brynna had changed him, even when his memory of her had dwindled to almost nothing.

He turned toward the door as Aileen rejoined him, and smiled at the lovely assistant trailing in her wake. "Good morn to you, Brynna."

Allowing the thought of early-morning lovemaking into his mind, he chuckled as she blushed a becoming shade of rose. She shifted the lengths of fabric she held and smiled. "And to you. Your mother tells me you're decorating."

"He's walking about the place scowling, as if that will get the job done," Aileen corrected her with a laugh. She dropped the material she carried on the bench at the foot of the bed and motioned for Brynna to do the same. "You know how men are."

"Aye."

Cocking his brow, Kieran grinned at Brynna. "Do ye, now? And how are we?"

"Stubborn, slow to ask for help with anything. And you never admit when you're lost."

He stepped closer and lightly kissed her lips. "The only time I'm lost is when I'm without you."

"Do you like this?" Aileen asked as she trailed emerald silk from a bedpost.

Drawing a length of it across Brynna's shoulders, he smiled. "Perfect."

"Kieran, I'm serious."

Ignoring her, he focused on his wife's enchanting eyes, watched them twinkle in response to his attention. "As am I."

"Only faeries wear green," Aileen reminded him, then laughed. "Forgive me, Brynna. I'm not yet accustomed to thinking of you that way."

"What think you?" Fingering the lustrous fabric, he allowed his touch to wander suggestively toward her breasts.

Parting her lips the tiniest bit, she made it clear she welcomed the idea simmering in his mind. " 'Twould make a beautiful dress, and I'd proudly wear it."

"Mother, I think Grania is calling you."

"That she is," she agreed without hesitation. "I can't imagine why I didn't hear her myself. Excuse me, will you?"

Kieran walked her to the door and bolted it behind her before turning to Brynna.

She began laughing. "Kieran, you dressed me— quite slowly, I might add—not two hours ago."

"And now I'll reverse it."

He worked open the buttons closing her bodice and slipped the deep blue day dress into a pile on the floor. Lifting a fold of the vibrant silk from the bed, he draped it across her breasts and brushed it over her cheek. "I want to see you in this."

"Now?"

"Now."

He removed the rest of her clothes one tantalizing layer at a time. The divine sight of her framed in sunlight nearly drove him to his knees, and he claimed her mouth for a kiss. Cupping her breast, he circled the budding tip with his thumb as she moaned into his mouth. He quickly shed his own clothes and laid her back on their bed.

Covering her body with his, he rolled 'til they were cocooned in silk warmed by bare skin.

"Soft," he whispered at her ear, nosing along her cheek to her graceful throat. "So soft."

Her murmur of agreement made him smile, and he pulled his head back to look at her. He kissed her lips, then each rosy cheek. "Did I thank ye for marrying me?"

"Earlier this morn."

"I seem to have forgotten," he teased, nipping at

her shoulder. "Because I'm feeling inclined to thank ye again."

"Are you, now?" She laughed. "And what if I have something to do besides lie abed with you half the day?"

Catching up a bit of silk, he trailed it along her neck to the hollow between her breasts, circling one and then the other. With a delectable sigh, she closed her eyes and tipped her head back into the pillows.

He mouthed her breast through the thin fabric, following the shape of it with kisses. Tightening a bit with each circuit, he slowly worked his way toward the peak. With a breath, the damp material puckered, and she arched her back in a command he understood perfectly.

Kieran filled his mouth with silk-covered flesh, rewarded by a heady moan of pleasure. She responded with the instinctive sensuality of a newly made woman, and it tested him sorely. Knowing the bliss that awaited him, he strove to master lust such as he'd never imagined.

He let his hand drift between her breasts, over her stomach to rest on her hip. At a gentle touch, her thighs parted for him. In the damp curls he found her cleft and gave a single stroke. With a gasp, she pressed into his palm. 'Twas all he could do not to bury himself inside her and rock them both into oblivion.

"Tell me, Brynna. Tell me what you want."

"Touch me," she whispered.

"Here?" He kissed her stomach.

"Nay."

"Here?" Now a nibble at her hip. She moved her head from side to side on the coverlet, and he chuckled. "I canna read your thoughts, lass."

"Kieran!"

Dropping kisses on her warm skin, he glided over her and lowered his mouth to hers. "Show me."

Hesitation shone in her eyes, but she took his hand and guided it between her legs. He stroked the wet edges of her, watched her eyelids flutter closed on a sigh. Delving inside, he moved in long thrusts, circling her tender nub with his thumb. She began to tremble, then writhed beneath him, her sensuous movements goading him beyond the limits of masculine endurance.

Kieran pushed himself up on his hands and sank into her liquid embrace. Groaning, he withdrew and plunged again, deeper each time, deliberately reining his pace so she might match him. Her breath came in ragged gasps, yet she arched greedily against him, demanding still more.

And he gave it to her. Everything he was poured from him, finding its home within her. Encased by her warmth, he rolled to his back and clasped her to his chest. Pressing his lips to her temple, he sighed. Simply, profoundly happy.

She lifted her head and grinned down at him. "You approve of my new gown, then?"

He grinned back. "Very much."

"I fear we've ruined it."

"I'll buy you bolts of silk. Velvet, brocade, whatever you fancy." He pulled the fabric away, baring her skin to the sunshine. "But none could compare with this."

"Such pretty words from a man of war."

"You'll find I learn quickly."

Rolling her over, Kieran set about proving what a clever student he could be.

"Kieran!"

He turned and was rewarded with a faceful of wet spring snow. It seldom fell this far south, and the bailey was teeming with children scampering about to enjoy the novelty before it melted.

"Samuel, mind your aim," he scolded with a laugh as he brushed off his woolen mantle.

Resuming his walk toward the stables, he felt a tug on his sleeve and found Lynette gazing up at him with imploring blue eyes. "Please, Kieran. Will you help us?"

He crouched before her so she'd not strain her wee neck looking up at him. "With what, little one?"

"We've only ten on our side." She pointed across the bailey to a stone trough currently serving as a bunker. "They have many more, and they're much bigger."

Kieran glanced over and found she had the right of it.

"Of course, I'll help you, Lynette. What do you need of me?"

"Ammunition," one of the lads answered. "Lots of it."

Aileen stood before a narrow window in the great hall, looking out at something she'd not seen in a very long time. "Brynna, you must see this."

Kieran sat cross-legged on the ground, scraping

up snow to pack into snowballs for the younger children. As quickly as he added to the pile, they snatched them up and fired them at the older boys, who retaliated with enthusiasm. Laughing and joking, Kieran kept his little compatriots well stocked for their raucous fight.

Brynna laughed. "What fun! Children do love the snow."

Her hands on either side of the window, Aileen drank in the sight of her son, happy and carefree. "I cannot remember the last time he did such a thing. Before he became chieftain, I suppose." Tears welled in her eyes, and she blinked to keep them at bay. "Before Magnus and Adam died."

She felt a gentle hand on her shoulder and gave it a grateful squeeze. "You should join them, Brynna."

The girl needed no prodding, but raced from the hall. Kieran looked up with a bright smile, catching her as she knocked him backward. Arms wrapped about her, he raised his mouth to hers for a kiss. Their laughter mingled with the shouts of children indignant over losing their best weapon.

They piled atop the kissing couple, pummeling them with snowballs and taunts, but to no avail. Kieran's new playmate eclipsed them all, and they resumed their fight without him.

"A fine lass Brynna is," Cavan said from behind her. "Full of all he's been missing."

Aileen turned away from the window and discreetly wiped her cheeks. "Aye. 'Tis good to see him so happy."

He stepped closer and tipped her face up to his. "Anything would I give to see you that way again."

"Young and in love?"

His hazel eyes warmed. "Love is not only for the young. We've much living yet to do. I see no sense in doing it alone."

He brushed her lips with a tender kiss that promised more should she desire it. She rested a trembling hand on his cheek, praying he'd not think her as clumsy as she felt. When he pulled away, he gave her a little smile.

"I did that badly," she chided herself.

" 'Twas a lovely kiss. I'd like many more of them."

Aileen's cheeks warmed with the unexpected praise. She'd felt awkward kissing him, enjoying it.

"I'm not Magnus," he said, as if sensing her disquiet. "Never will I be. But he's gone, and I'm here. With you."

She glanced about nervously, but no one stood near enough to hear them. "What are you saying?"

"I love you, Aileen. If you'll have me, I'll gladly marry you and care for you the rest of my days."

"This is so . . . so sudden." She stammered like a maiden, knowing it wasn't true. They'd been dancing about each other for months, but he'd not pressed for anything more until now. "I need time to consider it."

"Fair enough." He kissed her cheek and gave her a wink. "What say you?"

"A moment you give me?"

"What comes of waiting? More wasted time we could have together."

Aileen cast another look out the window, saw Kieran happily sitting on the steps with Brynna in his lap. Cavan's words brought to mind those she'd spoken to Kieran not long ago, begging him not to waste the second chance he'd been granted.

She turned to Cavan with a smile. "Very well. I shall marry you this evening."

"So soon?"

"Now you wish to wait?"

Chuckling, he rubbed a thumb over his scarred chin. "I could get word to Father William, I suppose. Are ye certain?"

"Very certain."

"Tonight it is, then. I'll come for you just before midnight."

Her heart light as a foolish girl's, Aileen smiled as she kissed him. "I'll be ready."

Brynna toyed with her stewed pears. Though it was one of her favorite dishes, this night it held little appeal for her.

Kieran, however, had dispatched his own and was now eyeing hers with great interest.

"You've no taste for fruit this eve?"

"Nay. Would you like them?"

Grinning, he opened his mouth, and she spooned some up for him. She went on to feed him the rest, one bite at a time. He finished the juice, then leaned in to kiss her. "Delicious."

"They're very nicely prepared."

"Aye, and the pears are good, as well."

She smiled at his jest, and he chuckled. "Tell me, Brynna: Does that smile taste as sweet as it looks?"

"You might prefer to decide for yourself." She returned his kiss. "What think you?"

"I think 'tis time I retired for the evening. Would ye care to come with me?"

"I might."

Motioning her closer, he whispered several suggestions, and she flushed hotter with each one.

The last made her giggle before she could stop herself. "I've never done that."

"Truly? 'Tis a favorite of mine."

"I don't believe it's possible."

"Do ye not?" Standing, he bowed and offered her his arm. "Then allow me to prove it to you."

Kieran glanced up from his noon meal when he felt a hand on his shoulder. Grania stood beside him, an odd expression lighting her eyes. "Your mother sent me to fetch you, lad."

He could scarce remember the last time she'd called him that. Panicked, he jumped to his feet and nearly toppled her backward. "Is she ill?"

"She's quite well," his aunt assured him with a mysterious woman's smile. "But she wishes to see you."

Curious and still more than a bit concerned, Kieran hastened up the stairs and knocked at his mother's door. 'Twas unusual for it to be closed so late in the day. When it opened, he blessed his wife's good sense in relating the gossip of the keep to him.

"*Fáilte,* Kieran." Cavan motioned him inside. "Thank ye for coming."

As the older man seemed quite uneasy, Kieran quelled a smile as he strolled over to kiss his mother's cheek. It held a lovely blush he'd not seen in a long time.

"You wanted to speak with me?" he asked as he settled on the stool beside her.

"Judging by that infernal grin you're trying to hide, you already know what we want to tell you."

Laughing, he smiled over her head at her new husband. "I've been expecting it, thanks to Brynna."

Cavan rested his hands on Aileen's shoulders in a protective gesture. "Do ye approve, then?"

He honestly felt it wasn't his place to do so, but out of respect for tradition, he nodded. "I could imagine no better match for either of you."

His mother gave him a trembling smile. "Thank you, Kieran."

Cavan echoed her, offering an enormous hand, as well.

" 'Tis I who should be thanking you," he teased with a wink. "For taking her off my hands."

Brynna wished Kieran would find something to do elsewhere in the keep. He'd spent the morning in his study meeting with several of his kinsmen, then bedeviled her with three games of chess. Which he excelled at, of course.

Just when she'd begun to consider feigning some lady's ailment, he took it into his head that 'twas a fine afternoon to take Gideon out for a ride. In truth, it had drizzled all morning, and the ground was most likely slick with mud, but she cheerfully escorted him to the door and bade him enjoy his romp. Once he was safely through the gates, she returned to their room as quickly as dignity would allow. After bolting the doors, she stood in the middle of their sunny bedchamber, hands folded imploringly.

"Shela, Rianne, if you can hear me, please come. I need you."

Several moments passed with no response, and she called to her sisters again. When they appeared, Rianne was but half-dressed, Shela still rubbing sleep from her eyes.

Despite her predicament, Brynna laughed at the disheveled sight before her. "Forgive me for disturbing you."

"I've only just gone to sleep," Shela grumbled as she stretched out on the bed. "What could be so important?"

Brynna took a deep breath and tried to speak calmly. "I think I'm with child."

Both turned to her with looks of astonishment on their lovely faces.

Rianne found her voice first. "Why do you think that?"

"I feel horrid. Everything I eat makes me ill. I can't seem to get enough sleep. My entire body aches as if I've walked for days. Mostly, it's a feeling I have. Can you tell me for certain?"

Her pleading roused Shela, who stood and came to her side. Hands framing Brynna's face, Shela looked deep into her eyes. A slow smile crossed her features. " 'Tis a small flicker, but a bright one. The light of a child."

"Kieran's child?" Brynna asked hopefully.

"That I cannot see."

"Even Mother won't know that until the babe is born. We must get back before Father misses us," Rianne added with a sisterly hug.

"Don't despair, little sister." Shela smiled and embraced her. "Your husband's mind is an accepting one."

With sympathetic looks for her, they vanished.

Kieran watched Brynna pick at her dinner. She'd eaten nothing, though she'd made a good show of sampling Grania's latest pork masterpiece. She wrinkled her nose at a cup of mead, asking Callie for cider instead. Even this seemed to displease her, and after a few sips she pushed it away.

He leaned closer so she'd hear him over the noise around them. "You're not feeling well?"

She merely shook her head, but he sensed 'twas more than a sour stomach that plagued her. She seemed dispirited, as if something weighed heavily on her mind. When he took up one of her hands for a kiss, he found it trembling. "Brynna, you've been like this for days. Tell me what's wrong."

Relief washed over her troubled features, but again she shook her head. "Not here," she said as she rose from her chair.

With growing concern, he followed her to his mother's library, the nearest chamber with a door. He closed it behind them, calling on his patience before facing his wife with a smile of encouragement. "Now then, tell me."

"I'm with child."

Kieran rushed forward to sweep her into an elated embrace, but she stepped away. Her reaction bewildered him, and he let his hands fall to his sides. "This doesn't please you?"

"If the child is yours, I welcome it with all my heart. But I detest the thought of birthing some Englishman's bastard."

Foolishly, he'd not considered that possibility. He'd been so impatient to wed Brynna, there was no way to know for certain who had sired her babe. Already he could hear the gossip, debating whether the chieftain's firstborn was of his own making or that of an enemy soldier.

He knew of only one way to meet such a challenge.

With a smile, he brought her into his arms and kissed her. "This child is no one's bastard. 'Tis mine."

"You don't know that."

"A child is more than those who created him." He kissed her again. "Surely you're proof of that."

"What are you saying?"

He held a hand to her waist. "I am the father of the child you carry. Say it."

"Kieran—"

"Say it."

A sigh escaped her, but she smiled. "You are the father of the child I carry."

"Not so difficult, was it?" He grinned. "And now, I think we should find Grania. No doubt she has a concoction that will ease your stomach."

CHAPTER FOURTEEN

As an early winter wind howled outside the windows of the hall, Dev was staring at the chessboard and muttering to himself. Kieran had given him ample time to decide on a move, and after a while his mind began to wander.

The customary raiding season had passed, the first he'd missed since becoming old enough to fight. Though he claimed it was his shoulder that kept him close to home, in truth it was his heart. He simply couldn't bear to leave Brynna.

When his opponent groaned, Kieran chuckled. "Do ye cede?"

"Nay." Dev leaned back with a grimace. "Aye. You've beaten me again."

" 'Twas a much better match this time," he commented as he reset the pieces.

When he got no response, he looked up to find his cousin considering him with a pensive expression. "What is it?"

"How did you fare with the chieftains this morn?"

"Things are improving, albeit slowly. A few months ago, some of them refused to even share a table, though they agreed we've been greatly successful in battle." He paused for a rueful smile. "Now they'll sit and talk more or less peacefully, so long as the food and wine hold out."

"I remember the first time all of ye met," Dev recalled with a laugh. "Took longer to disarm everyone than it did for them to devour an entire stag."

" 'Twill take persistence and determination to strengthen relations among the clans. Some of them have been feuding since before you and I were born."

"Ye have their respect, to be sure. When you speak, they listen."

"I hope so."

Dev nodded, glancing around as if searching for words. Clearly, something was troubling him, and Kieran waited for him to gather his thoughts.

With a sigh, Dev leaned forward and balanced his massive forearms on his knees. Looking Kieran dead in the eyes, he said, "It seems to me your shoulder is well mended."

Kieran couldn't lie, but if he admitted the truth, he'd look like a coward, sending his men into battles he refused to join. So he said nothing.

"If ye want to retire as commander, do it," Dev continued. "I'll continue leading them as I have been."

"I don't wish to dishearten the men."

"You're doing it now, leaving them so uncertain."

"I know." Kieran sat back in his chair and crossed a boot over his knee. "One day, I think to give it up, the next I think not."

" 'Tis not like you to be so indecisive."

"That I know, as well, but things are different now."

"For many of us." Dev rose and stretched his arms above his head. "I must be going. Carrick and Stephen challenged me to a wrestling match."

Kieran laughed. Such dares were common among the ranks. "They'd need a third to even come close to besting you."

"Easy money in the wagering, to be sure. Would ye care to join us?"

"Not today."

With a nod of understanding, Dev crossed the hall and headed down the corridor.

Left to his own thoughts, Kieran watched the children assembled before the mammoth central hearth, spellbound by another of Brynna's faery stories. As they laughed and squealed, he couldn't keep back a smile.

They didn't know the tales were true.

She mimicked a crooked troll, lumbering about as if she carried a large hump on her back. She sang like a wood sprite, danced like a nymph, popped up behind the older ones to startle them as a faun might do.

God, how he loved her. His wife, mother of the bairn making its presence known in the swell beneath her new gown. He longed to hold their child in his arms, look into a face that blended his rough features with Brynna's softer ones.

A flutter of motion on the mantel caught his eye, and he looked again to be certain he'd seen correctly.

Perched on a fat candle was a tiny figure that seemed made of spun sugar. She braced her hands on the edge, leaning forward as she swung her bare feet. Her gown shimmering like gossamer in the sunlight, she looked at him with a playful grin and a wink.

One moment she sat alone and the next a slightly taller figure joined her. Dressed in a similar fashion, this one seemed much more interested in him than in the story. She reclined on her side atop the candle, propping her head on her hand before granting him an inviting smile.

"Look!" Eyes wide, Lynette pointed toward the mantel. "Angels."

The two exchanged bemused looks, and the smaller one said, "Thank you for the compliment, but we're not angels." She turned slightly. "See? No wings."

"These are my sisters, Rianne and Shela," Brynna told the children as she walked toward the mantel. "Perhaps they'd care to join us."

Hand outstretched, she smiled at her wee guests. They returned the fond gesture, then lifted their skirts and stepped onto her palm. She bent to set them on the stone floor, and in a heartbeat, they grew to the same height as she.

One of the boys whistled his appreciation. "How do you do that?"

" 'Tis magick," the taller one said, tapping him on the nose. "Charles."

His eyes rounded with wonder. "You know my name."

"And so you shall know ours. I am Shela, and this is Rianne."

"Are you older than Brynna?" Charles asked.

Her luminous eyes crinkled with a smile. "Much older. Older even than your grandda."

Lynette overcame her characteristic shyness and approached the gracious *sídhe*. "Do you truly live forever?"

"We do."

Hands clasped, she gazed up at the smaller faery. "I wish I could live forever."

Kieran thought Rianne's smile a sad one, and she smoothed a hand over the girl's hair. "Which story is our little sister telling you?"

"The one about Clíodna, the most beautiful woman in the world. Do you know it?" When they nodded, she asked, "Would you like to hear it again?"

Lynette held out both pudgy hands, and for a moment the faeries stared down at her as though uncertain of what to think. In concert, they smiled and took her hands to follow her to a bench beside the hearth. Brynna glanced toward the archway and smiled, lifting her brow in a silent question.

Though he saw no one standing there, Kieran left his seat and strolled into the corridor. There he found Maire, hands held to her face while sparkling tears dripped through her fingers.

Without a thought, he took her in his arms and rested her head on his chest in the way that soothed Brynna so well. Shaking with quiet sobs, she gripped a fold of his tunic in her dainty hand.

After a bit, she raised her head and wiped her cheeks. "Forgive me, Kieran. 'Tis not my way to be so emotional."

"A mother is entitled to a few tears, I'd say."

She folded her arms between them, donning her customary regal bearing as she stepped away. Gazing through the archway, she smiled. "I seldom see them together. It brings me both joy and sorrow."

"The three of you are welcome here whenever you wish to visit."

She turned to him with a knowing look. "And Ronan?"

Kieran chuckled. "Of him I require fair warning."

"A wise policy."

"May I ask you a question?"

She held up a forefinger ringed in jewels. "Only one this time."

"What is it the king holds against Brynna? I've never heard him call her by name, and he insults her at every opportunity."

"She is the result of my love for another."

"But you have given Ronan many children of his own."

"None like Brynna." She cast a wistful look over her shoulder. "She has Donovan's strength, his courage. In her, I see the best of him, yet she possesses something he does not." The queen turned back to him. "A selfless heart."

" 'Tis what I love most about her."

"Such a good man you are. My grandson could ask for no better father."

She added an approving smile, and Kieran stared at her, unable to believe what he'd heard. Glancing about, he assured himself no one stood nearby.

"I'm to have a son?" When she nodded, he asked, "How many more will there be?"

"Always with you, more questions." She gripped one of his hands between her small ones with astonishing force. "For now there is one. I beg of you, Kieran, do not fail him."

Before he could ask what she meant, she was gone.

"Lord Ryan?"

Donovan looked up as a steward paused in the doorway of his study. "Aye?"

The lanky man swallowed visibly. "The Lord Deputy is here to see you."

"Is he, now? Well, show him in."

Donovan stood and smoothed his fine silk doublet over the waist of his trews. As he came around his desk, John Tiptoft, Earl of Worcester, strode through the door with two impeccably uniformed officers in tow.

Donovan greeted him with a dignified nod. " 'Tis an honor to have you here, Lord Deputy. Welcome to Ferndon."

"Thank you, Ryan." With a wave of his hand, the man known as the Butcher dismissed his guards and took a seat by the fire.

"May I offer you anything?"

"Thank you, no. I'm pressed for time as it is."

Donovan sat opposite his guest. "What help may I be to you?"

"I want the man you Irish call the Fearless One."

"Kieran MacAuley?"

"Yes, I believe that's his name," Tiptoft replied with a shrug.

The casual gesture did little to mask his intensity. The man knew precisely whom he sought. And it was clear he was out for blood.

No doubt, his revenge would be excruciating.

"What is it you require of me?"

"The king concurs with your assessment that MacAuley must be dealt with. My spies tell me he's not led any divisions yet this year."

"It seems he's retired."

"If only that were true." Tiptoft sighed deeply. "He continues to stir the chieftains with rhetoric, somehow convincing them to maintain their united front against the king. This simply cannot continue."

" 'Tis a problem, to be sure."

"Your experience with the clans will be quite valuable in designing a strategy for capturing and executing MacAuley. In return for your assistance, Edward pledges his ongoing support of you as High King."

Donovan stared out at the nearby hills of Tara as he considered the proposal. With Kieran gone, Edward's support might finally come to something. While the chieftains squabbled among themselves for bits of land, he would be in a position to command the entire Isle.

At last, the devastating wars would end, and Ireland would prosper once again.

Pleased with the prospect, he turned to face his visitor. "You may tell Edward that I shall turn my thoughts to this problem and devise a way to accomplish his end. I assume I'm free to enlist the aid of Major Hawlings and his men?"

"Yes, yes, of course," Tiptoft agreed as he stood. "I'll alert him of your intentions before I return to Dublin."

Donovan bowed respectfully. "Godspeed to you, Lord Deputy."

Grumbling a response, the man strode past him and gathered his guards with a commanding bark. As Donovan watched them go, a plan began forming in his mind.

"Forgive me, Brynna," he whispered into the silence. "Ireland is all I have left."

"Braeden."

Brynna looked up from her stitching to find Kieran watching her expectantly from his seat near the hearth in the great hall.

"What do ye think of Braeden?" he asked.

She could recall no one in the valley by that name. Then again, these days her memory was quite unreliable. "Have I met him?"

He looked puzzled, then laughed. "Not yet. I thought it might be a fine name for our son, a blend of your name and mine."

" 'Tis a good, strong name. I like it very much."

"What is it you're working on?" He eyed the snowy yarn she was knitting as if he expected it to disintegrate before his eyes.

"A coverlet for Maureen and Daniel. During her

last visit, she was bemoaning his house's lack of finery."

"She'll be as good for him as he will for her. She needs a solid man to manage her, and 'tis time Daniel ceased living like a wealthy hermit." Leaning toward her, her husband gave her a taunting grin. "No doubt you enjoyed seeing them wed."

"Kieran MacAuley, would you be trying to stir up trouble?"

"Never. I merely thought you'd be pleased that your rival is properly married off."

" 'Tis good to see them both happy." When he cocked his brow, Brynna allowed a slight smile of her own. "Beyond that, I have no rivals."

He didn't reply but studied her intently, his gaze heating with each flutter of her heart. Leaving his chair, he joined her on the small padded bench. He lifted her palm to his lips as his eyes remain locked with hers. His tenderness slowly consumed her as his mouth wandered up her wrist.

A chill skittered over her, and she tried in vain to quell a shiver. A frown chased his grin away, and he closed her hand protectively in his. "What is it?"

The visions flashing through her mind were too horrible to recount, even if she could somehow choke out the words.

"Tell me, Brynna. What did you see?"

One of the heavy main doors banged open on an icy gust of wind. Wild-eyed and drenched with rain, a young shepherd boy raced into the hall as if a banshee were chasing after him.

Recognizing Conor's son, Blaine, Kieran caught him about the shoulders to steady him. "What is it?"

"English, dozens of 'em," Blaine gasped between sobs. "They killed Da."

His voice broke, and Kieran pulled him close, knowing he offered pitifully little comfort. When the boy had settled a bit, Kieran held him away and forced a proud smile. "And ye slipped past them, did ye?"

"I was in the foothills herding sheep when they came. I hid behind a big rock 'til they left. They were bound for Daniel's farm."

Maureen was there as well—a beautiful, irresistible temptation. Kieran glanced about and found Dev where he always stood, solidly beside him. "Gather as many men as ye can find."

"Aye."

As Dev hurried off, Kieran turned his attention to Blaine. "Come with me, lad. Grania will find ye something to eat."

"I should go to the chapel." He swallowed hard. "To say a prayer for my father."

"I'll take ye there."

He reversed direction and began walking, but Blaine stopped him with a tug on his hand.

"You're going with Dev and the others?"

"Of course."

This time he couldn't stay behind. The English had invaded his territory, taking aim at those he'd sworn to protect. That he couldn't allow.

Brynna paced before the outer doors, awaiting Kieran's return. Jumbled and confused, her vision made no sense. All she knew was that she felt an urgent need to warn Kieran, but of what?

While she pondered that, he hurried through the doors. When he pulled her into his arms for a ferocious kiss, she knew. He was going with them.

His hand on her back, he walked her through the growing chaos toward the far stairs.

"How is Blaine?" she asked.

He motioned her into their bedchamber ahead of him. "Well enough."

The moment he'd touched her, she'd felt the rage simmering within him. Isolated from the keep and one another, the families farming the lush valley were easy prey. So easy, in fact, that it amazed her they'd not been attacked before.

"You know this isn't right," she began.

Kieran tested the edge of his *scian* with his thumb before sheathing it at his waist. "What do ye mean?"

"Have the English ever come here before?"

"They've not dared to." From the mantel he took Morgan's infamous sword. Drawing it from its scabbard, he smiled, as if seeing an old friend. "After this day, they'll never dare again."

She grasped his shoulders and forced him to stop moving long enough to look at her. "Have you considered this might be a way to lure you into the open?"

"And if it is? I'm far better able to defend myself than Maureen and Daniel or Conor, God rest him. 'Tis my responsibility to keep these people safe, Brynna. I'll not shirk it."

There was no time to convince him otherwise. As he buckled on his sword, she cautioned, "Listen to your instincts. If they tell you to duck, then duck."

"Always." He framed her face in his hands and kissed her soundly. "I love you."

"Then come back to us."

Resting his palm over the child nestled in her womb, he gave her a confident grin and kissed her forehead. "I will."

He hastened down the steps to join his men, and she followed him. She gripped the railing so hard, her knuckles went white. Grim-faced and furious, the hastily assembled force listened to every word their chieftain uttered. With a collective battle cry, they burst from the hall.

Holding back for a quick word with Devlin, Kieran was the last through the wide doors. When he looked toward her, Brynna swallowed her terror and forced a smile to her lips. Kissing her fingers, she held them to her heart. He returned the gesture, and then he was gone.

"They're running." Carrick motioned after the retreating soldiers with the bloody tip of his sword. "They'll think twice before coming back across those hills."

Dev wished he shared his cousin's confidence. They'd gotten to Daniel's farm just ahead of the English, and even now Maureen was tending the most serious wounds. But six other farms lay in ruins, smoke blotting out the pale sunshine. Many had died this day, farmers and members of their families. More to bury, more to mourn.

The men who'd rushed to the farmers' aid were banged up a bit, suffering cuts and bruises mostly, though there might be a broken bone or two in the mix. Still, his instincts told him something was wrong.

He surveyed the gathering men with alarm. "Where's Kieran?"

"At the flank," Carrick replied, frowning as he pointed to the empty position.

The two of them ran toward the spot where they'd last seen him. The handful of men arrayed with him had returned, but there was no sign of Kieran anywhere.

With his next step, Dev kicked something in the matted grass. He bent down to retrieve Morgan's sword from where it had fallen.

Clenching it in his fist, he swore in violent, heartfelt Gaelic, then filled his lungs with air.

"Keeerrran!"

Behind the biting gag, Kieran smiled at the sound of Dev's bellow. He was quickly rewarded with a backhanded slap that sent him sprawling across the bed of the road cart.

"I'd love to beat you senseless, Irish," his attacker hissed. "But my orders are to bring you in for a proper execution. The Butcher wants you in possession of all your senses when he separates you from your head."

Kieran knew which road they were on. Anyone with a drop of Irish blood in his veins knew the way to Tara. Even if he'd never been there, he could find it simply by delving into his memories and following the eastward wind.

The returning force entered the imposing gates of Ferndon Castle, and the cart pulled up before the heavily guarded keep. His father-in-law wasn't there to greet him. In fact, there wasn't an Irish face to be seen, only stiff-necked English soldiers and their officers. Still mounted and wearing a sour expression, Hawlings waited at the edge of the inner bailey. Kieran nodded to him, and the major's mouth curved in reply.

"Enough," the impatient one snarled, using the thong binding Kieran's hands to jerk him forward. "Into your pen, swine."

He and two others pushed and pulled Kieran by turns, shoving him down the last several steps to the dank dungeon level. The leather about his wrists was replaced with iron, and they shoved him into a cell before clapping a steel collar about his throat to shackle him to the wall.

Metal clanked as Kieran folded his arms and watched to see what they would do next.

He didn't have to wait long.

"They'll ransom him," Cavan said as Brynna held her breath to listen from the head of the stairs.

"Or they'll kill him," Devlin countered. "If it's the Butcher that's got him, God only knows what else they'll do."

"What are they saying?" Aileen whispered as she settled on the step beside Brynna.

She held a finger to her lips but grasped her mother-in-law's hand for a comforting squeeze. While they listened, the men postured and argued, offering one theory and another, clearly convinced Kieran was being held at the garrison in Westmeath.

But she knew otherwise.

Standing, she motioned for Aileen to follow her. In their bedchamber, she reached into Kieran's trunk for two small but deadly daggers. "The English don't have him."

Without so much as a blink, Aileen nodded. "Then who?"

"My father. He's at Ferndon."

"Sweet Mary. That place is better guarded than the Tower of London. We can't possibly get him out of there."

"We're not meant to." She went to the wardrobe and retrieved her heavy cloak. "But I'm going after him anyway."

"Not alone, you're not," Devlin growled from the doorway.

"Should anyone accompany me, my father will become suspicious. If I go alone, he'll allow me inside, and I can see Kieran."

"What's left of him, that is. How do you know he's not dead already?"

Kieran's heart beat within her, slow but strong. Trapped somewhere cold and without light, he was waiting to die. Alone.

"I know it. 'Tis enough."

Devlin considered her thoughtfully, then gave a single nod. "I'd wager you'll be needing a strong back to help bring him home."

"We haven't time to waste with this." She tried to push past him, but he caught her shoulders and gripped them hard.

"My cousin he is, and my friend, and I swore to protect ye if he could not. You'll take me along or ye won't go."

She found no support in Aileen's wise eyes, and she let out a frustrated sigh. "Very well, but on this raid, I'm in command. Storming in there will only get us both killed, so you must trust my judgment."

With a crooked grin, he bowed and offered her his arm. "Lead on, milady."

Kieran jerked awake as freezing water drenched him from head to foot. Every last bit of him ached from the beating he'd taken, and all he wanted was to slip back into his painless sleep. He heard a wooden bucket thud on the floor just before another wave of ice assailed him.

"Get up," a clipped English voice ordered from beyond the bars.

"Go to hell."

He was rewarded with a bout of derisive laughter. "Defiant to the last."

Kieran opened his eyes just enough to see the immaculate uniform of his tormenter. Though he'd never met the man, he knew 'twas none other than the Butcher taunting him.

"You should know you've been sentenced to die in the morning."

Kieran willed his parched lips into a grin. "Have I, now? I recall no trial."

"Your actions against the Crown speak for themselves. I shall gladly hear any pleas for mercy, however."

"Mercy from you?" From the back of his throat, he dredged up enough moisture to spit.

"As you wish." The Englishman moved away from his cell, then turned back. "If you're truly blessed, as the fables claim, one blow will be sufficient to remove your traitorous head."

Once the echoes of footsteps had faded, Kieran gave in to the shivering he'd quelled so he'd not give his enemy the pleasure of seeing his weakness. Thoughts of strength led him to Brynna, and he closed his eyes to conjure a vision of her to dull his pain.

He saw her at the top of the stairs, a hand over her heart as she sent him off with a smile she must have forced onto her lips. At that moment he'd hesitated, knowing he could be walking into a trap. But as always, he'd gone to defend those who needed his aid.

Baffled by the randomness of the English attack, he'd not sensed the soldiers behind him 'til they'd grabbed him and jammed a gag into his mouth. Never had his instincts failed him so completely.

Thank God for Brynna. She would see Braeden through to manhood while the bards filled his ears with tales of the father he'd never know, a warrior who gave his life for Ireland.

Please, he begged his unborn son, *be proud of me.*

"Kieran."

Brynna's sweet brogue drifted into his mind, caressed his name with a loving whisper. The warmth of the vision drove the chill from his aching bones, and he clasped her to his chest as she gave him a kiss that tasted of tears. Her features were obscured by the murky light, but in his mind's eye she was the most beautiful sight he could hope to see.

"Ye shouldn't be here."

The vision seemed to solidify, smiling at him. "Where else would I be? My place is with you."

Was this some trick his tortured mind was playing on him? How could Brynna be here? he wondered.

"Ronan came to visit me," she continued, smoothing the hair back from his brow. "He's given his word that he will free you if you agree to help him."

"What is it he wants this time?"

"The same." She grimaced, as if the thought of her father's death at her husband's hands pained her. Yet when she drew a dirk from beneath her cloak, she met his gaze squarely. "If you do it, Ronan will arrange your escape from here."

" 'Tis murder."

" 'Tis the price of your freedom," she corrected him, echoing the words she'd said to him in the woods beside her little hut.

Astounded, Kieran stared at her but saw no hesitation in her eyes. "Do ye know what you're saying?"

"I thought of nothing else the whole way here. For nearly three years, I ran from him. Then I found you and this wondrous new life. I cannot think of living it without you."

"But your father—"

"Cares only for himself, not the good he might do as king." She grasped his hand between both of hers, her eyes imploring him to listen. "You bind the chieftains together, make them strong. You've accomplished a great deal, but there is much left to do. I beg of you, accept Ronan's offer. Finish your last task and come home to us."

She guided his palm to her waist, and his honor wavered before emotion. Braeden deserved a flesh-and-blood father, Brynna a husband to cherish her.

But what of the cost?

While he'd lain in a broken heap, he'd come to accept his fate. Now, hope shimmered within him, enticing him with the choice Brynna had already made. As Kieran fingered the edge of the blade, he knew one slash would be enough to end Ryan's despicable life.

Brynna would be safe. Her father would no longer be a threat and, with him gone, Ronan's fury would turn elsewhere. At the back of his mind, he felt a tap, as if reason were trying to break through the fog clouding his thoughts.

Brynna bent to kiss him. "Rest now, Kieran. I won't be far."

When he closed his eyes, he saw the two of them walking near Lough Dunsmere. A sturdy lad toddled ahead of them while a pup romped about in the tall grass. Brynna laid a hand over her plump stomach, leaned her head against Kieran's chest with a contented sigh.

In his next heartbeat, the scene changed. Brynna and Braeden stood before his grave, somber in their dark clothes. The lad looked up at her, and she ruffled his hair with a sad smile. Even the pup was subdued, sitting quietly as it cocked its head and stared at the marker.

As the second vision faded from his mind, the other took its place, tormenting him with the promise of a long, happy lifetime with his family.

But to gain it, he must surrender his soul.

CHAPTER FIFTEEN

The evening had turned damp, and the fire did little to dispel the chill in Donovan's private study. He stared into the flames while he pondered the events of the day. As promised, he'd captured Kieran MacAuley. Soon, Ireland would know peace.

The price? Regrettable, but uncompromising men died uncompromising deaths. 'Twas the way of heroes and fools.

A commotion in the entryway drew him from his thoughts, and he glanced over his shoulder. Two guards were crossing the polished floor, a huge man held roughly between them. Before them strode a vision out of his dreams, and he stumbled to his feet, hardly daring to believe his eyes.

"Brynna?"

"Aye, Father, 'tis me."

The young woman who stepped into his study possessed a confidence the girl he remembered had not. When she pushed the gray traveling cloak back over her shoulders, his heart sank as he noted another difference. "You're with child."

"Kieran's child. We've come to plead for his life."

His eyes went to the giant, who looked as if he'd gladly rip Donovan's head from his body. "And this is . . . ?"

"My protector. I expect you to ensure his safety."

The man opened his mouth but snapped it shut when she glared at him. She had her mother's spirit, Donovan mused with a slight smile. "Your name, sir?"

"His name matters not," Brynna assured him.

"It matters to me. I wish to know whom you've brought into our home."

"*Your* home," she corrected in a quiet voice. "Mine is with Kieran."

Her words pierced his heart as surely as any blade, and he turned his attention to the man in question. "Your name."

"Devlin MacAuley."

"The chieftain's man at arms. You honor me." He addressed the guards in his sternest tone. "Accompany him to the library and see that he's made comfortable. Then lock the door and post yourselves outside."

The two exchanged puzzled looks, but one of them nodded. "As you wish, Lord Ryan."

"Brynna—"

"Go with them, Devlin. I'll be safe."

Hands still bound, he shook off the guards as if they were stripling lads and turned a menacing look on Donovan. "I swear, if anything happens to her, I'll hunt you down and carve out your black heart while it's still beating."

Donovan acknowledged the gruesome pledge with a raised brow and a nod. As Devlin was led away, a string of inventive Gaelic curses trailed behind him.

"Interesting choice for a second in command," Donovan commented as he took the poker from its stand and stirred the coals in the grate.

"Devlin is a fine man. His loyalty is beyond question."

And yours is not.

Though she didn't say the words, he understood them all the same. Approaching the hearth, she stopped an arm's length away and gazed up at him with the curious expression she'd so often worn as a little girl.

"You look well," he stalled, wanting to keep her eyes on him. Even lovelier than Maire's, they glowed like emeralds in the firelight.

She gave him a ghost of her beautiful smile and reached a hand to his cheek. "And you look tired. What troubles you?"

He drew her into his arms, held her close to assure himself she was truly there and not just another wishful imagining. After a moment she embraced him, and he nearly sobbed with joy.

"I thought I'd never see you again. I searched everywhere, sent men all over Ireland looking for you."

"I know."

He held her away and looked down at her.

"You've groomed your intuition, then. Is that how you found MacAuley within my walls?"

"Father, if you hand him over to the English, they'll kill him."

"I have given my word to Edward." He lifted his hands in a gesture of defeat. "I cannot go back on it now."

"Then let me see him."

Anything would he give to grant her wish, but he shook his head with a frown. "I cannot allow that either. He's an English prisoner, as surely as if he were in London."

"Foolish me." Retreating several steps, she gave an infuriating toss of her head. "I thought Ferndon belonged to the Ryans."

Kieran opened his eyes to find Brynna at the door of his cell. He didn't recall her leaving, but apparently she had, and now she'd returned. Once the door opened, she rushed through it and fell to her knees at his side.

She fingered the collar about his neck, curled her hand into a fist. "He's freezing and beaten half to death. How could you allow them to do this?"

Her words confused him, and he was bewildered to see Donovan Ryan standing in the corridor. What the devil was going on?

"They were not to harm him," Ryan said in a strained voice.

"Harm me?" Kieran choked out a laugh. "They mean to kill me."

Brynna removed her cloak and settled it over him, tucking it about him as if he lay in their bed and not sprawled across the stone floor of a dungeon. Her smile dispelled some of the darkness as she smoothed a hand across his brow.

"Father, get me some water."

When Ryan made no move to comply, she looked over her shoulder and repeated her command. Her touch began to soothe some of Kieran's pain, and it struck him that before he'd felt only her fingers, not their magick. Had he imagined her visit? When he felt the hilt of the dagger she'd brought earlier digging into his back, his addled mind grew even more confused. Something was wrong.

The chains about his wrist rattled as he stilled her hand. " 'Tis too dangerous for you."

"Trust me."

Somehow, he managed a smile. "How could I not when you've stayed with me this way?"

Again she frowned. "Kieran, I've only just gotten here. You must have been dreaming."

Ronan. Was he behind the earlier vision of Brynna?

Before Kieran could summon the breath for a proper curse, Ryan returned with one of the buckets that had soaked him earlier. This time Kieran was allowed to take water from the dipper, a blissful swallow at a time.

Brynna cupped some in her hands, warming it before bathing his face. Every touch bolstered him, and he felt the strength seeping back into his body. His limbs protesting, he lifted himself up on his elbow and ladled some water from the bucket for her.

She drank it and rewarded him with a brilliant smile. "Thank you."

Exhausted by the effort, Kieran rolled into her skirts with a groan. He wanted nothing more than to wrap his arms about her, but the irons prevented it. He whispered a few words to Braeden, ending with the kiss he'd envisioned placing on the lad's head at his birth.

And then, mercifully, the darkness reclaimed him.

Donovan watched Brynna pull her cloak more tightly around Kieran. Tears slipped unheeded down her cheeks, and he followed her gaze to the battered face pillowed in her lap.

He'd done this, as surely as if he'd led the forces that had taken the young chieftain.

He had destroyed the hope of Ireland.

Coming to the dungeons had been a grave mistake. Plotting strategy was one thing, witnessing its results quite another. The uncertainty that had been gnawing at him became more insistent as he watched his daughter lavish care on the man she loved.

She brushed the hair back from his face, began tracing each gash with a delicate finger. Even in the dim light, Donovan saw the flesh begin its mending. She did the same with his shoulders, reaching beneath his torn tunic to his chest. As Kieran's eyes opened again, she rested her head back against the wall with a weary sigh. Healing such serious wounds drained her own strength, and he marveled at her selflessness.

"You traded Kieran for Tara." Her accusation

settled hard, as if a heavy yoke had fallen onto his shoulders. "Your greed has cost hundreds of people their lives, and now this."

"Fighting the English is what killed them. If they'd bargained with Edward as I have, they'd still be alive."

"And under his boot."

"You sound like your husband," he scoffed. "Hardheaded and unyielding. See where it's brought him."

"Your treachery brought him here."

"I merely informed Major Hawlings where to strike for the best effect."

"How could you do such a thing?" Brynna demanded, her voice a mixture of anger and despair.

" 'Twas the only way."

Kieran made a derisive noise. "Ryan, your lack of vision disgusts me."

"I've put myself in a position to watch over Ireland. All you've managed to do is put your neck on the block."

"At least I've not destroyed innocent lives just to further my own ambition."

"Stop it, both of you," Brynna ordered in a hushed voice. "Do you want to bring the guards in here?"

Kieran let out a sigh. "She's right. We must work together."

Donovan snorted. "To what purpose?"

"Getting Brynna and me out of here without getting you killed."

"Devlin, as well," she added. "He insisted on coming with me."

"I must remember to thank him." Kieran smiled at her, then sent a querying look across the cramped cell. "What say you?"

"I'll not risk my head for yours. Why should I?"

"You need only give Brynna and Devlin safe passage to Dunsmere," a silken voice informed him. "I shall do the rest."

Maire stepped from the shadows, and they all turned toward her.

"Mother, what are you doing here?"

"Restoring the balance Ronan has upset with his scheming."

"What are you talking about?" Donovan demanded. "Ronan has nothing to do with this situation."

She regarded him with a sad expression. "Ronan has everything to do with it. Do you not know that he wants you dead for daring to love me? Ronan planned to use Kieran to kill you."

"Then he failed. MacAuley is the one to be executed, not I, and in his current condition he's of little threat to me."

"Mortal conditions can change quite rapidly," she retorted.

Maire knelt beside Kieran, rested her palm on his chest. Bowing her head, she whispered words so ancient only the *sídhe* still knew them. When she withdrew her hand, the shackles fell away, and very slowly, he sat up.

"Ronan blunted your instincts so you could be captured and brought here. He appeared to you as Brynna, hoping to sway you. He planned to free you this eve to kill Donovan," she said in a sorrowful voice. "But with so many English about, I feared you'd not escape with your life."

"How did you learn of this?" Brynna asked.

"While I was gone, he boasted to the court of his brilliance in manipulating the fates. My sisters were greatly insulted and granted me their blessings to straighten this twisted thread."

"But you told me you'd not interfere in Kieran's life again," Brynna said.

"Ronan's scheming has left me no choice but to break my word." Frowning, she turned to Donovan. "He will not be satisfied until you are dead. If you should die before one of his champions can kill you, he will attend your final breath so his laughter follows you into the next world."

" 'Twill be a long wait, even for him."

To his astonishment, she smiled. "I hope so."

Apparently, even a *sidhe* king hadn't the power to strip all her love away. Returning the smile, Ryan gave his attention to the problem at hand. "This changes everything. Have you a plan, MacAuley?"

The chieftain looked at Maire with a broad grin. "I do now."

"He'll be *what?*"

Devlin jumped from the striped chair, hands fisted as if to fight the idea she'd proposed.

"Please calm yourself." Brynna glanced over her shoulder when her father's guards appeared in the open doorway. "He's overwrought, nothing more. I can manage him."

"Are you certain, Lady Brynna?" one of them asked, a hand on the hilt of his sword.

"Most certain. Thank you for your concern."

They regarded her with dubious looks but retreated to their post outside the library. She turned back to Devlin, feeling guilty for distressing him. In the dungeons, they'd debated whether or not to divulge their plan to him, but she feared if he weren't included, he'd not agree to leave the castle with her.

" 'Tis not permanent," she assured him.

Clearly bewildered, he dropped back into his seat. "Pray tell me how death can be anything but permanent."

"Spells can be broken as well as cast." She sat on the arm of his chair, a comforting hand on his shoulder. "This spell won't harm him, merely put him to rest for a while."

His eyes narrowed. "How long is 'a while'? And how can ye be certain Maire will break the spell when he's safe?"

She bristled at his suspicious tone. "She's my mother."

"Aye, and Donovan Ryan is your father. Forgive me for not trusting in your parents."

He glared at her, and she glared back. "Kieran warned me you'd be obstinate about this."

"Then I'd say he was right." After a moment, his features softened a bit. "What do ye mean?"

"I felt 'twas only fair to tell you what would happen. He told me I'd be wasting my breath."

Devlin leaned back in the chair and considered her with a smile. "He knows me well, but I'm grateful to ye for arguing on my behalf."

"We must get him outside the walls if he's to have any chance at all of escaping."

"That I know, and it's a good plan." A shudder rattled his massive shoulders. "Aside from the dying part, that is. What's to keep the Butcher from beheading him for sport?"

"Didn't you know? A bad storm is brewing."

Folding his arms, he returned her smile with a mischievous one of his own. "Is it, now? Would Maire have something to do with that?"

"Aye. It's to last 'til the morn."

"And we'll disappear in the midst of it."

She snapped her fingers, and he laughed before taking her hand for a kiss. "Brynna, you've the cunning of a woman and the courage of a man. My cousin is truly blessed with you."

"Do you agree to your part in this, then?"

He looked out at the gathering clouds and sighed before turning misery-laden eyes on her. "If 'twill save Kieran, I'll do it."

"What do you mean, dead?"

Tiptoft shoved his own men aside and lunged at the prone figure on the floor. He shook Kieran several times, then kicked him onto his back. The only color in the prisoner's ashen face came from the dried blood and bruises Maire had restored. Donovan knew from his own inspection that not a single heartbeat could be felt, and the chieftain's limbs were as unyielding as the dormant spirit that still pulsed within his apparently lifeless body.

The earl brushed water from the sleeve of his immaculate uniform, scowled at the rivulets streaming down the wall. "It seems you have a leak, Ryan."

Donovan gave a careless shrug. "My prisoners have never complained."

"Damn and blast it," Tiptoft grumbled as he got to his feet. Hands at his waist, he kicked Kieran once more. "After all the trouble he's caused me, I did so want to watch him die."

"If you'd like, I could offer you a cart to take him back to Westmeath."

The Englishman's lips rose ever so slightly. "I would like that very much. Perhaps an example can still be made of him."

"If there is a way to accomplish that, you're the man to find it."

"Indeed, I am," the earl agreed with a mirthless laugh. "I shall gather my men and my things and be ready to leave within the hour. I've already dispatched a messenger with my latest report to the king. Your cooperation and hospitality have been duly noted."

Donovan bowed. "You are too kind."

He watched the soldiers fall into step behind their lord, then bellowed for his own guards. "Fetch a cart from the livery and put MacAuley in it for his journey to Westmeath."

The two exchanged puzzled looks, and the bolder one spoke up. "With respect, milord, the prisoner is dead."

"Load him in a cart and tie it to the back of the lord deputy's carriage," Donovan instructed in a tone that brooked no argument. "And find something to cover him. We don't want to be upsetting anyone."

"As you wish, Lord Ryan."

Once the guards had scurried off on their errand, Donovan glanced about to be certain no one was watching him. Then he leaned down and rested a hand on Kieran's shoulder. "Godspeed to you, Fearless One. *Erin go bragh.*"

As if from the stones themselves, Kieran's voice echoed the last three words back to him, and Donovan left the cell with a smile.

"Follow the eastern boundary of Tara to the edge of the forest," Donovan instructed Brynna while Devlin checked Boru's saddle. "Their usual route has been blocked by a treefall that should take them a while to clear."

Devlin nodded, turning to pat the forehead of the packhorse behind him. "I'll return the horse to you when it's safe."

Her father's face broke into a rare smile. "Keep him. Ferndon will not be safe for the MacAuley anytime soon."

"We're indebted to ye, sir."

He thrust a huge hand at Donovan, who regarded it for a moment before accepting the gesture. When he turned to her, Brynna saw something in his eyes she'd never seen before: tears. Though he said nothing, he drew her into a fierce embrace.

He pulled away slowly, as though it pained him to release her. "Take care, dear one."

"You've a story for the earl and his king?"

Uncharacteristic mischief lit his gray eyes. "I thought to tell them the faeries took him."

At her chiding look, he laughed and kissed her

cheek. "Off with you, now. Tiptoft will be on his way shortly."

Devlin mounted, and Donovan handed her up to him. Standing there in the rain, he suddenly looked ancient.

Once she was settled, she reached out a hand to him. "Thank you, Father. I'll not forget this."

"Nor will I."

With a sad smile, he kissed her hand, holding her palm to his wet cheek for a moment. Then he turned and walked up the steps into the hall.

Devlin shifted in the saddle behind her. "Shall we go, then?"

Still puzzled by her father's behavior, Brynna nodded her head, and the horses moved off at a brisk trot.

They followed the path Donovan had suggested and began searching for a place to hide. Fortune presented them with a small cave, and Devlin guided the horses inside.

"Your mother couldn't just take him out of the bleeding dungeon?" he groused as he dismounted and helped her down.

"If he disappeared from Ferndon, the English would start hunting for him—right after they executed my father for abetting an enemy of the king. If the earl loses him on the way to Westmeath, the blame will fall on him."

"Kieran's nigh a legend already. This should seal it."

"Hush, now. They're coming."

Devlin cocked his head like an attentive

wolfhound. "I don't hear—wait, there it is. Two horses in harness and four more under saddle, I'd wager."

From the packhorse he took a set of clothing stuffed with rags and rocks, then a woolen throw identical to the one that covered Kieran's body. "Your father's a crafty one, to be sure."

"His greatest talent."

" 'Tis time he used it to benefit his own." Grimacing, he shook his head. "Forgive me, Brynna. That was a heartless thing to say."

"But true enough."

He hefted the decoy onto his shoulder and turned to go. She stopped him with a hand on his arm.

"He looks dead, Devlin, but he's not. I swear it."

With a curt nod he strode from the cave.

In truth, Kieran looked worse than dead, his face covered with the evidence of countless English blows.

Dev's breath caught in his chest, and he glanced at the soldiers clearing the trees from the road to be certain he'd not been heard. The Butcher kept up a stream of caterwauling, cursing his men for the delay even while they strained to move the limbs made heavier by the steadily falling rain.

Watching them cautiously, he lifted his cousin from the cart and settled him over a shoulder. Then he put in the replacement he'd brought with him, covering it with the throw as Ryan's men had done.

When he reached the cover of heavy pine boughs, he braced his hand on a knobby trunk and took a moment to cool the fire in his blood. Battle rush, no doubt brought on by the sight of English soldiers. Once he felt calmer, he shifted his burden and continued toward the small cave.

He carefully laid Kieran on the hard-packed dirt and crossed himself. "Summon your mother, lass. Seeing him this way is giving me the chills."

Brynna's frown did little to ease his disquiet. "She'll come when she deems it safe."

"Do ye mean to tell me we're taking him back to Dunsmere as he is?" She nodded, and he muttered a curse beneath his breath. "I fear Aileen's heart canna stand it."

"That, or we can wait here."

She seemed perfectly content to do just that. But she was soaked to the skin, and he couldn't allow her to stay out in the cold awaiting the unpredictable pleasure of a faery.

"We'll go now, get ye back to where it's safe and warm."

Suppressing a shudder, he lifted Kieran onto the packhorse and covered him with the throw before tying him securely in place. Then he helped Brynna into the saddle and swung up behind her.

As they left the relative safety of the cave, he made certain no one followed them. Satisfied, he faced forward and resigned himself to the plodding gait of laden horses.

Brynna looked over her shoulder at him. "You're a fine man, Devlin MacAuley. Kieran chose his second well."

He smiled his thanks, pleased when she cuddled

against him the way she'd done with Kieran when they rescued her. He found himself envying the future his cousin would share with her.

"One must risk a great deal to know such bliss."

Sword already in hand, Devlin spun toward the unexpected sound. He barely swallowed a curse as Maire emerged from an overgrown thicket.

"Ye shouldn't sneak about that way," he snarled as he resheathed his blade.

With a smile, she approached Boru and stroked the stallion's wide forehead. "The *sídhe* have learned to move quietly through your world." She added a few unintelligible words to the gray, who tossed his head in agreement.

"I thought you'd meet us in Dunsmere," Brynna told her.

"And torment his mother with this sight?" She motioned to the burden atop the second horse. "Never. Fetch him down, if you would."

Dev gladly did as she asked, crouching beside Brynna as she settled Kieran's head in her lap. Maire knelt beside them and placed her hand on Kieran's chest while she chanted some archaic folk song. When she was finished, she sat back on her heels with an expectant look.

Nothing.

"What the devil is going on?"

"Give him a moment."

The queen's calm tone did little to soothe Devlin's nerves, and he glared at her. "What have ye done?"

"Devlin, please. Mother saved his life."

"By taking it from him?" Vexed by his helplessness, he jumped up and began pacing. "I could have gotten him out, but nay—ye wanted to talk to your father, convince him to help us. I should have taken a battalion to Ferndon and stormed the damned castle."

"The English would have killed him before you ever got through the gates," Brynna countered.

"It scarcely matters. Or have ye not noticed he's dead?"

"Am I?"

The sound of Kieran's weary voice ended their battle. While Brynna covered his face with kisses, Dev tried gamely to retrieve his jaw from atop his boots. Seeing a dead man sit up was the closest to a miracle he'd ever witnessed.

Kieran turned to the Queen of Meath and took her hand for a kiss. "Many thanks, Your Majesty. I pray you'll not have trouble with Ronan over this."

"He should be praying not to have trouble with me." She laid a hand on his shoulder and kissed his cheek. "The fates are with you, Kieran MacAuley, and I shall be watching. Be happy, my darling one," she added as she embraced Brynna.

"I am, Mother. Thank you."

When Maire's eyes swung to him, Dev forced himself to meet her unsettling gaze. "Remember, Devlin—sometimes to win a battle, you must be willing to surrender."

With a motherly smile for him, she swept a hand through the air and vanished.

Familiar with the *sidhe*'s unusual mode of travel, Kieran assumed Maire had disappeared from the small clearing. In truth, 'twas they who had vanished, horses and all, to reappear outside the walls of MacAuley Keep. Clever she was to drop them someplace no one would see them, yet he wondered why she'd not left them to make the short trip on their own.

When he tried to stand, he understood. Like a newborn colt's, his legs sagged beneath him, and he fell against Brynna. The gate stood only a few steps away, but it might as well have been leagues.

"I'll carry you." Dev bent to lift him.

"Nay, I'll walk."

"Stubborn," Brynna muttered. "I should have asked Mother to put you straight into bed."

Dev chuckled. "Difficult to explain his returning that way."

Despite his predicament, Kieran saw the humor in the situation and gave a weak laugh. "I only hope they haven't buried me again."

"Sweet Mary." He looked up to the wall walk to find Carrick hanging over the battlement like a lad ogling a brawl. Over his shoulder he called, "Samuel, go and fetch Aileen. I'll let them in."

The metallic grind of the portcullis invigorated Kieran's sluggish limbs. With Brynna on one side and Dev on the other, he walked through the gate and into the bailey. His mother flew down the steps and into his arms. Thank God Dev was bracing him, or he'd have dropped her in the mud.

"Word of your capture has spread like the plague." She touched his bruised face as if she mistrusted her eyes. "What happened?"

"Ronan."

Lips pressed tightly together, she took a deep breath. She'd not dare condemn the *sídhe* king aloud, but her thoughts blazed in her eyes. "Come inside, then. You're all half-drowned."

Kieran dragged himself up the steps and into the hall. The fire roared in welcome, tempting him with a warm seat at the hearth. But he feared if he sat down, he'd not stand again 'til morning. Loathe to worry his mother any further, he simply headed for the winding staircase.

"I'll send up some bathwater for you," she called after him.

He meant to thank her but lost his footing and nearly pitched onto his face. Trusting she'd overlook his lack of manners, he focused his waning strength on getting up those last few steps and into his rooms.

Dev and Brynna guided him to the bed, and he gladly collapsed onto the downy mattress.

Hands on his hips, Dev chuckled. "Will ye be needing my help getting up for your bath?"

"I'll help him," Brynna answered as she sat beside him.

Again, Dev chuckled. "Forgive me for saying so, but your talent seems to be for luring him *into* bed, not getting him out of it."

"Go find yourself a wench and some mead and leave me in peace," Kieran grumbled.

"That'd be an order, then?"

Kieran returned his cousin's grin. "I'm grateful to ye, Dev. I owe ye more than I can ever repay."

"We do, as well." With a hand on her stomach, Brynna added her loveliest smile. "Thank you."

"You're welcome. I pray you'll forgive me not trusting your mother."

"She thought nothing of it, and neither do I."

He grinned back at her. " 'Tis good to know. A pleasant eve to ye both."

Once he'd gone, Kieran closed his eyes and groaned. Though a few nicks and bruises were the only remnants of his injuries, every last bit of him hurt. Brynna's hands slipped beneath his shoulders, and she settled his head on her thighs. While she rubbed some of the ache from his arms, on his cheek he felt a fluttering movement. He thought it merely the rustling of her skirts; then he felt a rounded edge beneath the wool.

Though his muscles complained sharply, he reached a hand to her stomach. The spot came to life once again, a rolling motion followed by what could only be the jab of a tiny elbow or foot.

"Your son is welcoming you home," she said with a smile.

He might have missed it. Fulfilling his duty to his kinsmen, he'd ignored Brynna's warning and nearly left his own family without a husband and father. His promise to provide for her and their children rang loudly in his ears.

"Brynna, I swear—"

She silenced him with a hand over his mouth. "I'd have no choice but to hold you to such a vow. Only promise to love us for as long as you're given."

He removed her hand for a kiss. " 'Tis a promise easily made."

They both turned toward a polite noise in the doorway.

"Water for you, Kieran," Samuel announced as he hauled the buckets inside. "There's more behind me, as well. And this."

The neatly bound packet smelled of flowers and spice, similar to the soothing combinations Aileen mixed for him. But this one was different.

"You made this?" he asked his wife.

"Aye. Lavender, a bit of lemon balm and a few other things 'tis better not to know."

Kieran waited until the lads had closed the door behind them. He'd prefer they not see him struggle to his feet. His fingers refused to work properly, and he needed Brynna's help to undress. When her sleeve brushed his bare arm, he realized she was soaked.

"Ye need to get out of those clothes, Brynna."

"I'll see to you first."

"You'll do it now. I can manage."

When she hesitated, he spun her about and gave her a light shove toward the wardrobe. While she shed her sodden gown, he stepped over the side of the tub and sank into the water with a sigh. Slipping beneath the surface, his body gratefully soaked in the warmth. Then he heard Brynna's anxious voice.

He lifted his head and shook back his wet hair. "Aye?"

"Nothing. I only wanted to be sure you weren't drowning."

Her laughter sounded forced, and he smiled reassurance. "I'm not, but I'd do better if ye were to join me."

Clad in firelight, she was a vision to behold. Her rounded frame still fascinated him, and he allowed a bit of lust into his grin.

She tilted her head with a little smile. "There's not space for the three of us in there."

Always, she included Braeden. Her maternal instincts were so strong now, he could only imagine how she'd care for their son once he was born.

Her protectiveness made him love her all the more.

"I'll make room." He shifted to the back of the tub and offered her a dripping hand.

With a broader smile, she crossed the chamber and took his hand. Mindful of her balance, he guided her into the tub and sat back with her against his chest. She felt like ice against his warmed skin, and he berated himself for not seeing to her sooner.

He combed his fingers through her hair, then wet it with several ladles of water. Lathering his hands with the rose-scented soap she favored, he worked the suds into the mass of curls. He rinsed them, then turned his attention to the rest of her. When his hands glided over the swell of her stomach, she sighed, so he continued doing it. With each stroke, he felt her relax a bit more.

"That feels wonderful," she murmured in a drowsy voice.

"I'll do it as long as ye like. Or 'til the water gets cold."

She laughed, and he nuzzled the curve of her

shoulder. "I love that sound. It always makes me want to laugh with you." He wrapped his arms about her and held her close. "Please forgive me, Brynna."

"You did what you thought best. I understand."

"But you were right. It was a trap, set by Hawlings and your father. Conor and the others died because of me."

Though her girth made it difficult to move, Brynna lifted herself on her hands and turned to face him. He closed his eyes, but she'd seen the guilt deepening them to near black. Framing his face in her hands, she forced him to look at her. "English soldiers killed them."

"To get to me. How many did we lose?" She had no intention of telling him, but he gripped her wrists in his hands. "How many?"

"Eight. If not for Blaine, there would have been more."

"A brave lad, to be sure."

A happier thought entered her mind. "Daniel and Maureen wish to take him in."

Kieran stared at her a moment, then smiled. "Do they, now?"

"Maureen said it was the least they could do. She's always been fond of him." At her husband's blank look, she laughed. "You didn't know?"

"She was Adam's wife. I had no cause to know much about her."

"You never considered wedding her?" He shook his head. "Or Elizabeth?"

"Nay, but Regina . . ." He smiled appreciatively,

laughing when Brynna glared at him. "Not her, either. Ireland needed my full attention, and I had nothing to offer a wife."

"And now?"

Sobering, he lifted her hand and kissed the ring that sparkled there. "I have you and Braeden to care for. Ireland must make do with less of me."

His tender words shattered the last of her composure, and she lost her battle with the tears she'd been fighting. He drew her head to his shoulder, stroking her back while she sobbed. She was vaguely aware of him lifting her from the bath and settling her under the bedcovers.

As he gathered her into his arms, she resisted the fatigue trying to pull her into sleep. "I'm wet."

"You'll dry," he murmured with a kiss. "Rest now, sweet one. I'm here."

Kieran awoke, confused by the darkness that blanketed him. Then he realized he wasn't in a dank, unlit cell but the warmth of his own bed, his arms wrapped around his wife.

She lay with her back to him, cuddled against him the way he loved. He moved a hand to her waist, hoping Braeden could feel his touch. He felt a slight movement, then a sharper one. At the next jab, Brynna shifted position.

"Braeden, stop," she murmured sleepily, reaching to her stomach. When her hand brushed Kieran's, she rolled over to smile at him. "Strong, is he not?"

"Aye."

"Like his father."

He chuckled. "I daresay he could best me at the moment."

"You should get some more rest. You'll have a busy day explaining your latest escape."

"That I will. Perhaps my clever wife can help me conjure a story."

She gave him an implish smile. "Perhaps she can."

As she spun a tale filled with magick and courage, he lost himself in the melody of her voice. When she lifted herself on her elbow and gave him an expectant look, he realized she'd finished.

"Do you like it?" she asked.

"Forgive me, lass. I heard little beyond your voice. 'Tis a song all on its own."

Laughing, she leaned in to kiss him. "And when did the Fearless One become a poet?"

"When he met you."

Donovan glanced up as the door to his study banged open and John Tiptoft roared in like a furious bull.

"Where in hell is my prisoner?"

Feigning a scowl, Donovan capped his inkwell and stood to come out from behind his desk. "What are you talking about?"

"When I reached the garrison, I found this"—he threw the decoy sack on the floor—"in the cart behind my carriage. I ask you again, where is my prisoner?"

"One moment, Lord Deputy." He summoned the two guards who'd loaded the cart. "Did you substitute this for MacAuley's body?" he demanded, pointing to the sack.

The sentries' faces blanched, and they shook their heads as one.

"Nay, Lord Ryan," one of them replied. "As you ordered, we secured the corpse and covered it so as not to alarm anyone on the way to Westmeath."

Tiptoft rattled off several pointed queries, which the guards met with abject honesty. When he dismissed them, they looked at Donovan, who nodded for them to go. Once the door had closed, he poured two glasses of wine and offered one to his guest.

"Thank you." After a hearty swallow, Tiptoft asked, "What happened to that body?"

Donovan shrugged as he sipped his own wine. "Someone may have stolen it to bury in some secret location. There are those who believe if the body is not properly laid to rest, the soul will wander in torment forever."

"Nonsense. Little wonder your people are such a backward lot."

Donovan allowed a slight smile, but 'twas far from agreement. The earl's condescension supported Donovan's belief that only a native son could effectively rule Ireland. With no understanding of Irish history and beliefs, how could the new deputy hope to succeed in the mission Edward had set for him?

"I promised my king I would bring him the head of a traitor," Tiptoft went on, considering his empty wineglass with a thoughtful expression. "It would seem I must find another way to fulfill that pledge."

*   *   *

Kieran found Brynna in his mother's library, a book open in her lap while she stared out the frosted window. Though no tears marred her cheeks, never had he seen her look so sad. He closed the door and joined her, looking out on a day as bleak and cold as a demon's heart.

"My father is dead."

Her voice devoid of emotion, she continued her outward staring. Only when he took her hand did her eyes lift to his face. "He's gone, Kieran."

Such news traveled swiftly, but he'd heard nothing that morn. When he said as much, she shook her head with a frown. "You will."

He didn't even consider doubting her. While she'd been in Dunsmere, Brynna's remarkable skills had grown stronger, more controlled. She wielded them with great care, yet he couldn't help being awed by the magick she carried within her.

A quiet knock at the door interrupted his thoughts. "Aye?"

"Kieran, is Brynna with you?" his mother asked.

Pain flashed in Brynna's eyes, and she turned back to the window. Kieran opened the door for Aileen, who looked at his wife with a sympathetic expression. "You know, don't you, child?"

"I know," she replied listlessly. "But thank you for coming to tell me."

A great cheer sounded from the hall. Turning to Kieran, Aileen motioned toward the corridor.

"Wait here," he said with a kiss for Brynna's cheek. "I won't be long."

A slight nod was the only indication that she'd heard him. Wishing to leave her alone for as short a time as possible, he hurried into the hallway to join his mother. "What is it?"

"Already the stories have begun," she said in a hushed voice. "They say you killed Donovan Ryan and escaped right under the noses of fifty English soldiers."

Grimacing, Kieran shook his head. "They'll turn me into a legend even before I'm dead."

"Did you kill him?"

"Nay, but I've a fair idea who did. The Butcher must have been quite vexed to find me missing when he reached Westmeath."

" 'Twould be logical to blame Ryan," she agreed with a nod. "But why kill him?"

"Revenge. 'Tis a shame that all his deceit brought him great wealth, but an act of honor brought about his death."

"He was no fool. He must have known the risk he took in helping you."

"Aye, he knew, but in the end he loved Brynna more than Ireland. That is what I wish for her to remember of her father."

CHAPTER SIXTEEN

It had been ages since Brynna had last celebrated Christmas. The aromas wafting up from the kitchens were heavenly. Cinnamon and mulled cider mingled with the scents of the clove wreaths and evergreen boughs decorating the hall. Mistletoe hung over doors and windows to ward off evil spirits who might wish to spoil the celebration.

When she saw her mother and sisters descending the spiral steps with Kieran, Brynna barely contained a squeal of delight.

She rushed to greet them, laughing with the joy of seeing them on such a festive occasion. The MacAuley had grown accustomed to their visits, just as the *sídhe* had become more at ease within the clan. The children flocked to them, vying with one another to gain the attention of their fascinating guests. For their part, the fae showed admirable patience, talking with each child before turning to the next.

She and Kieran moved through the crowded hall,

exchanging tidings of peace, pausing to speak with each person for a few moments.

When at last they reached an empty pair of chairs near the hearth, Brynna felt ready to drop. Sensitive to her as ever, Kieran sat and guided her onto his lap. She rested her head on his shoulder with a little sigh.

"*Nollaig shona,* Kieran."

"And a Merry Christmas to you, sweet one," he replied, kissing her cheek. "Thank you for all you've given me."

When she made no response, he looked down to find she'd fallen asleep.

"Such rousing company y'are," Dev joked as he took the chair next to them. "Bored your own wife to sleep, have ye?"

"'Twould seem so." Kieran stood carefully to avoid waking her. "I think it best if I put her to bed."

Dev's eyes twinkled as he sipped his mead. "I suppose you'll be following after her, then."

"Aye." Kieran chuckled. "Good night, Dev."

"Sleep well, Kee."

Stabbing pains jerked Brynna from a restless sleep. Rolling to her side eased them a bit, but they returned with more force, and she realized 'twas not the baby's movements disturbing her. When the sensation moved to the small of her back, the cause of her distress became clear.

"Kieran." He mumbled a drowsy response, and she nudged him. "I think your son is coming."

In the near darkness, she saw the glint of his eyes. "What?"

"I've been having pains the last few days—"

"And ye said nothing?" he interrupted, bolting upright.

"This night, they've gotten worse," she continued, hoping to soothe him with a calm voice. "And Braeden seems to be in a different place."

"Wait here." He rushed from their bed, cursing as he bumped into something. Through the gap in the curtains, she saw a flicker of light, then more as he pushed the rose-covered tapestry aside and set a taper on the table beside their bed.

He passed a hand over her stomach, and his eyes widened. "By the saints, you're right. He's dropped a good bit since yestreen, has he not?"

Anxiety girded the excitement in his voice, and she smiled to reassure him. "Perhaps being early is a good thing, considering how large he is."

And how small you are.

She heard his thought as if he'd spoken it aloud but could think of nothing to ease his concern.

Then another pain crept up her back, and she resigned herself to a long, sleepless night.

"Mother, I canna leave her this way." Kieran cast a worried glance at his wife, who was drenched in sweat, her face contorted with pain. He feared Brynna hadn't the strength to bear much more. In truth, he had no idea how she'd endured the grueling hours since midnight.

"Women have been bearing their men's babes for centuries," Grania reminded him.

But the look she exchanged with Aileen showed her concern, and he strode between them, back to

Brynna's side. He took her hand in his, and smoothed a cooling cloth over her forehead while another spasm wracked her body. Birthing was foreign to him, to be sure, but he had an abiding knowledge of pain.

"Breathe, lass." He took a deep breath with her. "That's it. Think of something ye love, something that brings ye joy. 'Twill help ease the pain."

She cried out and arched her back, crushing his fingers in a deathly grip. Gritting his teeth, he reached behind her and rubbed his other hand along the tightly clenched muscles of her back. After a few strokes, he felt her relax, and she granted him a smile.

"Thank you."

"I'll keep doing it, if ye like."

"Oh, aye." Rolling so her back was facing him, she rested her cheek on his open palm and closed her eyes with a weary sigh.

Each time a pain hit her, he administered the same treatment. Before long, he could sense them before they struck and cut them off as he would an advancing opponent.

After the birth waters came, the pains grew even more intense. Brynna scarce had time to catch her breath before another wave shuddered through her body.

He tended her as best he could, adding his clumsy efforts to the practiced efficiency of the women. Dozens of bairns had entered the world in their capable hands, and he was grateful his son would be among them.

But as dawn broke, so did Brynna.

"I can't," she sobbed in a despairing whisper. "Kieran, I can't do any more."

"There's no time for rest, Brynna," Aileen told her in a sympathetic tone from the foot of the bed. "Come now, try again."

She did as she was bade, but her effort was weak at best. Grania and Aileen stepped away to confer in whispers. Kieran dragged his attention from them and lifted Brynna's shoulders to offer her a sip of water. Tears flooded her eyes, mingling with the sweat on her face as they coursed down her cheeks.

When her eyes drifted shut, he knew she was on the verge of surrender. If he didn't do something, he could lose them both.

Acting on instinct, he shifted so he sat behind her. He settled her head on his crossed legs and dropped a kiss on her forehead, then the tip of her nose. He trailed his hands along her sides, over the straining muscles and back up again. The rhythmic movement seemed to calm the spasms, and at last she took a deep breath. Then another. When her eyes opened, they were a listless green, but he forced a smile.

"That's it, Brynna. Look at me while I tell you a story."

"A story?" Her voice was little more than a whisper, but a feeble spark lit her eyes.

"Aye, about an enchanting nymph who lived in the forest."

As he recounted the dreams he'd had of her, he felt the quiver of exhausted muscles and followed their movements with his hands. He glimpsed a blur at the foot of the bed, but he dared not glance away while he held Brynna's gaze. Somehow, staring into his eyes, listening to his voice, was helping her.

"Brynna, you're doing it," Aileen approved as she rolled up her sleeves. "A fine mop of MacAuley hair he has, too. Come, now, Braeden, and meet your grandma."

Grania lifted Brynna as near to sitting as possible and rested her back against Kieran's chest. As he cradled her in his arms she felt like a rag doll, but from somewhere she summoned the strength for another push.

"Look at you!" Tears streaked down Aileen's face as she supported her grandson's head. "You have mischief written all over you, just like your father."

Brynna was saying something, and he leaned closer to hear. "I want to see him."

He lifted her a bit so she could see their son, and she fell back against him with a wan smile. How she could smile baffled him, especially when another spasm erupted under his hands.

"Fine broad shoulders he has," he told her when it was over.

She laughed weakly. "That I know."

With determination such as he'd never seen, she gathered herself for a final effort.

In the muted golden light of dawn, the newest MacAuley made his entrance into the world, kicking and squalling like a netted troll. Then Aileen placed him in Brynna's arms.

His eyes slitted open, widened as he considered her with great interest. When she opened the front of her gown and guided him to her breast, he latched on with a contented murmur.

"So, that's the trouble, is it?" Kieran chuckled. "You're hungry."

"And early, thank God," Aileen added.

"Though that could be a problem, as well." Grania frowned as she ruffled the lad's hair, but then a smile lit her features. "Then again—"

She pushed the fine hair aside to expose his temple. Clear as day, it bore the same star-shaped whirl Kieran's did.

"Mother must have been here." Brynna kissed the faery mark. "No doubt your very wise Grandmother Maire gave you that mark, so none would question who fathered you."

Kieran glanced about the chamber. "I didn't see her."

"She'd not intrude that way. Neither would she leave 'til she knew for certain she wasn't needed." She tipped her head back and kissed him. "You knew just what to do, Kieran. Thank you."

Grania pinned him with a curious look. "Which brings to mind a question, lad: How did you know?"

His chest swelled with pride as he kissed his son's wrinkled brow. "It seemed there was little I could do to make things worse."

She chortled as she rose from the bed. "When word of this gets out, every woman within ten leagues will want you at her birthing."

Kieran felt the color drain from his face, then laughed when he realized she was teasing.

Aileen put a hand on his shoulder and smiled. "For now, you should go."

"Ye mean there's more to this?"

"Aye." She artfully steered him out the door. "Some things even a husband shouldn't see."

"He's beautiful." Rianne sighed, running a hand over the dark hair peeking out from the sheepskin wrap. "And so tiny."

"Not when 'tis you doing the birthing," Brynna countered with a tired laugh. "Would you care to hold him?"

Rianne pulled away her hand and cast an uncertain glance at Shela.

"Go on if you wish, little sister. He's a sturdy lad. You won't harm him."

After another moment's hesitation, she held her arms out awkwardly, smiling as she took the baby. She lifted him to her face and rubbed noses with her nephew.

As Shela fluffed his hair, he stirred and reached for her hand. He grasped her smallest finger in his fist, and she laughed. "He has his father's grip, to be sure. And I see Mother's been here," she added, brushing a fingertip over the star at his temple.

Like his father before him, Braeden embodied the hope of Ireland. As Brynna bent to kiss him, she prayed his path wouldn't be fraught with the danger Kieran had faced.

She didn't feel the tears on her cheeks until she felt Shela's arms come about her.

"Don't cry, Brynna. He has a wondrous life ahead of him, your Braeden."

Lifting her head, she studied her older sister for a moment. Shining in the faery's aquamarine eyes she saw the past and into the murky future. Though she shouldn't, she asked, "Can you tell me?"

Shela looked about, then at Rianne. "Go on, Shay. 'Twill ease her worry."

"Mind, now, that the future is always in motion."

"Yes, yes, I know," Brynna huffed impatiently. "Tell me what you see for Braeden."

"He's quick and bright, full of mischief. His heart is always light, and darkness cannot touch him. For this one"—she smiled down at him—"to be loved is enough."

Sensing Shela had neglected something important, Brynna looked at Rianne, who frowned.

"Of course, one such as he is marked with more than a star. With the blood of a *sídhe* and a warrior in his veins, he will be different from the mortals around him. Some will admire those differences, some will revile them."

"But already he's strong," Shela said. "You and Kieran must teach him to hold his head high and be proud of who and what he is."

Fresh tears sprang into her eyes while she considered her son. "I want only for him to be happy."

"He will be." Rianne handed him back and wiped away Brynna's tears. "But 'twill not come easily. He must create his own happiness, as his parents have done."

Recognizing the truth in their words, she sniffled a bit and nodded. She would help Braeden learn to treasure his unique qualities as Kieran treasured hers.

He shifted in her arms, stretching as he yawned. Mouth wide open, he turned and began rooting for her breast once more. When it eluded him, he reached out a tiny yet determined hand, grabbing at the front of her gown.

"Hungry again, are you?" Laughing, she loosened the ties. "Is this what you're after, then?"

His hand grasped her wrist, and his eyes held hers while he suckled. The tug reached far beyond her skin, deep into her heart, where love had already put down roots nothing could destroy. Smiling, she brought his hand to her lips, kissed each of his perfect little fingers in turn.

'Twas only then she noticed her sisters were gone.

CHAPTER SEVENTEEN

Just before dawn, two-month-old Braeden began to fuss, banging his wee fists on the sides of the oaken cradle in a bid to escape it.

Brynna groaned, burying her head under a pillow. "I've only just fed him."

"Then he's not hungry." Kieran burrowed in to kiss her cheek. "Perhaps a walk will soothe him."

She gave him a weary smile and closed her eyes. "Thank you."

After another kiss, he slipped from their bed to rescue Braeden from the offensive cradle. Holding him at arm's length, he chuckled at the toothless grin that lit the chubby face. "Come with me, lad. Let your mother have her rest."

He strolled into his study and closed the door behind him. With Braeden in one arm, he stirred the coals and added several logs to the fire. Outside the windows the February sky held an ominous gray cast that sent a chill through his blood.

Looking down, he found his son studying him

with wide eyes. " 'Tis the warrior's sense, I've been told. I'm not certain if 'tis a blessing or a curse, but I'd wager you have it, as well. I pray you'll not need it as I have."

A knock at the outer door interrupted him. "Aye?"

Dev poked in his shaggy head, a grim look on his face. "You'd better come."

"What is it?" he asked as Brynna appeared in the doorway behind him.

"We've news from the parliament at Drogheda."

Braeden began struggling, and Kieran realized he'd tightened his hold a bit too much. He handed the boy to Brynna and summoned a patient tone. "Tell me."

"Desmond has been judged a traitor to the Crown. The English beheaded him yestreen."

Braeden's lusty wail matched the howling of Kieran's heart. With Desmond had died their best chance at forging a dignified peace with England. Beyond that, Kieran would miss the wise and generous man who'd been a true friend to Ireland.

Rage and grief tightened his throat so he could barely speak. "The messenger is still here?"

"Aye."

"Gather everyone together. We'll join you in the hall."

Dev hurried off, and Kieran held an arm out to his wife, hoping to add her strength to his own.

"Kieran, I'm so sorry. He meant so much to you, to your family."

"To Ireland." Resting his chin atop her head, he

gazed out at the lough shrouded in fog. "I dread the chaos that will come of this."

He expected her to ask him if he would join it. Instead, she tipped up her face and granted him a lovely smile.

"Ireland is never far from your thoughts, is she?"

"Brynna, I—"

"Don't apologize. 'Tis who you are, and I love you for it."

With Braeden cuddled between them, they walked down the steps to join the bewildered crowd milling about the great hall. Dev's nod told him all were present who could come, and Kieran signaled for quiet.

"I'd like to extend the gratitude of the MacAuley to our visitor"— he nodded at the tired messenger— "who has traveled hard to bring us news from Drogheda. Please read your message."

He knew Devlin's terse account of Desmond's trial and execution was only the half of it, and he braced himself for the rest.

"The Grand Council of Clans will assemble with all possible haste at Tara. Men, horses and arms are needed from every quarter to avenge the murder of our great ally. *Erin go bragh*."

"*Erin go bragh!*" the throng shouted in return, adding several other chants before allowing him to continue.

"Chief MacAuley?"

"Aye?"

"Will your clan join the campaign?"

Kieran's gaze roamed over his kinsmen, met with

determination from the men, resignation from the women. For generations, war had raged on Irish soil. With all likelihood, it would do so for generations to come. The MacAuley had lived in the thick of it, peacefully when they could, fighting when they must.

There was a time when he'd have ridden off without a thought to take revenge on the bastards who had murdered one of the finest men he'd ever known. But as he'd told Dev not long ago, things were different now.

"Such a decision is not mine alone." He swept the crowd with another glance. "I shall abide by the will of the MacAuley."

They reacted as he'd anticipated, with raucous support for the Grand Council's plan. He turned to the messenger with a grim expression. "I believe you have your answer."

"Shall I tell the other chiefs to expect you at Tara?"

He looked at Brynna, at the precious child in her arms. Not a trace of fear showed on her face, and her lovely smile answered the question in his mind. Whatever choice he made, she'd not oppose it.

Her acceptance eased his dilemma, and he nodded. "I'll be there."

Kieran dismounted and handed Gideon's reins to a stable boy. A quick count totaled two score of his kinsmen on the steps leading into the hall, every one of them dressed for battle. He approached the impromptu war council with great trepidation. "Come to welcome me home?"

A few laughed, and Dev asked, "What happened at Tara?"

"We're to send all the might we can spare. Already the fighting has begun. The Earl of Kildare fears for his own life and has pledged funds as well as soldiers."

"A messy business, this throwing in with the lords," Cavan muttered, shifting in his seat.

"The English have left us no choice," Carrick retorted. "Thieving, murdering bastards, every last one of 'em. At the least, we can show them we'll not be trampled into the mud."

"The clans are mustering near Newgrange," Kieran told them.

Carrick jumped to his feet, turned to the others with arms held wide. "If we leave now, we'll arrive just before the evening meal."

His enthusiasm evoked more laughter, and they all stood, making ready to depart.

Dev came down the steps and paused beside Kieran, a hand on his shoulder. "Will ye be joining us?"

A slender shadow appeared just inside the doorway, and this time the path before him was clear as a summer sky. Meeting Brynna's gaze, Kieran smiled as he slowly drew Morgan's legendary sword.

And plunged it into the ground.

Created at the dawn of time to protect humanity, the ancient warriors have been nearly forgotten, though magic lives on in vampires, werewolves, the Celtic Sidhe, and other beings. But now one of their own has turned rogue, and the world is again in desperate need of the

IMMORTALS

Look for all the books in this exciting new paranormal series!

THE CALLING by Jennifer Ashley
On sale May 1, 2007

THE DARKENING by Robin T. Popp
On sale May 29, 2007

THE AWAKENING by Joy Nash
On sale July 31, 2007

THE GATHERING by Jennifer Ashley
On sale August 28, 2007

The Reinvented Miss Bluebeard

Minda Webber

When your father is not only an infamous pirate but the husband of six vanished wives, respectability's hard to come by. That's why Eve invented herself a husband. How else was a nineteenth-century gal to follow her dreams and become one of those newfangled psychiatrists? Certainly she will never run The Towers, London's preeminent asylum for potty paranormals. But now, wackier than the werewolves and loonier than the leprechaun she's treating, something new takes shape—and he has the name of her never-before-seen husband and the body to drive a girl absolutely batty....

ISBN 10: 0-505-52706-5
ISBN 13: 978-0-505-52706-6 $6.99 US/$8.99 CAN

Connie Mason

Highland Warrior

She is far too shapely to be a seasoned warrior, but she is just as deadly. As she engages him on the battlefield, Ross knows her for a MacKay, longtime enemies of his clan. Soon this flame-haired virago will be his wife, given to him by her father in a desperate effort to end generations of feuding. Of all her family, Gillian MacKay is the least willing to make peace. Her fiery temper challenges Ross's mastery while her lush body taunts his masculinity. Both politics and pride demand that he tame her, but he will do it his way—with a scorching seduction that will sweep away her defenses and win her heart.

SANDRA SCHWAB

CASTLE OF THE WOLF

Celia Fussell's father is dead, and she reduced to the status of a poor relation in the house of her brother, the new baron, and his shrewish wife. A life of misery looms ahead.

But there is hope. Deep in the Black Forest stands Celia's inheritance, The Castle of Wolfenbach. It is a fortress of solitude, of secrets, of old wounds and older mysteries. But it is hers. And only one thing stands in her way: its former master, the hermit, the enigma…the man she is obliged to marry.
